HALLOWEEN KILLS

THE OFFICIAL MOVIE NOVELIZATION

HALLOWEEN KILLS

THE OFFICIAL MOVIE NOVELIZATION

BY
TIM WAGGONER

TITAN BOOKS

Halloween Kills – The Official Movie Novelization
Print edition ISBN: 9781789096019
E-book edition ISBN: 9781789096194

Published by Titan Books
A division of Titan Publishing Group Ltd
144 Southwark Street, London SE1 0UP
www.titanbooks.com

First edition: October 2021
10 9 8 7 6 5 4 3 2 1

A CIP catalogue record for this title is available from the
British Library.

Printed and bound in the United States.

This one's for Dennis Etchison who,
as Jack Martin, wrote the novelization
of *Halloween II.* It's an honor to follow
in his blood-soaked footsteps.

PROLOGUE

The Shape stands motionless at the foot of the stairs, looking up at the three women who have imprisoned him in this trap. Their faces display a range of emotions: anger, disbelief, fear... but most of all, triumph. This is most prominent on the face of the oldest woman, although when the Shape looks at her, he sees a different face, a much younger one. The face of She Who Will Not Die. The Shape is incapable of feeling anything as he gazes into her eyes, but something stirs inside him, a need for... what? Completion? Closure? Perhaps. Or maybe it's simply a need to see the life fade in those eyes—those stubborn, stubborn eyes—to watch them become cold and empty, like his.

Iron bars separate him from the women, and orange flames flare to life around him. He feels heat on his back, smells smoke in the air, but neither sensation alarms him. They mean no more to him than the pain of the injuries he's sustained this night, during his hunt. Some prey go down easy, some go down hard, but they all go down in the end.

Except Her.

The women leave, but not before She gives him one

1

last look, as if she wants to etch this moment into her memory so she might relive it over and over. The Shape understands this desire.

Then the women are gone, and the Shape stands alone in the basement, still staring up through the bars of his prison, at the empty space where those faces had been. He thinks nothing, feels nothing, is nothing.

The flames grow hotter, the smoke thicker, and he waits for whatever will come next.

1

HADDONFIELD, ILLINOIS

Halloween night, 2018

Cameron Elam walked through the park in his bare feet. It was late October, and the grass was cold, but no way was he going to try to walk home in high heels. He'd only worn them as part of his costume, and he'd taken them off soon after he and Allyson had arrived at the dance. Not only did the damn things pinch his feet, he could barely keep his balance in them. And given how much he'd had to drink tonight, he figured he was unsteady enough as it was. So he carried the shoes, although why he hadn't simply dropped them in the trash before leaving the high school, he couldn't say. It wasn't as if he was ever going to use them again. Maybe carrying them was a small way of punishing himself for having been such an asshole tonight. It wasn't much in the way of penance, but it was a start.

He and Allyson had gone to the dance dressed as gender-swapped versions of Bonnie and Clyde, the infamous bank-robbing couple from the 1930s.

Cam's outfit consisted of a tan beret, brown scarf, yellow short-sleeved cardigan—now beer-stained—brown plaid skirt, lipstick, and those damn heels. Instead of a blond wig, he'd decided to go with his own brown, shoulder-length curls, and he hadn't shaved his legs, figuring that would make the outfit funnier. The costumes had seemed like a good idea at the time, but once they were at the dance, no one had a clue who he and Allyson were supposed to be. The 1930s were ancient history as far as his generation was concerned. Practically prehistoric.

He walked through a small neighborhood park—oak trees, playground equipment, soccer field—rather than on the side of the street. The last thing he wanted right now was for someone to see him like this. He didn't need people honking their horns and laughing at him as they drove by, shouting through open windows. *Hey, baby! Looks like you had a rough night!*

He couldn't believe he'd screwed things up with Allyson so badly. Things between them had been going well lately, so much so that she'd even introduced him to her family. Her mom and dad seemed nice enough—for parents, that is—but her grandmother was an absolute headcase. Still, he had no room to criticize. His dad was pretty messed up, too. That was something he and Allyson had in common: nuts growing on the family tree. She hadn't been thrilled about Oscar tagging along with them tonight, though. He could be obnoxious sometimes... okay, *most* times, but she'd put up with him because he was Cam's friend. What she *hadn't* put up with was Cam's drinking. He'd brought a hip flask with him to the dance. *It's an accessory*, he'd told her, *that's all*. What he hadn't told her was that he'd filled his "accessory" with gin. Not only had he drunk liberally from it every chance he got, he also had a couple of the beers that Oscar had snuck into the dance. He'd known Allyson didn't like it when he drank, and to make matters worse, when she'd gone off to answer a call—most likely from Vicky— his former girlfriend Kim had approached him on the dance floor. They'd spoken for a couple minutes, making small talk. *You having a good time? What's the most ridiculous costume you've seen so far?* And then, out of nowhere, she'd kissed him. Yeah, he'd kissed her back, but he'd been drunk and hadn't realized what he'd been doing. Or maybe that had just been his excuse. Allyson had seen him kiss Kim, and when he'd tried to explain what had happened and how it hadn't meant anything, not really, they'd argued. He'd ended up snatching her phone out of her hand and dropping it into a bowl of nacho cheese sauce. He *hated* her phone—it seemed she was always on the damn thing, interrupting their time together— but it had been a stupid, childish thing to do, and he'd instantly regretted it. But before he could apologize, Allyson had stormed off and he'd been too ashamed to go after her right away.

When he'd finally worked up his courage—and sobered up a little—he'd gone in search of her, but he hadn't been able to find her. She'd left, and he couldn't blame her. He'd looked for Oscar then, but he hadn't been able to find him, either. The three of them hadn't driven to the dance, and he hadn't felt like bumming a ride off anyone, didn't want to explain why he was on his own, so he'd started walking. The night air was cold on his bare arms and legs, and he wished he'd thought to bring a jacket with him to the dance. He shivered, and figured he'd probably end up getting a damn cold. God, could this night get any *worse*?

He wished he could call or text Allyson, but of course she didn't have her phone. For all he knew, it was still back at the high school, submerged in cheese sauce. He *could* call Oscar, however. Maybe he knew where Allyson was, and even if he didn't, at least he'd listen to Cam's tale of woe. Oscar could be a jerk sometimes, but he was a good guy underneath all the smarminess.

He carried his own phone tucked into his skirt. He took it out now and called Oscar's number. He listened as it rang on the other end. And rang. And rang.

"Pick up, *pick up*..." he muttered. "Where are you?"

A click, and then Oscar's voice.

"Hey there, sassy lover. This is Oscar—"

Voicemail.

"—I'm not able to come to answer your call right now because... I'm standing right behind you. BOO!"

A beep, then Cam began speaking, the words coming out in an anxious rush.

"Oscar, call me when you get this. I messed up with Allyson. I gotta find her. Gotta fix it. If you

6

guys are together, if you know where she is, let me know, okay, bud? Be safe."

He disconnected.

"Dammit!"

In frustration, he tore the beret off his head and hurled it away from him as hard as he could. It spun through the air and landed soundlessly in the grass near the high chain-link fence that separated the park from the street. He was about to throw the high heels too, when he saw something lying on the other side of the fence, not far from the curb. There weren't any streetlights close by, but the moon was full tonight—how appropriate was that?—and Cam could see that the object was human-shaped. At first he thought it was a scarecrow or a dummy, a Halloween decoration that someone had stolen and left in the street. But then the decoration stirred and let out a soft moan. Christ, it was a *person*!

"Hey, you okay?" Cam called out nervously.

Another moan, louder this time.

Cam didn't think. He tucked his phone back into his skirt, dropped the heels, and ran toward the fence. There wasn't an exit to the street here, so when he reached the fence, he began climbing, fast as he could. The metal links were cold on his hands and they hurt his already aching feet, but he barely registered the discomfort. The fence wasn't all that high—maybe seven, eight feet—and when he reached the top, he swung his bare legs over and dropped. He landed with a jolt on a small strip of grass that lay between the fence and the street, and nearly lost his balance and fell. Goddam gin! He stood, turned, and hurried toward the man, reaching him in three quick strides.

The first thing Cam noticed was the blood. It lay on the asphalt near the man's head, inky black in the moonlight. Then he saw the vicious wound on the side of the man's neck, and he understood where all that blood had come from, was *still* coming from. He knew that if he didn't do something, and fast, the man would bleed out within minutes, maybe seconds. He tore the scarf from around his neck and crouched next to the man. When he saw the wound close up—flesh torn and ragged, wet meat visible inside—his stomach lurched. He almost vomited, but he gritted his teeth and swallowed. *Keep it together, Cam. This guy needs you.*

"I'll get help," he told the man. He raised his voice and shouted, "Somebody help! Help us!"

He lifted the man's head, wrapped the scarf around his neck, pulled it tight as he dared—eliciting a sharp intake of breath from the man—then tied it. He couldn't use the scarf as a tourniquet, couldn't risk cutting off the flow of blood to the man's head, which meant this makeshift bandage was a temporary solution. This guy needed a paramedic, not some drunk high school kid. Although Cam didn't feel very drunk right now. He felt stone cold sober.

His voice echoed in the night, but there was no answer.

He looked at the man, registering his features for the first time. He was older than Cam had first thought, in his fifties or sixties, with short, gray hair and a high forehead. He wore a dark jacket with a gold badge on the front and the Haddonfield Sheriff's Department emblem stitched onto the shoulder. Cam wasn't a fan of cops—what teenager was?—and he was uncomfortably aware that he still carried his flask, *and* that it wasn't empty. But he told himself to forget about that. Who gave a damn if he got in trouble for underage drinking tonight? A man's life was at stake.

"Hold on, man. Hold on. Officer…" He took a quick glance at the nametag on the man's uniform. "Hawkins. Take it easy. C'mon, *please*. You got it!"

Up to this point, the man's eyes had been closed, as if he were hovering on the brink of unconsciousness. But now his eyes flew open and his hands lunged toward Cam. He flinched, thinking the man was attacking him in his delirium. But instead he grabbed hold of Cam's sweater with surprising strength and pulled him closer. His eyes were wide and wild, and when he spoke his voice was a harsh rasp.

"He must die. He *needs* to die."

Then all the strength drained out of the man, and he let go of Cam's sweater. He lay back, face pale, but he didn't close his eyes, and while his breathing was rough, it remained steady. The man wasn't ready to check out yet. He was a tough one.

Cam had no idea what the man was talking about. *Who* needed to die? But right now it didn't matter. He grabbed his phone and called 911. And while Cam frantically explained to the operator what was happening, Officer Frank Hawkins gazed up at the full moon—which looked too much like an expressionless white mask to him just then—and remembered another night, another Halloween, long ago...

2

HADDONFIELD, ILLINOIS

Halloween night, 1978

Frank Hawkins, twenty-five years old, ran through shadows cast by tall leafless trees, revolver in his right hand, flashlight in his left, feet pounding, heart racing, lungs heaving. When he'd joined the sheriff's department a few months ago, he hadn't anticipated running hell-bent for leather through quiet neighborhoods, desperately searching for a madman, yet here he was. And he sure as *hell* hadn't expected that madman to be little Mikey Myers, all grown up and returned to Haddonfield to shed more blood. So far, Michael had killed three people during his homecoming—including Sheriff Brackett's teenage daughter—and the entire department was out in force, determined to make sure Michael didn't claim any more lives.

There weren't any streetlights in this part of town. The residents here liked it dark and peaceful at night, wanted to preserve a cozy small-town atmosphere. Streetlights, with their cold garish illumination, were for cities—impersonal, crime-ridden, *dangerous* places. Not little old Haddonfield. And while some people had a habit of leaving their front porchlights on at night, most were off now, a signal to any late trick-or-treaters that the homeowners' candy supplies had been depleted. No one had their back porchlights on, though, which was why Hawkins searched their yards. The darkness made a perfect hiding place for things that preferred to go about their work unseen—things like Michael Myers. He kept his flashlight off, though. He didn't want to give away his location to Michael, didn't want him to flee—or attack.

Hawkins had been ten, only four years older than Michael when the boy had, for some twisted, unfathomable reason, slaughtered his teenage sister Judith on Halloween night in 1963. Michael had been institutionalized ever since, his family home long abandoned. Hawkins had no idea what had happened to Michael's parents. One day they were simply gone, their house empty. People gossiped about what had happened to them—some said they'd had another child and left town to start their family anew—but no one seemed to actually know. Hawkins figured that remaining in town, and especially in *that* house, had been too painful for Michael's parents, and they'd gone somewhere they could, if not forget, at least not be constantly reminded of the tragedy that had struck their family.

In the fifteen years since Michael had killed Judith, Haddonfield's children had turned him into folklore, telling stories about Michael, saying his family had kept him locked in the attic where they tormented and tortured him until he'd been driven insane. Or that he had been possessed by a demon that had forced him to commit murder—a demon that still remained in the Myers house and which would possess any child foolish enough to cross its threshold. Hawkins wondered what stories children would tell after this night was done.

He stopped running, as much to catch his breath as to listen and see if he heard anything suspicious. At first there was nothing, but then he heard the sound of a vehicle racing down a street a couple blocks over. He turned and saw the blue lights of a sheriff's department cruiser flickering between the dark silhouettes of houses as the officer hauled ass down the street. Had Michael been spotted somewhere else? God, he hoped so. He wasn't afraid of encountering the lunatic, but it wasn't something he wanted, either. He'd never fired his weapon on the job, had never had cause to even *draw* the damn thing, and while he hoped his training would take over if and when the time came to take a shot at someone, the truth was he didn't know if he could do it—and he wasn't in a hurry to find out. Besides, rumor was that Michael had *already* been shot, six times as a matter of fact, point-fucking-blank. But that had to be bullshit. No one could take that many rounds to the chest and live, let alone go on the run. If Michael *had* been shot, which Hawkins seriously doubted, he was most likely lying dead in some alley or ditch and his body wouldn't be found until the sun rose.

Where were the other deputies? This was a lot of area for one man to search, so he'd called for backup a while ago. And while he didn't want to admit it, he was spooked out here by himself. He could use the reassurance of having more experienced officers with him. But so far he'd seen no sign of them.

He'd finished with this street, and he considered heading back to where they'd parked the cruiser. Maybe the other deputies he'd ridden with had finished searching and regrouped back at the car. Maybe they'd gotten word that Michael had been located somewhere else. But his job was to continue searching until he received orders to stop, so that's what he'd do. Besides, what if Michael *was* lurking somewhere around here? Hawkins wouldn't be able to live with himself if someone died because he'd gotten scared.

He decided to head west, and he jogged toward an alley between a pair of two-story houses, intending to use it as a shortcut. But he only made it a few yards before he froze. A tall, almost robotic figure was crossing the alley fifty yards in front of him. The man had just appeared, as if he'd emerged from the shadows, and he moved silent as a ghost, his feet making no sound. It was difficult to make out much detail from this distance, but Hawkins saw the man wore dark clothes—as if he was garbed in shadow itself—and his face was an eerie, spectral white. If Hawkins hadn't known better, he might've thought the man was nothing but a disembodied head floating serenely through the night air.

He knew at once that he had found Michael Myers. Or perhaps Michael had found him.

Instinctively, he dropped his flashlight and fell into a shooting stance, feet apart, revolver raised, left hand gripping his right wrist.

"Stop right there!"

His voice came out strained and he winced to hear himself. He thought he sounded like a little boy playing police officer, but he didn't tremble and his gun hand held steady. He didn't expect the man—*Michael*—to obey his less-than-authoritative-sounding command, but he stopped walking at once. He stood there for a second, still as a statue, before turning to face Hawkins. Then, again moving like a machine instead of a creature formed of flesh and blood, Michael started walking toward him. Hawkins couldn't tell if Michael was carrying a weapon, but he had a feeling the man didn't need one to be a threat. Michael was a weapon all by himself.

Hawkins spoke again, his voice whip-crack strong this time.

"Stop! Haddonfield Sheriff's Department!"

Michael kept coming, moving with a deliberate, mechanical stride. As he drew closer, Hawkins could make out the features on his mask. He'd seen it before, or one like it, in the display window of a hardware store downtown, but on Michael's face, the mask's features seemed to have taken on a strange life. They didn't move, of course, but it looked as if the rubber had sealed itself to Michael's flesh, forming a second layer of ivory skin. So lifelike were the features that he wouldn't have been surprised to see the eyes blink, the nostrils flare, the lips tighten. Speaking of eyes, a black line ran from the left one down to the chin, like the track of an ebon tear. Was that blood? Had one of his eyes been injured? Hawkins looked to see if there were any bullet wounds on Michael's chest, but the fabric of his coveralls was too dark for him to tell in this light.

Michael continued toward Hawkins, pace relentless, arms held tight at his sides, hands open, fingers stiff and curled like claws. Hawkins was overwhelmed by sudden atavistic fear, a profound sense of *wrongness*, as if the thing coming for him wasn't only inhuman, it was something that couldn't, shouldn't exist. Terror in human form, darkness solidified, death—the great Nothing itself—given *shape*.

Hawkins had been trained to give warning before discharging his weapon, but he was so frightened that he acted without thinking. He squeezed the revolver's trigger, one, twice, three times in rapid succession. The gun roared and bucked in his hand, and the flash of its muzzle flare—so bright in the night's blackness—temporarily blinded him. He blinked furiously, expecting to feel Michael's hands grab hold of him any second, but he felt nothing. When his vision began to clear, he saw that Michael was gone. He ran to the spot where he judged

Michael had been standing, looked left, right, turned back the way he had come. Nothing. It was as if Michael had returned to the shadows that had birthed him. Obviously, all of Hawkins' rounds had missed his target; perhaps not by much, but as the old saying went, a miss was as good as a mile.

Hawkins squatted to examine the ground. He retrieved his flashlight, turned it on, and shined its beam downward. The alley wasn't paved, and he saw depressions in the moist dirt. Boot prints—proof that Michael was human after all. Hawkins reached down with his right hand and ran his fingers over one of the prints. They came away wet and sticky with blood. *Michael's* blood. The man could bleed, and what could bleed could die.

"Hawkins! You okay?"

Hawkins' ears were ringing from the sound of his weapon discharging, and the voice sounded muffled, far away. Still, it startled him, and he sprang to his feet, revolver raised, ready to defend himself. Three men ran toward him, all carrying lit flashlights and wearing sheriff's department uniforms and brown jackets. They too had their guns out, but they carried them at their sides, and Hawkins, embarrassed, quickly lowered his weapon. The three men weren't that much older than him. Tobias and Sullivan were in their thirties, and McCabe was around the same age as Hawkins. As veterans of the sheriff's department, they delighted in busting the rookie's balls, but Hawkins was glad to see them now.

Deputy McCabe, the one who'd asked if he was okay, reached him first, but Sullivan and Tobias were close behind. The men might be veterans of the sheriff's department, but right now they all looked as scared as he was.

"Did you see him?" Tobias demanded. "Where did he go?"

Now that the encounter with Michael was over, Hawkins lost control of his emotions. He began to tremble with fear, and when he spoke, he practically yelled.

"Where have you guys been? I called for backup ten minutes ago!"

"Easy, rookie," Sullivan said, an edge of irritation in his voice.

"Slow dance in the big city," McCabe added.

Hawkins was unfamiliar with the phrase, but he got the gist of it. He took a deep breath, let it out, and forced himself to speak calmly.

"He crossed right here. Saw him from fifty yards away. Then he just… disappeared."

The three older deputies exchanged looks.

"Loomis said he shot him multiple times in the chest," McCabe said.

So it's more than a rumor, Hawkins thought, and he shuddered.

"No one could survive that," Tobias said dismissively. He shined his flashlight on the ground. "Hey, footprints."

"Always late to the chase, Tobias," Hawkins said. He knew Tobias would be angry with him later, but right now he didn't care. Michael was out there somewhere, and they—

"Shut up," McCabe said, then he shushed them. "Shhh!"

Without speaking, the four deputies moved to stand back to back and directed their flashlight beams outward. They saw nothing. A siren wailed in the distance.

"He just disappeared," Hawkins repeated. His voice held more awe than fear now.

McCabe began barking orders. "Sullivan, you and Tobias search Chestnut, south to the bypass. Hawkins and I will track Market Street to Lampkin. We'll catch him."

"*Catch* him?" Hawkins said in disbelief. "You kidding me? That asshole just killed Sheriff Brackett's daughter Annie. You see Michael Myers, you shoot him, got it?"

Hawkins knew it wasn't his place to give orders—especially when they countermanded McCabe's—but he couldn't help it. He'd *seen* Michael, had felt the vast emptiness that was shaped like a man. They hadn't.

Sullivan and Tobias shared an uncomfortable look, then they turned to McCabe.

"Go," McCabe said, and the two men started jogging down the alley. When they were out of earshot, McCabe turned to Hawkins.

"Jesus, Frank. You can't be barking orders like that. Our badge says *Protect and serve*, not *Shoot to kill*."

Embarrassed, Hawkins looked away from

McCabe. A moment later, McCabe began walking, and Hawkins fell in line beside him.

"I used to know him, you know," McCabe said, his voice subdued. "Michael. When we were kids."

This surprised Hawkins. McCabe had never said anything about this before.

"He one of those weirdo freaks who'd pull the wings off butterflies, that kinda thing?" Hawkins asked.

McCabe shook his head. "Not that I ever saw. He was just—"

"He killed his sister when he was six years old," Hawkins put in. He immediately felt stupid for saying this. Everyone in town knew this fact, and McCabe surely did. But Hawkins was nervous and had felt as if he had to say something. If McCabe was irritated by Hawkins' interruption, he gave no sign.

"Yeah. My mom used to make me go to his house to play. Sometimes Michael would just stare out his sister's bedroom window. I always wondered what he was looking at. And then one day... he just snapped."

Hawkins tried to imagine Michael—an ordinary little boy—standing at Judith's window, gazing outward, seeing... what?

"He was looking at Haddonfield," Hawkins said. "A simple town where nothing exciting ever happened. Until now."

They continued their hunt in silence.

*

On a street corner several blocks from where Hawkins and McCabe searched, eleven-year-old Lonnie Elam was in trouble. Three teenagers in Halloween costumes—one girl, two boys—had surrounded him, and they were *pissed*. Worse, they were all Mullanys, which meant they were Conrad Mullany's siblings.

Up until ten minutes ago, Conrad had been Lonnie's trick-or-treat partner. Neither of them wore costumes. Costumes were for little kids. They each wore jeans and sneakers, but while Lonnie wore a boring plain T-shirt beneath his red jacket, Conrad had on a kick-ass Kiss concert T-shirt under his blue puffer jacket. It wasn't as if Conrad had actually *been* to a concert. One of his brothers had brought the shirt home for him, but that didn't make it any less cool.

At the last house Lonnie and Conrad had stopped at they'd each only gotten a single piece of candy from stingy old Mr. Harrison: a tiny brick of rock-hard bubblegum for Lonnie, but for Conrad—the lucky jerk—a full-sized gobstopper.

As they headed back toward the sidewalk, Lonnie had said, *"Wanna trade that gobstopper for my bubblegum?"*

Conrad had laughed. *"Are you crazy? Did you see how big it was?"*

Lonnie had. What's more, Lonnie *hated* bubblegum—*and* Conrad had been getting better treats than him all night. He'd get a dumb lollipop while Conrad got a peanut butter cup. He'd get a stale popcorn ball while Conrad got a brownie

21

wrapped in cellophane. It wasn't fair, and Lonnie had decided to do something about it. He pushed Conrad hard, and when the boy fell onto the grass in Mr. Harrison's front lawn, he dropped his bag of candy. Lonnie snatched it up, jammed his hand inside, and rummaged around until he found the gobstopper. Grinning, he dropped the bag—he only wanted the candy, it wasn't like he was a *thief* or anything—and started running. Conrad shouted after him, calling him names, some of them cusses that Lonnie had never heard before and which he decided to file away for later use. Lonnie kept running until he was sure Conrad wasn't following him, and then he slowed down to look at his prize, still gripped in his hand.

Once he'd examined it more closely, he saw that the chocolate bar wasn't *that* big. But even if it had been jumbo-sized, he knew he shouldn't have taken it. And now that he'd stopped running and had a chance to think about it, he wasn't sure *why* he'd stolen it. Conrad was supposed to be his friend, and friends didn't steal from each other. Lonnie sometimes did things out of... what was the word his mom had used? *Impulse.* She'd said that meant he did stuff without thinking first. Later, when he did have a chance to think, he'd regret what he'd done. Well... sometimes. He'd decided to go back to Mr. Harrison's, give Conrad his chocolate, and tell him that it had all been a dumb joke, and that he was sorry. He'd been on his way when Conrad's siblings came running down the sidewalk toward him.

Conrad wasn't with them, but Lonnie had no doubt Conrad had told his brothers and sister what he'd done. He wouldn't have been surprised if Conrad was watching from a hiding place somewhere close by. He *was* kind of a wimp.

Conrad's siblings evidently didn't think costumes were for kids. Maybe costumes became cool again once you got older. Marcia Mullany was dressed as a witch—pointed black hat, cape, short black skirt. She was blond but tonight she wore a frizzy black fright wig. Glenn Mullany was dressed as a soldier—mottled green combat fatigues, big black boots, black greasepaint striping his face. A plastic toy rifle completed his look. Ian Mullany was decked out as Frankenstein's monster—green makeup, scars painted in red, plastic bolts affixed to his neck, black turtleneck, black pants, and even bigger boots than Glenn's.

"He's gonna get you, he's gonna get you," Glenn chanted.

Lonnie knew Conrad's siblings... kind of. He'd been over to their house a number of times, and they'd nodded to him, said hey, but that was about it. They were teenagers. They viewed Conrad and Lonnie as little kids and wanted nothing to do with them. But that didn't mean they intended to let anyone get away with picking on their little brother.

Marcia leaned in close to his face. When she spoke, her voice was tight with anger.

"Lonnie, if you touched Conrad's candy, I swear to *god* I'll beat your ugly ass."

Lonnie's first instinct—his *impulse*—was to lie. "I didn't take it. Wasn't me. It was Richie!"

Richie Castle sometimes hung out with him and Conrad. The three of them had been messing around earlier tonight at the Myers house. Conrad and Richie had dared him to go in, but he'd only made it as far as the front porch before someone— probably another damn teenager out to scare some kids—had whispered for him to get his ass out of there. All three of them had run after that. Richie hadn't stuck around to go trick-or-treating with him and Conrad, though. Every year his mom and dad dragged him to his aunt's annual Halloween party. But Marcia didn't know that Richie hadn't gone with them—Lonnie hoped.

Ian sneered, making him look even more like Frankenstein's monster than he already did.

"Then *show* me. Show me what's in your hand! Why don't you open your hand?"

Lonnie gripped the gobstopper tightly.

"No, I don't want to."

Glenn stepped toward him then. Glenn was big and strong, and from what Conrad understood, he intended to enlist in the army for real when he graduated high school. Before Lonnie could run, Glenn grabbed him and put him in a headlock. He was none too gentle about it either, and Lonnie drew in a sharp hiss of breath.

Ian pried the gobstopper out of his right hand while Marcia yanked his bag of candy out of his left. Glenn continued holding him in a headlock as Ian inspected the piece of hard candy.

"It's all sweaty," he said, then tossed it over his shoulder.

Marcia dug through Lonnie's Halloween haul and pulled out a chocolate bar filled with caramel and covered with nuts. One of Lonnie's favorites. She then turned and hurled his bag of candy into the front yard of the house on the corner. It landed with a thud, and candy spilled onto the grass.

Glenn laughed. "*That's* what you get when you fuck with the Mullanys."

He gave Lonnie's neck one last squeeze before releasing him. Lonnie knew he'd deserved this, but he felt like he wanted to cry. He fought to hold back the tears, though. He didn't want to give Conrad's siblings an excuse to pick on him further.

Before any of them could do or say anything, they heard the *whoop* of a police siren. They turned to look in the direction of the sound and saw a blue-and-white sheriff's cruiser—lights flashing—approaching swiftly. The officer pulled up to the curb in front of them, leaned over, and rolled down the passenger side window. Lonnie didn't recognize the man, but he was damn glad to see him.

"Everything all right with you kids?" the officer asked.

Ian smiled and answered in a fake-polite voice. "No problems. Just trick-or-treats with our new old friend Lonnie."

As if to bolster her brother's statement, Marcia also smiled and put an arm around Lonnie's shoulders. Her grip was tight and Lonnie got the message. *Don't even think about narcing on us.* His eyes were watery, but he fought even harder to hold back tears and managed a smile of his own, although he doubted it looked very convincing.

The officer looked at each of their faces in turn, scowling, as if he was shooting some kind of truth rays at them from his eyes. In the end, he must've decided they were okay, because his features eased.

"Be on the lookout for a man in a white mask," he said.

The Mullanys exchanged bemused looks.

"It's Halloween," Ian said. "Halloween masks."

"That's right. I need you all to go home right now. Go home to your parents…" He paused, then added, "and lock your doors."

The way the officer said those words—*lock your doors*—sent a chill shivering down Lonnie's back. The man sounded scared, and Lonnie wasn't used to adults being scared, let alone a sheriff's deputy. Deputies carried guns, *real* ones. What did they have to be afraid of?

"Why?" Marcia said. She sounded frightened as well. "What did he do?"

The officer hesitated, as if he wasn't sure whether or not to answer her. Finally, he said, "He murdered three teenagers down the street."

Lonnie and the Mullanys stood there, stunned, as the officer hit the gas and sped away. Lonnie watched the vehicle skid around a corner, and then it was gone.

"C'mon," Glenn said. "Let's go get Conrad."

Lonnie hoped the Mullanys would let him tag along, but Marcia shoved him away from them.

"Don't get murdered, Lonnie!" Ian said.

Marcia started chanting then, and her brothers quickly joined in.

"He's gonna get you, he's gonna get you, he's gonna get you!"

The three teenagers laughed, turned, and starting walking away. Lonnie considered running after them so he wouldn't be out here alone, but he'd had enough of being bullied for one night, whether he deserved it or not. And he was still too ashamed of what he'd done to face Conrad. Besides, his house lay in the opposite direction from where the Mullanys were going.

He retrieved his bag of candy from the yard and started walking.

3

The sidewalks in this part of town were not in the best condition. In fact, they were overdue for replacement, but the neighborhood kids didn't mind. They liked playing Step-on-a-Crack-and-Break-Your-Mother's-Back, and they also enjoyed prying up bits of concrete and throwing them at targets—usually each other. Lonnie had only made it halfway down the block's cracked and broken sidewalk when he began to get the creeps. He heard a dog barking furiously off in the distance, and wind blew through the trees in the yards he passed, rustling those few leaves still clinging to their crooked and twisted branches. He didn't like trees when the leaves were gone—they looked too much like large alien hands stretching up from the earth, hands with too many fingers, too many joints. He imagined those hands coming to life, extending toward the sidewalk, reaching for him, reaching... reaching...

The image made him shiver, and he zipped up his jacket, more for the comfort of it than because he was cold. He thought about what the Mullanys had chanted at him before they'd left. *He's gonna get you, he's gonna get you, he's gonna get you!* He knew they were just trying to mess with him. They wouldn't have left him to walk home alone if they really thought there was a killer running around out here somewhere. Would they? He looked over his shoulder, hoping to see the Mullanys walking toward him, prank over, ready to make sure he got home safe.

No one was there. He'd never felt so alone in his life.

He faced forward once more and continued walking. He wanted to run, but he restrained himself. He was eleven, practically a teenager himself. He was too grown up to run home scared like a little baby. Sure, there was nobody around to *see* him run, but *he'd* know he did it. Plus, not rushing home was a way of punishing himself for what he'd done to Conrad. It was… *penance*. Yeah, that was the word. Lonnie liked words. He liked the way they made his mouth feel when he spoke them, liked how they looked on a page. He wasn't the greatest student in school, but he got high grades on his essays. Mrs. Haney had even suggested he might be good enough to be a writer one day.

The two houses at the end of the block were separated by a large hedge that, in the dark, looked like a wall made entirely out of shadow. He stopped several yards before he reached it, and gave it a long hard look. The hedge was tall enough for someone— someone *big*—to hide behind. It was a perfect place

29

for a killer to lay in wait for some dumbass who wasn't paying attention to their surroundings to come by. And when they walked past the hedge— *bammo!* Dead meat. Lonnie considered turning around and heading back the way he'd come. If he did that, he might still catch up to the Mullanys. But if he didn't, he'd have to walk a lot farther to get home. Alone. In the dark.

There's nobody there, he told himself. *It's just your imagination. Like the way you imagined those trees as monster hands. There's nothing to be scared of.*

He tried to swallow, but his throat was so dry he couldn't manage it. Slowly, step by step, he moved closer to the hedge. He could hear his pulse thrum in his ears, and beads of sweat broke out on his forehead. Still, he continued on. Another step… and another… When he reached the hedge, he drew in a breath, held it, and quickly looked around to the other side.

No one was there.

He released the breath he'd been holding in a shaky sigh of relief.

See? What did I tell you? Just your imagination.

Feeling slightly more confident, he continued down the sidewalk. He was going to be okay, he knew that now. All he had to do was keep walking… He felt a disquieting prickle on the back of his neck then, and his gut muscles clenched tight.

Someone's behind me.

He didn't know how he was aware of this, but he was. He stopped walking and began to turn around slowly. He knew he should just take off running and keep running as fast as he could and not let up until he made it home, but he couldn't make himself do it. It was like he was no longer in control, as if his body had a mind of its own, and it wanted, *needed*, to see whatever it was behind him. He hoped that it would be like with the hedge, that his imagination was getting the better of him, and when he finished turning all the way around, he'd see that no one was there.

But someone *was* there—a tall man in dark clothes, with a face so white it almost gleamed in the darkness. No, not a face, Lonnie realized. A *mask*.

He stood there, unable to move, frozen, a small animal that had suddenly found itself in the presence of a large—and *hungry*—predator. The man in the mask didn't move at first, and Lonnie had the impression that the man was examining him with cold detachment, like a scientist peering at a specimen under a microscope. Trying to figure out what he was, trying to figure out what to *do* with him.

Then, decision evidently reached, the man started walking toward Lonnie.

Lonnie's paralysis broke then, and he decided to do as the disembodied voice at the Myers house had told him earlier that night: get his ass out of there. He turned and ran like hell.

His right foot came down on a divot in the sidewalk, his ankle rolled, he lost balance, and he fell forward. He lost his grip on his bag of candy and it went flying. He was able to get his hands out

31

in front of him to protect himself, but he still hit hard, and the breath was driven from his lungs. The tender flesh of his palms hurt, too, and he wondered if they were bleeding. Gasping for air, he rolled over and was shocked to see the man in the mask was standing over him. He hadn't heard him run. It was like the man had teleported from one place to another in the blink of an eye. Then again, maybe he *wasn't* a man…

White-Mask gazed down at Lonnie, and he saw a dark line extending from the left eyehole down to his chin. The man stood motionless—so still that Lonnie wasn't sure he was even breathing—but he felt the weight of the man's regard upon him, felt the sheer, vast malignance of his presence. This wasn't a man… This was a *monster*.

Lonnie curled into a ball, covered his head, squeezed his eyes shut, and screamed as loud as he could.

"Help! Help me! Hellllllllp!"

Time passed then, probably only a few seconds, but it seemed to Lonnie like a goddamn eternity as he waited to feel White-Mask's hands latch onto him. But that didn't happen, and then he heard a voice shouting from a distance, along with the sound of boots pounding on pavement.

"Hey! Are you okay? You okay, kid?"

A man's voice. Hesitantly, Lonnie opened his eyes and saw a pair of sheriff's deputies looking down at him. He was still too gripped by terror to process the deputies' arrival, and he said nothing as the men reached down and helped him rise to his feet. His ankle hurt, but not too bad. He didn't think it was twisted. That was good. His parents would give him hell if he came home hurt. They'd never let him go trick-or-treating without adult supervision again.

"Take it easy," one of the deputies said. "Take a deep breath."

The man's coat was unzipped, and Lonnie could see his nametag. Officer Hawkins.

Lonnie did take a deep breath, and when he let it out, he felt a little better. He looked around for White-Mask but saw no sign of him. But that was impossible... wasn't it? He'd just been here a few moments ago.

"Where did he go?" Lonnie asked.

The other deputy—his jacket was zipped and Lonnie couldn't see his nametag—frowned.

"Who?"

Lonnie felt a cold sensation move across his body, as if the autumn air had, just for a second, become a wintery blast. He answered the deputy in a small, almost inaudible whisper.

"The Boogeyman."

The deputy looked at him quizzically for a moment, and then his attention was caught by something on the other side of the street. He pointed.

"That's it," the man said. "That's the Myers house."

Lonnie turned to look in the direction the deputy had indicated. He'd been so caught up in running away from Conrad and then getting away from his siblings that he'd had only the most basic idea of his location. But now he knew exactly where he was. He'd been on the other side of the street only a couple hours ago, had stood on that porch, the other kids taunting him to go into the house. *Chicken! Go ahead, Lonnie, go in!* He had shaken like a leaf as he reached for the doorknob, had heard that voice— *Lonnie! Hey, Lonnie! Get your ass out of here!*—and he had, hadn't he? It had seemed like an excellent idea then, and it seemed like an even better one now.

Not caring what the deputies thought about him, he turned and ran in the direction of his home. He'd had enough Halloween for one night—hell, enough to last him a lifetime.

*

Hawkins turned as the boy fled, but McCabe said, "Let him go. He'll be all right. We know where Myers is."

Hawkins looked across the street at the house. *Michael's* house.

"That's where it happened," McCabe said. "Halloween, 1963."

Two-story colonial, weathered wood siding, gray shingles. Stone steps leading to a wooden porch with columns and banisters. Windows boarded up, second-story gutter hanging halfway off. *No Trespassing* sign taped to the outer wall to the left of the front door, and stuck in the lawn—in front of a row of overgrown bushes—a metal sign for Strode Realty. Hawkins couldn't imagine anyone wanting to buy this goddamn spook house. *Strode must be one hell of an optimist,* he thought. *That, or a damn fool.*

McCabe stepped into the street and started walking toward the house. After a second's hesitation, Hawkins followed, jogging a couple steps to catch up. Both men still had their weapons out and held at their sides. Hawkins had seen the Myers house numerous times throughout the years, of course, but he'd never really looked at it closely. It always had been part of the scenery, a dark bit of Haddonfield history which most people did their best to ignore. He was surprised by how... *ordinary* it looked. There was nothing especially sinister about it—no gothic spires or stone ramparts, no dark cloud overhead unleashing white-hot bolts of crackling lightning, like in the low-budget monster movies he'd loved watching on Dr. Dementia as a kid. No, the Myers house looked like what it was: an abandoned house that had been left to rot. But that didn't mean it was empty. Not tonight.

Hawkins tightened his grip on his revolver.

The two men stepped up onto the porch. Sagging wooden boards creaked beneath their weight, and Hawkins wouldn't have been surprised if the entire porch collapsed beneath them. McCabe activated his flashlight, and Hawkins did the same. McCabe shined his beam right, then left, making sure they were alone on the porch, and then he tried the front doorknob. It was unlocked. McCabe gave Hawkins a look that said, *Ready?* Hawkins didn't know if he was, but he nodded, hoping he looked more confident than he felt. McCabe pushed the door open, and — revolvers raised — they stepped inside.

The smells of mold and mildew hit Hawkins like a slap in the face as they entered. The atmosphere inside the house felt heavy, oppressive, like a great weight settling onto his shoulders. This was a place where bad things had happened — and maybe more bad things would happen before the night was over. The deputies' flashlight beams punched through the darkness as they moved further into the house. The lack of furniture, along with cobwebs clinging to the ceiling, created an overall sense of desolation; the decaying shell of a place where a family had once lived. Now it was nothing more than a dead, dry husk. Beige wallpaper had been torn away from the walls to expose the drywall beneath, and the floorboards here creaked even more than the ones on the porch had. If Michael was in the house somewhere, they sure as hell weren't going to be able to sneak up on him.

McCabe led the way as they moved through empty rooms — dining room, kitchen, living room… Every shadow was a place where Michael Myers could be hiding, and Hawkins swept his flashlight beam back and forth, trying to drive away the darkness. But once his beam moved on, the shadows returned, flowing into place again like thick, black water.

"What the fuck?" McCabe said. He stopped abruptly and shined his flashlight at the floor, almost at their feet. Hawkins did the same.

Their flashlight beams illuminated a dog — some kind of scruffy mutt — lying on its side, fur matted with blood. Its belly had been ripped open and the organs removed. Hawkins crouched down and reached out, intending to put his hand on the poor thing's head. But he stopped when he saw the animal had no eyes—and no tongue. Goddammit! What kind of a monster could *do* something like this? Anger flared bright inside him, the fire partially stoked by fear. He rose to his feet, and turned to the stairs that led to the second floor.

"Haddonfield Sheriff's Department!" he shouted. "Let yourself be known!"

Silence.

Hawkins' hands began to shake, causing the beam of his flashlight to jitterbug around the room. McCabe looked at him, sent another unspoken message. *You good?*

Hawkins took a deep breath, let it out. His hands still shook, but they were steadier now, and he nodded. McCabe nodded back, then turned and headed for the stairs. Hawkins followed.

The steps creaked as they slowly ascended, and Hawkins felt a line of sweat run down his spine. As freaked out as he was being here, it had to be worse for McCabe. The man had come to this house to play with Michael when he was a kid. What was it like for him to be here now, reliving those memories while hunting a childhood friend who'd turned out to be a psychopathic killer? He supposed it was the kind of thing that could fuck a man up for life. Good thing McCabe was a tough bastard.

*

When they reached the second-floor landing, the deputies split up without discussing it. Hawkins checked the room on the left, McCabe the right. There was a small closed door next to the room McCabe had chosen—Judith's room—but he figured it for a linen closet and ignored it for now.

McCabe hesitated at the open bedroom door, as if he was afraid to step inside. He didn't believe places retained the negative energy of terrible acts that had been committed there, and he sure as *hell* didn't believe in ghosts. The room was nothing but an empty space. That's all. Gun raised, flashlight beam leading the way, he stepped inside.

He'd never set foot inside Judith's room when he'd come here as a kid, but several times he'd stood in the doorway and watched Michael stare out the window when his sister wasn't home. The last time he'd visited was little more than a month before whatever dark switch flipped inside Michael's diseased brain, causing him to take a butcher knife from the kitchen and plunge it into Judith's tender flesh nine times. That had been fifteen years ago, but in many ways, it seemed like yesterday.

Moonlight filtered through the grime-streaked window, giving the room a soft blue-white glow. Blotches of mold covered the floral wallpaper in Judith's room to the point where the flowers were almost unrecognizable. He found this almost unbearably sad.

He checked behind the door. Clear. There was

a side doorway, and he was about to check that when his attention was once more drawn to Judith's window. Unlike the other windows in the house, this one hadn't been boarded up. No, that wasn't right. There were pieces of broken wood lying over in one corner. Someone had removed the boards from Judith's window—and McCabe had a damn good idea who that someone was.

"All clear!" Hawkins shouted from the room across the hall.

McCabe jumped at the sound of his partner's voice, but then he forgot about Hawkins, his attention drawn once more to the window. Without thinking he began walking toward it, moving forward as if compelled by some unknown force. When he reached the window, he looked down and saw a pair of footprints on the dust-covered floor.

"Someone's been in here," he said softly to himself. *Not someone*, he thought. *Michael.*

He stepped into the footprints and stood where Michael had when they were kids, where he'd stood after breaking out of Smith's Grove and coming home. McCabe gazed out the window, trying to see whatever Michael saw when he looked out, but the glass was streaked with grime, and all he could make out was a smeared, distorted version of his own reflection. He tried rubbing the glass with his jacket sleeve to clean it, but it didn't help much. The worst of the grime was on the window's other side. But he managed to clear a tiny spot somewhat, and he leaned toward it now. He peered through the window, through fifteen years of dirt clinging to the outer glass. He thought he saw something out there, an indistinct shape that he couldn't quite make out. Was this thing—whatever the hell it was—what Michael had been looking at all those years ago? What he'd been looking at tonight? Maybe.

"Haddonfield," McCabe said, drawing back from the glass. "Where nothing exciting ever hap— *Shit!*"

He caught a flash of movement from the corner of his eye, and he spun around to see Michael coming toward him from the side doorway. Michael held a length of rope, the ends coiled tight around his hands. The psychopath charged McCabe with his stiff-legged gait, and before the deputy could get off a shot, Michael wrapped the rope around McCabe's neck and pulled it tight. McCabe's eyes bulged, and he couldn't breathe. He dropped both his gun and flashlight and reached up to frantically claw at the rope, hoping to loosen it so he could pull in a breath. But it was no use. Michael was too damn strong. McCabe didn't intend to go down without a fight, though.

Michael had maneuvered himself so that he stood behind McCabe, so the deputy threw his weight backward. The action knocked Michael off balance, and the two men slammed into the wall next to Judith's window. Michael pushed forward, and they stumbled into the center of the room.

"Drop him!" Hawkins shouted. "Let go or I'll shoot!"

McCabe couldn't turn his head, but he flicked his eyes in Hawkins' direction. The rookie had entered the room, no doubt drawn by the sound of fighting, gun raised and pointed at Michael. But since Michael stood behind McCabe, that meant Hawkins had a bead on his partner, not the killer. Hawkins held his revolver in one hand, flashlight gripped in the other, light focused on the two of them.

"Michael, let go! I'm warning you!" Hawkins sounded scared, and McCabe didn't blame him. He himself was fucking *terrified*.

McCabe continued pulling at the rope, but with no more success than before. His hands grew weak, began to shake, and his lungs felt like they were on fire. Tiny dots of light danced in front of his eyes, and he was finding it increasingly hard to think. He gazed at Hawkins and tried to send him one last unspoken message between partners.

For fuck's sake, SHOOT!

*

Michael paid no attention to Hawkins' words. He didn't even seem to be aware of the officer's presence. All of his attention was focused on choking the life out of McCabe. The officer's face had turned dark red, and wild panic shone in his eyes.

"Goddammit!" Hawkins said.

McCabe's body almost entirely blocked Michael, leaving Hawkins with only one clear target — Michael's face.

He dropped his flashlight, braced his right hand with his left, and tried not to think about how badly he was shaking.

He took the shot.

The round struck McCabe in the neck, passed through, and shattered the glass of the window behind him. The impact knocked McCabe and Michael back against the wall, and blood gushed from McCabe's wound. Michael rebounded off the wall and let go of the rope. As McCabe dropped to the floor, Michael turned and, moving with eerie mechanical grace, passed through the open side door. Hawkins fired again, but he had no idea whether or not this round had struck Michael. He ran out the bedroom's main door and into the hallway. The side door, which he'd thought led to a linen closet as well, was open. The bedroom was larger than they'd thought, and it had *two* entrances. How could they have been so damn careless?

He ran to the stairs and looked over the balcony just in time to see Michael disappear into the darkness on the first floor. He hesitated, momentarily torn. Should he pursue Michael or tend to his wounded partner? If Michael escaped, he'd undoubtedly kill more people. But if Hawkins left McCabe—the man *he'd* shot—he'd surely die. In the end, he had no choice. He ran back to the room, laid his revolver on the floor, and knelt next to McCabe.

Blood pooled on the floor around the man's head, mixing with dust. His eyes were still open, but his face was deathly pale. The rope was still wrapped around his neck, but now that Michael wasn't holding onto the ends, it had slackened, allowing McCabe to breathe. For all the good it would do. Hawkins pressed his hand to McCabe's neck wound, attempted to put pressure on it, but the man's skin was so slick with blood, it was hard for Hawkins to keep his hand in place.

McCabe spoke then, voice weak.

"Did you get him?"

Before Hawkins could answer, McCabe coughed, and blood splashed from his mouth. The flow from his neck wound increased, became a miniature crimson river, and there was nothing Hawkins could do to hold it back.

"Oh god. Hang on, McCabe. *Hang on!*"

McCabe's eyes went wide, and as Hawkins watched, something passed out of them, and they became dull and glassy. A last hiss of breath filtered from the man's lungs, and then he fell still. McCabe was dead.

Hawkins grabbed hold of McCabe, half-lifting him into an embrace. He closed his eyes.

"I'm sorry, Pete," he whispered.

He heard sirens then, a lot of them. It sounded as if the whole goddamn sheriff's department had arrived. Cars skidded to a stop, and through the broken bedroom window, he heard an older man shout, "Stay where you are! It's him! Michael, stop!" He recognized Dr. Loomis' voice, Michael's keeper for all the years he'd spent in Smith's Grove.

Hawkins gently placed McCabe back on the floor. He then grabbed his revolver, jumped to his feet, and ran out of the bedroom.

Moments later, he was out on the porch, staring at the tableau spread out before him. Seven cruisers were parked in the street, blue lights flashing in the night. Michael Myers stood at the end of the sidewalk, motionless as a mannequin, surrounded by deputies, guns drawn and trained on him.

"Holy shit! It's *him*!" Sullivan said.

"Hold it right there! *Freeze!*" Tobias shouted.

Hawkins stood on the porch, unable to make himself go any farther. All he could think about was the look of surprise on McCabe's face when the bullet had ripped through his neck.

Loomis saw Hawkins and came running toward him, spry for a man in his sixties. He stepped onto the porch and stood directly in front of Hawkins.

"Officer Hawkins, tell me what happened in there."

Hawkins said nothing.

"You *must* tell me what happened," Loomis insisted. He sounded almost frantic. "Did Michael kill? *Did he kill again?*"

No, Hawkins thought, a tear running down his cheek. *Not Michael.*

4

HADDONFIELD, ILLINOIS

Halloween Night 2018

Mick's Bar and Grill might not have been the fanciest place in town, but it *was* one of the most popular—especially on Halloween. Or rather, as the sign taped to the bar's front window proclaimed, *Hallowine, Open Mick Night*. Mick was, as one might surmise, not known for his finely honed sense of humor. Outside, the bar looked more like a VFW than a tavern; a plain, unassuming building, complete with the stars and stripes flying from a flagpole in the parking lot. As for inside... it was kind of a dump, to be honest. The wooden floor was deeply stained from years of spilled alcohol of various types, and the tables and chairs were long overdue for replacement. The tabletops were scored with graffiti—much of it filthy—and the chairs were so wobbly you felt drunk the moment you sat down. The design of the place was simple: bar on one side, stage on the other, the rest of the floor for patrons to drink, dance, and do whatever they felt like as long as it didn't bring the cops to Mick's door. Flatscreen TVs were mounted at intervals on the walls, normally for patrons to watch sports. But tonight they were tuned to *The Thing*, a horror movie about a shape-changing alien terrorizing the increasingly paranoid personnel of an isolated Antarctic base. Hallo*wine* was in full swing, and the place was packed with working-class men and women, many in costume, having a good time as they got sloppy drunk. On the stage, illuminated by lights mounted on metal stands, the identical Garcia triplets—dressed in matching mermaid outfits—sang karaoke. Well, they *tried* to sing. Mostly they kept messing up the lyrics and breaking into laughter, to the delight of their audience.

New arrivals Marcus and Vanessa Wilson made their way through the crowd, searching for an empty table. Marcus thought they were going to be out of luck, but they found a small table for two in the back, near a raised section enclosed by a wooden railing. Marcus and Vanessa were an attractive African-American couple in their late thirties, and tonight Marcus was dressed as a doctor, with a white lab coat and a stethoscope draped around his neck. Vanessa's costume was "sexy nurse"—a choice Marcus approved of wholeheartedly. He especially liked how she'd put her hair into pigtails, tied with curly black ribbons that dangled down to her bare shoulders. Cute as *hell*. He smiled as he pulled a seat out for her. She took it, but not before giving him an upset look. He sighed and sat down next to her.

"Don't be mad at me, Ness. I thought that was gonna be like a holiday pizza party with a bunch of coworkers, not a threeso—"

"Your vulgar-ass boss acted inappropriate," Vanessa said. "You gotta stand up for yourself in these situations."

He sighed again, more deeply this time. "That's right. *You're* right. Stand up for myself. First thing tomorrow morning, I'm gonna walk into work and quit that job and punch Mr. Mathis in the damn stomach. You've got me real fired up now."

She gave him a skeptical look, but she had the grace not to comment.

The table closest to theirs on the raised level was a high-top with four seats around it. Two women and a man—all white—sat there, leaving one seat empty. Marcus glanced up at them, curious. The man looked to be in his late forties, maybe early fifties, as did one of the women. The other woman was older, though, closer to seventy, he suspected. None of them wore costumes tonight. After the fiasco at Mathis' house—seriously, whose boss invites a colleague and his wife over to have sex with him?—Marcus had convinced Vanessa to come to Mick's and try to salvage something of the night. He hadn't thought about stopping at their house so they could ditch their costumes and get into regular clothes, like the people sitting next to them. Now he wished he had. After what Mathis had tried to pull, Marcus doubted Vanessa enjoyed wearing her sexy nurse outfit. Worst of all, Mathis had been the one to suggest their costumes! *They'll be ironic because you really* are *a doctor and nurse!* he'd said. *It'll be a hoot!* He wondered how long Mathis had been fantasizing about seeing Vanessa decked out as a sexy nurse? The more Marcus thought about it, the angrier he got. Maybe he really *would* punch the sonofabitch in the stomach tomorrow.

A middle-aged white man approached the group at the high-top table above Marcus and Vanessa. It seemed the fourth member of their party had returned, carrying a bottle of what looked like champagne by the neck. When he reached the table, he set it down, then took the empty seat. Marcus didn't mean to eavesdrop on their conversation, but the group was seated so close it was hard not to. Plus, it was a lot better than listening to the triplet mermaids attempting to sing, *attempting* being the operative word.

The fiftyish woman—pretty, straight brunette hair hanging past her shoulders, wearing a light gray jacket over a black top—picked up the bottle to examine it.

"Nice one, Lonnie," she said. "Champagne?"

The man who'd fetched the bottle—thick brown hair, beard that was showing signs of gray, dressed in a red flannel shirt—poured a measure in the woman's glass. They all had champagne glasses, and Marcus had a feeling this wasn't their first bottle.

As the man poured, a woman wearing a cow costume—with four plastic breasts on the front instead of an udder—tried to squeeze past their table. She bumped his elbow, which caused him to jerk to the side. A bit of champagne sailed through the air and splashed Marcus' shoulder. Marcus scowled up at the man, but he went back to pouring, seemingly unaware of what had happened.

"It's like a white peach Cristal," he said. "Very *sous bois*, which is a French term that suggests there's a vegetative mushroomy quality—"

The other man at the table—hair cut close to his scalp, severe features, dark gray sweater, black T-shirt—had been on his phone. He put it down next to his currently empty glass, and when he spoke, he sounded worried.

"Hey, guys. Laurie's not answering. Straight to voicemail again."

The woman with the shoulder-length hair was nervously picking apart a paper napkin. She wasn't paying attention to what she was doing, and some of the pieces drifted down to land in Vanessa's hair. Vanessa quickly brushed them out and glared up at the woman. She didn't notice.

"She struggles," the woman said. "Depressed then suicidal then paranoid. Every now and then I get a Christmas card—"

The man with the buzz cut interrupted. "And with all the shit happening today… I mean, two *homicides* at a gas station…"

Marcus was startled by this bit of information. He hadn't been aware of any murders. He looked to Vanessa, and she appeared just as surprised as he was.

The man with the champagne had moved on to filling the rest of his companions' glasses.

"Stop it, Tommy," he said. "We don't know if he was even on that bus. Probably just a bunch of lunatics and pedophiles."

The older woman—reddish hair, maroon cardigan worn open over an olive-green shirt— had been silent up to this point. Now she removed a metal cigarette case and a classy lighter from her purse. She took out a cigarette, placed it between her lips, and ignited the lighter.

Before she could touch the flame to the cigarette's tip, Champagne Man said, "You can't smoke in here."

Smoking Lady gave the man a sour look, but she killed the lighter's flame and put the cigarette back in the case. She then spoke, her voice raspy from decades of sucking on cancer sticks.

"Even if he *was* on it, Smith's Grove has their patients sedated and bound for transfer. He couldn't escape."

Champagne Man filled his glass last, then he set the bottle in the middle of the table and took his seat.

"Not anymore," he said. "Eighth amendment violations. It used to be an eye for an eye. Now it's political correctness. Too many lawsuits after patients swallowed their tongues and shit themselves."

Vanessa winced at the man's words.

"Can you imagine?" the brunette said. "If he did escape, Haddonfield would self-destruct."

Marcus let out a loud theatrical sigh, hoping that the four of them would take the hint and keep it down. But they kept on talking loudly.

Buzz Cut raised his head and cocked it to the side.

"I hear more sirens out there…"

Smoking Lady shook her head. "You're paranoid, Tommy. He's not coming for you. He's not trying to murder any of us."

Champagne Man drained half his glass in a single gulp. "And, brother, if he is, I'll be the one to catch him. I'm gonna put his neck in a noose. Been waiting my whole damn life. *Am I right?*"

He let out a loud braying laugh that had more than a tinge of hysteria to it.

Vanessa had had enough. *More* than enough. She gave Marcus a look that said *Do something—now!*

He remembered what she'd said when they'd first sat down. *You gotta stand up for yourself in these situations.* There had been an implied criticism in those words, and Marcus had to admit it was a valid one. He'd never been an assertive person. All his life, he'd gone along to get along. He'd go to the mat for his patients, but in his personal life he *hated* confrontations, would do whatever it took to avoid them. But he didn't like this about himself, and he sure didn't like the way Vanessa was looking at him, as if she expected him to wimp out and do nothing. Again. So he did stand up—literally. He rose from his seat and turned toward the group at the high-top table.

"Hey, guys, would you mind dialing down the volume a tad?" he said. "My wife and I are trying to watch the talent show." He tried to keep his tone pleasant. Being assertive was one thing, but he didn't want to be a dick about it.

He braced himself in anticipation of the group being defensive, maybe even belligerent. But they were genuinely apologetic.

"Sorry about that, man," Buzz Cut—Tommy—said.

The others gave Marcus embarrassed smiles.

"Appreciate it," he said. He turned to Vanessa, feeling flushed with victory. What he'd done might not have been a big deal for someone else, but for him it was huge. "I'll get us a drink. You relax."

She smiled and gave him an approving nod.

As Marcus maneuvered his way through the crowd toward the bar, he thought maybe tonight would turn out to be not so bad after all.

The sister mermaids had finished their act before Marcus had left the table, and now a man dressed as a cowboy—complete with spurs—had taken the stage. He leaned close to the mic and said, "Tonight I'm gonna recite some of my poetry for y'all."

There were some groans in the audience, along with a smattering of polite applause. Marcus tuned the man out as he began reciting. Amateur poetry was definitely not his thing.

Marcus and Vanessa weren't exactly regulars, but they came here often enough for him to recognize the bartender—Mick himself. He was a beefy white guy in his early fifties with shaggy blond hair, a goatee, and intricate sleeve tattoos. He wore an orange T-shirt with black letters on the front that said *This IS my Halloween Costume*.

Marcus' eyes were drawn to a mounted baseball

bat hanging on the wall behind the bar. Every time he saw it, he wondered why it was there. Had to be some kind of story to it, but he didn't feel as if he knew Mick well enough to ask. Maybe someday.

"Two session IPAs, please," Marcus said.

"Sure thing." Mick didn't move off right away, though. Instead, he glanced in the direction of Marcus' table. Or more precisely, to the group sitting nearby.

"Don't be bothered by those motherfuckers, Doctor. They're friends of that crazy lady that survived Michael Myers in the seventies."

"Really? No shit." He shot a look at the group before turning back to Mick. "You mean Laura Stropes?"

"*Laurie Strode*. They get up in here every year on Halloween, and you know… tears in their beers. Don't sit too close."

As Mick poured two beers for Marcus, he noticed a small cardboard donation display on the bar top— *Tips for Treatments*, it said. The display featured photos of kids with spinal muscular atrophy, and above their smiling faces in a cheerful font were the words *Love Lives Today!* Marcus paid for the beers with cash, and after leaving Mick a few dollars for a tip, he slipped what remained of the change into the donation slot. As a doctor, he could never pass by a donation display raising funds to treat medical conditions without giving something, even if it was only a little—especially when the money went to help kids. Vanessa teased him about this sometimes, told him he had a bleeding heart, but he knew she felt the same way.

He carried the mugs back to their table and sat down. The cowboy recited one more of his deathless works—titled "Ode to a Lost TV Remote." When he finished, people applauded—more enthusiastically than Marcus expected—and he stepped down from the stage. Then to Marcus' surprise, Champagne Guy came down from the raised level, glass in hand, crossed the bar, and hopped up onto the stage. He leaned into the mic and began to speak.

"Ladies and gentlemen, I'd like to introduce our next thespian. I used to bust his balls when we were kids, but now he's all grown up, and he's become a most captivating bird whistler!"

The crowd applauded and Tommy—looking more than a little reluctant—came down and joined his friend on the stage. He too brought his champagne glass, his full almost to the top. The two men gave each other a quick hug, and then Champagne Guy left the stage and headed back to their table.

Now it was Tommy's turn to lean into the mic. He looked uncomfortable as hell. Marcus had read somewhere that public speaking was people's number-one fear. He didn't know if that was true, but it sure seemed like it was in Tommy's case. The man was pale, he fidgeted nervously on stage, and when he spoke, his voice was shaky with emotion.

"Oh, jeez. Lonnie put me up to this. I'm not here to whistle, though. I'm gonna… I'm gonna tell you a story."

"Oooo! Ghosts and goblins!" someone in the crowd shouted out. This was instantly followed by someone else shouting, "Turn out the lights!"

There were scattered groans and snickers among the audience, but the lights dimmed—probably thanks to Mick—and the crowd grew quiet. Tommy took a gulp of champagne to bolster his courage and then began speaking.

"Any of you know the story of the Haddonfield Boogeyman? Too young to remember? Too drunk to give a shit?"

People shouted from the crowd.

"Bring back them mermaids!"

"Lookin' good, Tommy! Lookin' *real* good!"

"Freebird!"

"Show us your tits or get off the stage!"

Tommy closed his eyes, as if to center himself, and then took a deep breath. Something about his manner got through to the crowd, and everyone grew quiet once more. When the room was silent, Tommy opened his eyes and began talking. He was nervous at first, but his voice grew stronger and more confident as he went on.

"Forty years ago… a madman escaped from a mental hospital after being institutionalized for fifteen years. It was the night before Halloween. Three innocent teenage girls were walking home from Haddonfield High. They had sightings of a ghostly figure creeping through the town. A man in a white mask—or was it more than a man?—watching them. And before the night was over, three people would be murdered in this very neighborhood. And in the house next door, a babysitter and a young boy and young girl were brutally attacked by this stalker with a power beyond any mortal man. My name is Tommy Doyle. And I was that young boy."

The bar remained silent for a moment, as if the patrons had no idea how to react to Tommy's words. Finally, there was a smattering of applause which Tommy acknowledged with a brief nod. He then spoke once more.

"Tonight, join me in commemorating the victims and the survivors of Michael Myers."

He reached for one of the stage lights and turned it to illuminate his friends sitting at their table.

"Lindsey Wallace. Her babysitter Annie Brackett was executed."

The fiftyish woman with the brunette hair stood. She nodded to Tommy and wiped a tear from her eye.

"Marion Chambers. A nurse at Smith's Grove, the hospital from which the Boogeyman escaped. Survived an assault."

Smoking Lady stood, chin raised almost defiantly, as if she was daring the audience to judge her. Tommy continued.

"Lonnie Elam. Ghost hunter and historian of the legend of the Boogeyman. Escaped a face-to-face encounter."

Champagne Man stood, glass in hand. He gave Tommy a smile and a wink.

Tommy went on, emotional now, fighting back tears. "It's Halloween night in Haddonfield. When terror is supposed to be fun. When we hide behind masks and pretend we aren't what we are. I'm an astronaut, King Arthur, Tarantula Man. You're a werewolf, a skeleton… or a maniac in a white mask."

Marcus had gotten so caught up in listening to Tommy's story that he was startled when Vanessa reached over to take his hand. Her attention was also fixed on Tommy, and there were tears in her eyes as well.

"I've lived my life in fear," Tommy said, "and watched others in this once-peaceful town plagued in different ways. Is he real? Who knows? Who's next? Maybe not tonight and maybe not tomorrow, but the Boogeyman's coming for me. He's coming for *you*. But he's not going to get us. Not this time. Because we will *never* succumb to fear. *Never!*"

He shouted this last word, and the crowd went crazy, clapping, cheering, crying. As Tommy stepped off the stage, patrons rose from their tables to shake his hand or clap him on the back. Marcus and Vanessa, without consulting, stood, turned toward Tommy's companions, and reached out to shake hands with Marion and Lonnie, the two nearest to them.

Tommy raised his glass and turned his gaze to the ceiling. He didn't shout his next words, but Marcus had no trouble hearing them.

"This is for you, Laurie! Wherever you are!"

5

At that precise moment, Laurie was sitting in the bed of a pickup with her daughter and granddaughter. The driver was hauling ass, and Karen and Allyson braced Laurie to keep her from being jostled too badly. Laurie wore a khaki-colored tank top and jeans, and Karen—still wearing that godawful Christmas sweater she'd donned as a fuck-you to Halloween— held Laurie's overshirt in her hand, pressing it to her mother's stomach. At first, Laurie was puzzled why Karen would be doing something like this, but when she saw the worry and fear on her daughter's face, it came back to her. She'd been stabbed. In the gut.

By Michael.

Michael, who was right now riding a fiery—and she hoped excruciatingly painful—express elevator to hell. The thought brought a smile to her face. Now that Michael was dead, she could rest. For the first time in forty fucking years. Who knows? Maybe she'd rest forever. She thought she might like that. Yes, she might like that very much. She sighed contentedly and closed her eyes.

"C'mon, Mom," Karen said, voice frantic. "Stay

with us… We'll be at the hospital soon."

Let me go, baby, she thought. *You're safe. Allyson's safe. And Michael will soon be nothing more than charred and blacked bones—if he isn't already. My work is done, and I just want to sleep…*

She could feel herself slipping away, and she was ready to give herself over to the great dark, slide into the oblivion of its shadowy waters gently, peacefully…

She was almost gone when a sound—distant, shrill—cut through her cocoon of tranquility as violently as Michael had sliced into her gut. She tried to shut out the noise, told herself that whatever it was, it wasn't important. Nothing was important, not anymore. But the sound grew louder, louder, and she heard Allyson say, "Oh no, what are they doing?"

Laurie instantly returned to full awareness. Her eyes snapped open in time to see flashing lights as a pair of firetrucks roared by, sirens blaring.

Laurie leaned forward, as if by doing so she'd be heard more easily. The movement caused her own miniature fire to blaze in her wounded stomach, but she ignored the pain and called out to the firefighters, shouting with surprising strength for someone who seconds ago had been on the verge of checking out for good.

"Let it burn. *Let it burn!*"

*

Laurie must've passed out after that, because the next thing she knew, she was being helped out of the back of the pickup by a pair of nurses and strapped onto a gurney. Karen and Allyson—who still gripped the bloodstained knife Laurie had given her—stood off to the side, watching with concern. The driver of the pickup had pulled in front of the ER entrance, and Haddonfield Memorial Hospital loomed over her, all six stories of it. As she gazed up at the building, and the stars and full moon beyond it, she remembered that night forty years ago when she'd been brought here after Michael's attack. Had there been a full moon that night? Funny, but she couldn't recall. She'd spent some time here recovering from her wounds, and after leaving, she'd only returned once: to deliver Karen. She decided to focus on the latter memory—her very best one—now. It gave her comfort.

There were three sheriff's department cruisers parked near the ER entrance, and for a moment Laurie wondered why they were there. Then she realized—Michael had been busy tonight before she'd caught him in her trap. Who knew how many people he'd hurt or killed before coming to her house?

The pair of nurses rushed Laurie into the emergency room, Karen and Allyson following close behind. It was busy inside, people sitting in the waiting area, standing at the reception desk, or just milling around, as if uncertain what to do.

"Another victim!" one of the nurses shouted. "This one's alive!"

A doctor over by the reception desk turned around and rushed over to the gurney. The woman—tall, thin, curly black hair, probably a decade younger than

Laurie—examined her with efficient speed. As she did so, she gave a running tally of Laurie's injuries.

"Patient is semi-conscious with at least one severe stab wound, left anterior chest, possibly penetrating. Multiple contusions, possible fracture in her left ankle, lost a lot of blood."

The doctor leaned over and looked at Laurie. She had a kind face, Laurie decided. A good asset in her line of work.

"Ma'am, can you tell me your name?" the doctor asked.

Laurie tried to reply, but she simply didn't have the strength. Instead, she gave the doctor a weak smile, closed her eyes, and let unconsciousness take her.

*

While the doctor examined Laurie, Karen hurried over to speak to the clerk behind the reception desk. She was glad to have something to do. Attending to the mundane details of checking her mother into the hospital would help her focus on something other than her own emotions.

"Her name is Laurie Strode," Karen said. When the woman—thirtyish, African-American, with a round face and soft brown eyes—showed no sign of recognition, Karen repeated her mother's last name, louder and with emphasis. "*Strode*."

An older man in a security guard's uniform sat in a chair close to the reception desk, staring down at his phone. When he heard Karen say her mother's last name, he looked up and turned toward her. She wasn't surprised. For good or ill, her mother was a celebrity in Haddonfield.

Karen went on, voice strained. Her emotional control was failing. "She was attacked. Multiple stab wounds. Possible concussion. She needs *help*."

Karen was a therapist, not a physician, but she knew if Laurie didn't get medical attention ASA-fucking-P, she wasn't going to make it.

The desk clerk gave Karen a sympathetic smile and started typing on her computer.

"They're taking her back now, ma'am."

Karen turned to see the doctor and nurses wheel her mother's gurney through a set of double wooden doors marked AUTHORIZED STAFF ONLY. An instant later, her mother was gone. She looked up at Allyson, who, suddenly left alone, stood there for a moment, as if unsure what to do next. She gripped her grandmother's bloody shirt—evidently the nurses had given it to her before taking Laurie back—but she no longer held the bloodstained knife Laurie had given her. *She must've wrapped the knife in the shirt,* Karen thought. *Smart.* Allyson's expression was blank, as if she was in shock, and she was covered in so much blood that she looked like she needed medical care as badly as her grandmother did. Karen figured she probably looked just as bad, if not worse, since she'd been the one tending to her mother's wound during the frantic ride to the hospital. Allyson started walking toward Karen, and she reached out as Allyson drew near, intending to put her arm around her shoulder, to give comfort and receive it in turn. But at the last instant Allyson veered off to avoid the contact. Instead, she took an empty seat in the waiting area and looked down at the floor so she wouldn't have to meet her mother's eyes.

Karen was hurt by this rejection, but she understood. For Allyson's entire life, Karen had told her that her grandmother wasn't mentally well, that she suffered from untreated PTSD, and had wasted her life preparing for an attack which would never come. Yes, Michael Myers had nearly killed her. But the key word there was *nearly*. Laurie had survived. She should've gone on with her life, tried to make something of herself. But instead she became the crazy old woman who lived alone in what amounted to a survivalist compound, taking target practice on featureless white mannequins whose smooth, white faces resembled Michael's mask. Karen was surprised her mother hadn't bought dark coveralls to put on the mannequins to complete the resemblance.

Karen had done everything she could over the years to keep Laurie away from Allyson. She'd told herself that she hadn't wanted her daughter to become contaminated by her mother's sickness, but at least part of the reason was to punish Laurie for being such a shitty mother to her. She'd been raised to be terrified all the time, to continuously look over her shoulder because one day the Boogeyman would be there, large gleaming knife in hand, ready to rip her to shreds. Maybe things would've been better if Karen's father had been around. Maybe, just maybe, he would've been a stabilizing influence on Laurie. But her father hadn't been in the picture. In fact, she had no idea who her actual father was. Laurie had been married—and divorced—twice, but neither of those men had been Karen's father; at least that's what Laurie told her. Maybe Laurie's... *intensity* had driven off Karen's father. Or maybe he'd been just as unstable as her mother, and his leaving had been a good thing. She'd likely never know, and she'd long ago made her peace with that. But that didn't mean she didn't resent the hell out of her mother because of it, and for brainwashing her into believing the world was a malicious, chaotic, and above all dangerous place.

Death gets us all in the end, Laurie had once told her. *But some of us it comes for personally.*

Tonight Allyson had seen for herself that her grandmother wasn't deluded in her belief that Michael Myers would return to finish what he'd started forty years ago. She'd had a front row seat to the goddamn horror show, during which Michael had claimed her own father—Karen's husband—as one of his victims.

Ray... Jesus, I'm so, so sorry...

In Allyson's view, if Karen had just believed Laurie, had *listened*, they'd have all been better prepared for this night. And then maybe, just maybe, her father would've survived.

Karen finished giving the clerk the data she needed to check Laurie in. Then she slowly, calmly walked toward the nearest women's room. When she saw her reflection in the mirror over the sinks, she was horrified. There was blood all over her! Her *mother's* blood.

She grabbed a handful of paper towels from a metal dispenser on the wall, then turned on the tap to wet one. When she raised it to her face to begin cleaning herself, her hand froze. She stared at her reflection for several moments, trying to tell herself that nothing that had happened tonight had been her fault. Michael Myers—the goddamn freak psychopath—was responsible, no one else.

She couldn't make herself believe it, though, and she began sobbing.

*

Allyson felt like a shit for not going to her mom, but after everything that had happened in the last few hours—Oscar dead, her *dad* dead, both at the hands of Michael-fucking-Myers—she needed some time alone, to process. But that wasn't the whole truth. Right now, she didn't want to look at her mother, let alone talk to her. She knew it wasn't fair to blame her for what had happened tonight, even partially, but she couldn't help it. Sure, in the end, the three of them—mother, daughter, and granddaughter— had stood together as a family against Michael and kicked his ass. But how much more effective might they have been if her mother had allowed the three of them to be a *real* family all these years? Would they have been even stronger, maybe strong enough to take out Michael before he killed her dad?

She became aware that people were staring at

her—no surprise considering her white shirt was almost completely covered with blood—and she was glad she'd had the presence of mind to hide the blade by wrapping it in her grandmother's bloody shirt. She held the bundle on her lap, but she wasn't sure why she'd kept the knife. Her grandmother had told her to hold onto it when they'd first gotten in the back of the pickup, and she supposed she wanted to honor Laurie's wish. Hopefully not her *last* wish. There'd been too much death this night already. Far too much.

The desk clerk that her mother had spoken to came over to her. She held a small disposable cup of water, and she smiled at Allyson as she offered it to her. Allyson looked around for her mother, but didn't see her. She figured she'd probably gone back to check on her grandmother. She took the water, grateful, but she didn't return the clerk's smile. She didn't have it in her right now.

"Ma'am, you really should let a nurse look at you," the clerk said, concerned. "All that blood…"

Allyson didn't mean to snap at the woman, but she couldn't help it. "*I'm fine.* Just save my grandmother so this nightmare will finally be over."

If the woman took offense at Allyson's attitude, she didn't show it. Allyson figured she was used to seeing people in all kinds of emotional states in her line of work. The woman just smiled, turned, and began walking back toward the reception desk. As she went, she shook her head slowly, and Allyson heard her repeat, "All that blood."

Allyson downed the water in a single gulp. Her

throat was raw from screaming and from inhaling smoke from the flames as her grandmother's home burned. The water helped, but not much. She was about to get up and find a drinking fountain so she could get a refill when an old man in a security guard's uniform came walking toward her. When he reached her, he stopped and regarded her for a moment. He didn't look at the blood on her clothes. Instead, he looked directly into her eyes, as if assessing her.

"It's him again, isn't it?" the man asked. "Michael Myers."

Allyson didn't know who this guy was, and her first impulse was to ask him to leave her the hell alone. But she saw sadness in his gaze, along with anger, and she thought that if he couldn't know exactly how she felt right now, he came damn close. And so she answered him.

"It was."

She thought of her grandmother's home. The violence, the blood, the fire... It seemed like it had all happened a lifetime ago, but it probably hadn't been more than twenty minutes.

The guard frowned. "What do you mean, *was*?"

"She did it. My grandmother. She killed him." There was pride in Allyson's voice as she responded. Laurie Strode—her "crazy" grandmother—had not only been proven right in her obsessive preparation for Michael's return, she'd gotten the motherfucker in the end. She remembered speaking to her grandmother in the high school parking lot earlier, when she'd given Allyson the fee she'd collected from the two podcast journalists who'd briefly interviewed her. When the conversation ended and Laurie headed for her car, Allyson had told her to "Just get over it," meaning get over *him*—Michael— and start living life for herself. At the time she'd thought she was trying to help her grandmother, but now she knew she'd let her frustration with the endless emotional conflict between her mom and her grandmother get to her. And she was ashamed.

Her words seemed to stun the guard. His eyes widened with disbelief, and he actually took a step back, as if the news had struck him with physical force. He then spoke in a voice thick with emotion.

"He murdered my daughter Annie."

She looked down at his nametag. The man's name was *Brackett*. It seemed familiar, but she couldn't quite... And then it came to her. *Leigh* Brackett. He'd been sheriff in Haddonfield in 1978, during Michael's original killings. His daughter had been one of the girls the Boogeyman had slaughtered that night. She felt a sudden connection with this man. They'd both lost someone they loved to that madman.

"We burnt him alive in her basement," she said. "Michael Myers is dead."

Brackett's mouth stretched into a slow, satisfied smile.

"I would have loved to watch him fry," he said wistfully.

Me too, she thought. *Me too*.

6

Neil Benton was an eleven-year veteran of the Haddonfield Fire Department, and during that time, he'd been on the scene of more house fires than he could remember. But one thing that he'd never gotten used to was how goddamn *fast* fire could spread. It only took thirty seconds for a small flame to become a life-threatening blaze, and residents had two to three minutes to get out before it was too late. That time limit was for modern structures, though. Because synthetic materials were used in their construction, they burned much faster and released deadlier chemicals into the air. Structures thirty years or older used natural materials that burned more slowly, giving residents additional time to escape: between fourteen and seventeen minutes. When every second counted, that was a *huge* difference. So when the call came in that Laurie Strode's house was on fire, the first thing Benton thought was that the woman had lived there for almost forty years— or so the gossip around town went—which meant her place should be a slow burner. And *that* meant if anyone was trapped inside, there was a decent chance of getting them out alive.

When the two engines arrived on the scene, flames were visible from outside the house, surging from windows and licking at the roof. The firefighters immediately implemented an aggressive attack strategy, blasting jets of water onto the blaze. Their goal wasn't to extinguish the fire immediately—that would take time—but rather to cool the burning debris inside and limit oxygen's ability to feed the flames, giving an entry team the opportunity to go in and conduct a search for survivors.

Benton was part of that team, along with Hudson, Alvarado, and Zhang, and they suited up while the hosemen sprayed the house. Benton and Hudson would go in first, while Alvarado and Zhang remained outside, ready to relieve them when they got tired or, if they got in trouble, rescue them. The team's equipment consisted of fire helmets, turnout pants and jackets, self-contained breathing apparatus, thick leather gloves, rubber boots with reinforced steel in the toes, radios, and personal alert safety systems. All four also carried Benton's favorite friend, the Halligan bar—a multipurpose tool designed for forcible entry. The Halligan resembled a crowbar, with a claw on one end, and a blade and pick on the other. Its design was simple, elegant, and extremely effective. Benton thought of it as an oversized Swiss army knife for firefighters.

The hosemen soon managed to beat back the flames issuing from the windows on the house's left side, so that's where Benton's team chose to make their entry. As they approached the burning structure, the department's smaller fire truck arrived. This vehicle carried auxiliary tools such as ground ladders, spreaders, cutters, and rams, and that crew would unload them while the others continued the initial assault.

The entry team stepped onto the porch and made their way to their chosen window. Most of the glass had been shattered when the flashover occurred inside, and Benton used his Halligan bar to knock out the remaining shards to make it safe—or at least safer—to climb through. He gave Hudson a look to check if he was ready. The man nodded, and Benton began climbing through the window, moving as fast as his heavy protective gear would allow. He had a ritual whenever he walked into hell, one that he'd never shared with his fellow smoke eaters. He would close his eyes—only for a second—and silently make a promise to his wife Miriam and young son Joey, a promise that consisted of three simple words. *See you soon.*

And then he was inside.

Benton moved through the house with confidence. A thermal-imaging camera was mounted on the side of his mask, and a small screen was located inside, near the eye.

Benton turned back to the window in order to assist Hudson if necessary, but the man made it through by himself. Benton then made his first assessment of the scene. The flames in here—a side room, he thought, maybe one used as a home office—were scattered, thanks to the dousing the hosemen had given the room. But those that remained were still going strong. There was a lot of white in the thermal image, indicating the fire was burning damn hot—hotter than he would have expected at this point, especially after the room had undergone a good soaking. And he thought he knew why that was.

The firefighters' radios—set on an open two-way channel—were worn on a strap under their turnout coats. All Benton had to do to be heard by his companions was speak aloud. No need to fumble awkwardly with handheld controls.

"We've got a gas-fed fire in here," Benton said.

A moment later, a voice came over the radio. "Copy that. Utilities are being shut down." And then a few seconds later, "Assignment complete. Utilities are disengaged."

"Good deal," Benton said. "Let's get to it, Hudson."

The two men walked out of the room together, then split up. Hudson moved into the main living area, and Benton started toward the kitchen. Both periodically called out to any potential survivors. *Anyone here? Where are you? Are you hurt?* But they received no replies. Water streamed from large cracks in the ceiling, falling like intermittent rain. This place was old, and who knew how long ago the roofing had been replaced? Plus, the fire had already caused a lot of damage before they'd got here. By now, it had surely gotten into the spaces between the walls, floors, and ceilings, weakening the entire structure. The house was a goner for sure. Benton hoped the same couldn't be said for any occupants still inside, but given the state of the fire, he feared they'd arrived too late. Still, he and Hudson wouldn't leave until they'd checked every inch of the place. If there was a chance—no matter how small—that someone in here still lived, he intended to do everything in his power to save them.

The kitchen was in better condition than he'd expected. Flames still burned, but the ceiling had partially collapsed, allowing a great deal more water to stream inside. The water had extinguished the worst of the fire here, though there was still a lot of smoke. He caught glimpses of what the room looked like: cabinets, shelves, countertops, walls— all blackened, making it look as if the kitchen had been constructed entirely from charcoal. Water pooled on the floor, but he wasn't worried about slipping. The soles of his boots had been designed to provide greater traction to allow firefighters to move more easily on wet surfaces.

"Anyone in here?" he called out. He listened, waited, heard nothing but water streaming from the ceiling.

As he moved farther into the kitchen, the smoke cleared a bit, and he saw a large, rectangular-shaped object lying on the floor. At first, he didn't know what it was, but then it came to him. It was a kitchen island, one that had been knocked over on its side. Had there been an explosion in here? A lot of home fires started in the kitchen. Maybe something had gone wrong with the gas stove, and ka-boom! That *could* account for the island's position, although the stove looked intact, and from what he could tell, there weren't any other signs of an explosion in here. There was a square opening in the floor—a basement entrance, he assumed—although why in the hell someone would put one in the middle of the kitchen like this, he... He broke off his train of thought and frowned. Were those metal *bars* across the entrance? What the fuck was—

Benton didn't feel the floor give way beneath him. One moment he was staring at what looked like the door to some kind of goddamn cage, and the next he was lying on his back amidst a jumble of debris, looking up at the kitchen ceiling, which was now much farther away from him than it had been an instant ago. The impact had stunned him and he wasn't sure what had happened at first. But then he realized: the kitchen floor had suffered both fire *and* water damage, rendering it no stronger than tissue paper. A goddamn rookie mistake. Water streamed over the edge of the hole he'd created, pattering all around him, as if he were the centerpiece of some fucked-up kind of fountain, a statue titled *Dumbass Firefighter*.

The wind had been knocked out of him when he'd fallen, and he tried to take a deep breath. He could draw in air, but it was difficult, and more, the air smelled... off. He realized then that he wasn't getting any O2. The fall had damaged his tank somehow, or maybe the mask's connection to it

74

had been severed. Whichever the case, he was now breathing the air in the basement, and that was bad. Fires released deadly chemicals into the atmosphere, chief among them carbon monoxide and hydrogen cyanide. More people died from inhaling these gases during a housefire than perished in the flames themselves. Benton was in trouble—big time.

He tried to sit up, hoping he might be able to make a quick field repair to his SCBA unit, good enough to keep him breathing until he could get out of here, but his back screamed in agony when he attempted to move. Cold terror jolted through him. Had he broken his back? Was he paralyzed? On the verge of panic, he tried wiggling his toes in his boots. They moved, and that came as such a relief that he almost laughed. He was hurt, sure, but not as seriously as he could've been. He'd maintained his grip on the Halligan bar when he'd fallen. Maybe he could use it to brace himself as he got up? No, better to remain still and not risk injuring himself any further. He spoke into his radio.

"Mayday, mayday, mayday!" he said, and one of the captains outside responded.

"Radio silence. We have a mayday alert."

Now that the comm channel was cleared, Benton went on, pausing between sentences to catch his breath.

"This is firefighter Benton with Engine Eight. There has been a structural collapse. I entered with attack team on Alpha Beta side. My air supply has been compromised. PASS alarm has been activated."

The captain spoke once more. "Central, we have a firefighter down. RIT Team One commence rescue."

"Roger that," Alvarado said.

Then the captain added, "Hold tight, Benton."

Benton didn't see that he had much choice but to do as the captain suggested. Hudson's voice came over the radio then.

"I've found zero survivors. I'm heading your way."

Hudson would be here soon, and Zhang and Alvarado would be close behind. All he had to do now was lie here and breathe as shallowly as possible. With nothing else to do, he took in his surroundings.

He was in a basement, a small one. More like a storage area, really. There was a set of wooden stairs—or rather, the charred remnants of them— leading down from the kitchen. The metal bars he'd seen covered the entrance to the stairs, making it impossible for anyone to get in or out. Not that anyone needed stairs, now that there was a gigantic hole in the kitchen floor. There were shelves set against brick walls, and while flames still flickered here and there, the water streaming between the bars had taken care of the worst of the fire. A corrugated metal door was set into the wall directly in front of him. It resembled the sort of door you might find in a self-storage facility, except there was an image painted on it. Fire had blackened the metal, making it difficult to tell for sure, but the image looked like… flowers. Green stems, red blooms. It struck him as the sort of thing a child might paint. Almost as if he or she had wanted to bring a piece of the outside world down here, since there weren't any windows.

Benton was musing on what might be behind that door—and whether this mini-basement had been designed to be a shelter of some sort—when the door began to roll upward. Benton's pulse picked up speed. There *was* a survivor! Someone had managed to hide down here and...

His thoughts slammed to a halt when the door finished rising and he saw who—or more precisely *what*—had been concealed in the small recessed area behind it. A tall, pale-featured man dressed in soot-stained coveralls, strange ivory face darkened from smoke, hair singed. He was missing the last two fingers from his left hand, and the wounds looked fresh.

The man didn't move right away. He stood rigid, so absolutely still he barely seemed human, as he observed the downed firefighter before him. Benton had the sense that this apparition, this demonic *thing* that seemed born of smoke and flame, was studying him the same way a scientist might study an intriguing new type of insect. But then Benton realized the man—was that a mask he was wearing?—wasn't looking at him so much, as what he held gripped tight in his hand. The Halligan bar.

The man started forward, and Benton sat up, gritting his teeth as his injured back exploded with pain. He intended to rise to his feet and defend himself, but he was unable to move fast enough. The masked man tore the Halligan bar from Benton's hand. He looked at the Halligan for a moment, as if appreciating its design, then he turned back to Benton. The firefighter tried to stand, but the ivory-faced man kicked him hard in the chest, knocking him back onto the floor. Benton tried to draw in a breath, but his ribs hurt like hell, and his lungs were on fire.

The ivory-faced man spun the Halligan bar around in his hand so the spiked end was on top, and Benton—knowing what was coming—shouted a wordless cry of horror. And then the man brought the spike down onto Benton's protective face mask. The plastic shattered, but the tip of the spike only scratched the skin on his nose. The ivory-faced man withdrew the Halligan and made ready for a second strike. As the spike descended toward Benton's unprotected face, he had time for one last thought: he wondered if his son had enjoyed Halloween this year. He hoped so.

And then the Halligan found its mark, and he was gone.

*

Hudson had almost reached the kitchen when Benton's yell came blasting over the radio. The sound startled him so much, it almost made him piss his pants. He'd never heard anyone so scared before, and he *never* would have imagined Benton could be that frightened. Benton was as tough as they came. Hudson had worked alongside the man for years, and they'd walked into more dangerous situations together than he could remember. The man wasn't a cowboy—he didn't race into fires because he wanted people to think he was a hero. Benton was a pro. He knew the risks, he accepted them, and more than that, he *respected* them.

But now Benton sounded fucking *terrified*, and Hudson feared the worst for his friend. Had he been impaled on a sharp piece of wood when he'd fallen? Was he trapped with no way to escape the flames drawing ever closer to him? His O2 wasn't working. Had he breathed in too much toxic gas and wasn't thinking straight, was maybe hallucinating? Hudson didn't know, but he knew Benton needed help, and he needed it now.

The flames in the kitchen were mostly out, thanks to the water streaming from open areas in the ceiling, but a lot of smoke remained and visibility was poor. Hudson wanted to run into the kitchen and start shouting for Benton, but he forced himself to move slowly. The last thing he wanted to do was accidently fall into the goddamn hole and land on top of his friend, potentially injuring him further. He kept his gaze focused downward as he slowly made his way into the room, and the smoke cleared enough that he was able to make out the edge of the hole. He headed straight for it and peered inside, careful not to get too close. There was smoke down there, too, so it was hard to tell, but it looked like the debris from the floor collapse had landed in a pile large enough to climb up onto. Which meant Benton could get out—with a little help.

Hudson knelt at the edge of the hole, placed his Halligan bar on the floor, and reached downward.

"Take my hand!" he shouted.

No reply. Hudson tried again.

"Benton! Take my hand! Take my hand! *Now!*"

Hudson stretched his hand farther, willed his buddy to take hold of it.

What if he's too hurt to move?

But then Hudson felt a hand wrap around his, the grip so strong it was painful, and he laughed. Benton was a tough old bastard, all right. Hudson slowly stood, pulling Benton up through the hole and onto the kitchen floor. At first, he couldn't see his friend due to the smoke, but it cleared some, and he saw the face of a man wearing a horrifying mask.

The masked man looked to be in poor condition: soot all over his clothes, dark smudges on the chalky skin of his face, hair singed close to the scalp. And then Benton noticed one more thing—the man was holding a Halligan bar, presumably Benton's, gripped in his right hand. Hudson glanced at his own Halligan, lying on the floor where he'd left it. It might as well have been a million miles away. He looked back to the chalk-faced man just in time to see the spiked end of Benton's Halligan come streaking toward his face.

*

Hudson is dead before the Shape throws him into the hole, and, just as Hudson feared, his body lands on top of Benton's with a dull thud. The Shape forgets about them both the instant their corpses are out of his sight. In his world, there is only meat, and meat is divided into two types: *that which moves and that which doesn't*. Once he has transformed the former into the latter, it ceases to exist for him.

The Shape leaves the kitchen, walking swiftly. The smoke is too thick for him to see well—plus it makes his good eye water—but he doesn't need vision to find his way through the house... *Her* house. He is a thing of darkness, and wherever there is an absence of light, for whatever reason, he is home.

The air is hot, and breathing it sears his nasal passages, burns his throat, makes his lungs ache. These sensations are of no importance, and thus he ignores them. Water streams from cracks in the ceiling, but it does not occur to him to question why it is raining inside a house. Inside *Her* house. But he does alter his path so that he walks beneath the water, allowing it to cool him. Protect him.

Along the way, he encounters Alvarado and Zhang. He makes quick work of them.

He avoids the flames still burning in the living room and reaches the front door. He doesn't put his hand on the knob—thanks to the fire, it's far too hot to touch. Instead, he uses the Halligan bar to force the door. Wood cracks, splinters, and when the door has been weakened enough, he breaks it open with a single, savage kick. He then steps onto the porch, stops, and surveys the scene before him. Flames blaze through the windows on either side of the door, framing him in orange-white. Water streams down from the roof, forming a curtain in front of him. He sees parked fire engines, firefighters spraying water onto the house, smoke everywhere, like thick fog.

The men are so intent on their work that at first they don't notice him. The Shape sees a pair of hosemen, raining water onto the burning house, a firefighter holding an axe, another a chainsaw. There are other men as well, at least a dozen, but these four are the closest. He will begin with them.

The firefighters stop what they are doing, and—as if sharing some kind of primitive warning instinct—turn in unison to look at the Shape. They stare at each other for a moment, these men and this thing on the porch, then the firefighter with the chainsaw starts it, and the engine roars to life, a signal that battle is about to begin. The Shape tightens his grip on the Halligan bar and steps off the porch.

Five minutes later, the Shape is the only one on the Strode property still breathing.

7

Lonnie stood at the bar, watching as Mick served a couple dressed as zombie versions of Elvis and Marilyn. *Dead celebrities*, he thought. *Can't go wrong with the classics.* Marcus and Vanessa came to fetch a fresh bottle for the table. Lonnie gave them both a smile and a nod, and when Mick gave the couple the wine, they paid, smiled at Lonnie, then headed back to the table. He'd join them in a few minutes, but right now he was enjoying standing here and watching the talent show. On stage, a ventriloquist and his dummy were singing the old novelty song "Shaving Cream," the dummy messing up his lines. The crowd laughed and applauded their antics, but not Lonnie. Ventriloquist dummies were just too damn creepy.

He felt good. Relaxed. And that was only partially due to the amount of alcohol he'd had this evening. This night—when he and his fellow survivors got together for their yearly booze-soaked group therapy session—was one of the things that kept him going. And when Tommy had gotten on stage and told his story… that had been powerful stuff, cathartic in the best possible way. He only wished Laurie could've been here tonight. He didn't like the idea of her holed up in that fortress of hers right now, alone and brooding. Maybe he'd stop by tomorrow, see how she was. Assuming she'd answer the gate intercom when he got there. With Laurie, you never knew.

Not that he had any room to criticize how Laurie chose to live her life. None of them did. Yeah, they'd all survived encounters of one kind or another with Michael Myers, but each of them had lived pretty fucked-up lives ever since. Marion had continued working as a nurse, although not at Smith's Grove. She'd gotten the hell out of there as soon as she could after Michael's original rampage. These days she did in-home healthcare for the elderly and disabled. She'd never been the warmest person, but she'd grown cold and brittle over the decades, developing a shell to protect her from the world and its evils. She'd never been married, had no kids, had no friends aside from her fellow survivors. She didn't talk much, and he had the sense she was burdened by untold secrets. She continued to smoke even though she knew how bad it was for her. Lonnie thought she did so as a slow means of committing suicide, not that he'd ever tell her that.

Lindsey was a florist, with her own shop in town called Flowerworks. She said she liked flowers because they represented both life *and* death. *We grow them until they're at their most beautiful*, she'd once told him, *then we cut them from their roots and put their corpses in water to slow down the inevitable process of decay. That's how existence is, right? We're all dying, and we just do what we can to postpone the big event*. She'd had two failed marriages, suffered from extreme anxiety—for which she was highly medicated—and had a college-age son in California who rarely called her.

Tommy... In some ways, he was the worst of them, including Laurie. Ever since the night that Laurie saved him and Lindsey from Michael, he'd had difficulty controlling his anger. *A headshrinker once told me that my real problem is redirected fear. I attack before I can be attacked*, he'd once told Lonnie. He had a hair-trigger temper, was quick to take offense at any perceived slight, no matter how mild, and he could be irritable, impatient, and impulsive. He'd gotten into a lot of fights in high school, and even more after he'd graduated. He drifted from job to job, unable to hold on to one for any length of time without blowing his top at someone—usually his boss—or taking a swing at them. He'd gone through a series of relationships, but they never lasted long either. No one wanted to be the partner of someone with such a volatile emotional state. He wasn't trustworthy, wasn't *safe*. Lonnie had no idea if Tommy had ever been physically abusive with any of his partners, and he'd never asked. He did know that Tommy had been in therapy on and off since his late twenties, and while he'd picked up a lot of psychological tools to help him deal with his anger, it was by no means fully under control. He was so obsessed with Michael and all things Halloween that he'd gotten a tattoo of a Thorn rune on his left arm, and when he was anxious, he rubbed his hand over it subconsciously.

And Lonnie? He'd taken the most clichéd route. He'd become obsessed with bizarre crimes and the paranormal, begun visiting sites of infamous murders and investigating reported hauntings. He didn't need a therapist to tell him that by doing these things, he was trying to understand how something like Michael Myers could possibly exist in this world, and through that understanding, gain some measure of control over the fear which had lain coiled inside him like a venomous serpent since the night he'd encountered Michael. He'd started writing about his experiences, first in articles, then later in books. Eventually, he'd written the definitive account of Michael's murders, simply titled *The Boogeyman*. It hadn't become a *New York Times* bestseller, but it had done all right.

His interest—some might say obsession—with the dark and macabre had branded him a weirdo in Haddonfield. Still, he'd gotten married, and Cameron had been born. The boy's mother couldn't take living with a man who was more interested in death than life—and who had a tendency to drink a little too much, a little too often—and eventually they had split up. She'd taken a job in St. Louis, and Cam had opted to stay with him to finish high school in Haddonfield. Lonnie had done his best not to influence Cam's decision, but he'd been damn glad when the boy had told him he was staying in town. Lonnie loved his son dearly, and he believed Cam loved him, even if he did find his old man's profession to be more than a little embarrassing.

Mick finished serving zombie Elvis and Marilyn, and Lonnie raised his hand to catch the man's attention. But before Mick could come over, Lonnie's phone vibrated in his pants pocket, and he waved the man away. He took out his phone, checked the display, and saw it said *Cameron*.

Think of the devil, he thought, and answered.

"Hey there, Bonnie. You and Clyde need a ride?"

Cameron's words came out in a frantic rush. "Dad, you gotta come get me. I'm at the park near the school. A cop was attacked."

Lonnie heard another man's voice in the background. "Do you know where you are right now? I'm going to touch your leg and you let me know if it hurts. Stay with us."

Who the fuck was that? An EMT? An attack, Cameron had said. A cop. Lonnie felt a sudden rush of fear for his son. He didn't know what the hell was going on, but Cam needed him, and that was all that mattered.

"On my way."

*

Sheriff Barker sat in the passenger seat of his cruiser as Detective Graham—who was performing chauffeur duties at the moment—raced up the driveway toward Laurie Strode's house, lights flashing and siren whooping. A squad of cruisers followed in their wake, lights and sirens going as well. *We must make a hell of a sight*, Barker thought. *Like we're headed off to war.* He supposed in a way they were.

Deputies on scene at Haddonfield Memorial had called in a report that Michael Myers had attacked Strode in her home, and while the specifics weren't clear, evidently the woman had set fire to her whole goddamn house in order to stop the masked killer. *A badass move,* Barker thought. *Batshit crazy, but badass.* Fire engines had been dispatched to deal with the blaze before anyone realized Myers was involved, but no one at the fire station had been able to get in touch with the crew since they'd left. Hence the reason why Barker had ordered every man and woman in the department to accompany him out to the Strode compound, as people in town liked to refer to it. He knew they'd be walking into a grade-A shitstorm, and he wanted to bring the full force of the sheriff's department down on top of Michael Myers' latex-covered head like the proverbial hammer of the gods.

As Graham pulled up to the house, Barker could see that the fire was mostly out, leaving Strode's place a smoldering ruin.

Barker was a broad-shouldered African-American man in his mid-forties with a neatly trimmed goatee. As *the* sheriff, he chose to wear a suit and tie on the job instead of a uniform. His clothes immediately identified him as a supervisor, and he added a dark brown cowboy hat to his ensemble because it made him easy to spot when at a scene. His people never had any trouble finding him when they needed him. Plus, the hat looked good on TV.

Graham was a white man around the same age as Barker, with a squarish head and a face that could generously be described as rugged. As a detective, he too wore a suit and tie, but no hat. The only person allowed to wear a goddamn hat in Barker's department was him.

Fire vehicles were present on the scene, but the firefighters themselves were now nothing more than bodies—and body *parts*—littering the grounds, along with copious amounts of blood.

"Fuck me," Barker breathed. *One man did this. One. Man.*

There was a cruiser already on scene, parked away from the house. Barker pointed at it and Graham parked next to it. As soon as he had, both men got out. Graham drew his revolver, while Barker carried a megaphone. Graham moved quickly to check out the parked cruiser, and Barker joined him. The air was filled with the sound of tires screeching to a halt and doors opening and closing as deputies parked and piled out of their vehicles.

The cruiser's driver's side door was open, and Graham was the first to see what lay inside. The man was an absolute pro, so Barker was surprised to see him swiftly turn away from the cruiser, eyes squeezed shut as if he couldn't bear what he'd just seen. He was about to tell Graham to grow a pair, but then he got close enough to see into the cruiser, and his words died in his throat. Richards and Francis—the two deputies who'd been assigned to watch the Strode residence earlier—were both dead as fucking doornails. Richards' throat had been cut and he'd been stabbed in the head with what looked like a fucking penknife, while Francis' head had been removed entirely, hollowed out, and turned into a grisly mockery of a jack-o'-lantern, a lit flashlight shoved up through the neck hole to serve in place of a candle. The Francis-o'-lantern sat on the front seat, next to Richards' body, light spilling out of its wide empty eyes and silently screaming mouth.

"Jesus," Barker muttered and looked away as swiftly as Graham had. He hadn't felt like vomiting at a crime scene since he'd been a green-ass rookie, but it was all he could do to keep from puking now. How the *hell* had the firefighters not noticed these bodies? None of them had called in to the sheriff's department to report them. Then again, he supposed a blazing-hot inferno would take priority for firefighters over everything else.

Barker started walking toward the smoking blackened husk of Strode's house, Graham following alongside. They were soon in the midst of unspeakable carnage, and Barker found himself trembling with rage. He turned to address Graham.

"We got a massacre on our hands, Detective. Establish a perimeter!"

Barker wasn't watching where he was going, and he tripped over a dead firefighter lying on his back. The man no longer had a face. Barker stumbled, but he managed not to fall on his ass.

"Motherfucker!" he cursed.

The assembled deputies fanned out behind

Barker and Graham, flashlights and guns drawn. A dog team was present as well, and Barker hoped the mutts would track Michael's scent and run the bastard to ground. And if they chewed that maniac up in the process, that would be just fine with him.

Barker stopped walking and gazed at the deputies, saw them looking at the killing field around them, disgust and fear on their faces. But there was anger too, as well as determination. They wanted to bring down Michael as much as he did.

He turned to Graham and gave him a nod.

"Attention all responders!" Graham called out. "Be advised, we have a violent criminal at large. Armed and dangerous. We will deploy all units of frontline and tactical officers to search the area. Additional resources have been notified. This fugitive is on foot. I want a sweep of Highway 17, west to the causeway! Get to work, people!"

The deputies broke into different groups and hurried to carry out their orders. Barker watched them go, wondering how many of their lives Michael might claim before this long night finally ended. They'd get him eventually, though. No way the psycho bastard could take them *all* out. He lowered the bullhorn and looked once more upon the bodies of the dead firefighters scattered across the ground. Then again…

"What do *we* do, boss?" Graham asked.

"What else?" Barker drew his revolver from his shoulder holster. "We join the hunt."

And try not to get our asses sliced and diced in the process.

8

Sondra Dickerson, clad in jeans and a University of Illinois sweatshirt, stood in her kitchen, remote control unit in her hands, eyes fixed on the toy drone buzzing in the air in front of her. She was sixty-two, African-American, gray hair so short it was almost a buzz cut. At her age, the last thing she felt like doing was messing with her damn hair every morning. This way, she could just roll out of bed and get her day started. The drone—which to her mind resembled a robotic bug with tiny helicopter blades on its legs—had been a birthday gift from Phil. Their daughter Crystal piloted real drones for the army, and Phil thought Sondra would get a kick out of the toy—and he'd been right.

One of the nice things about being empty nesters was that Sondra and her husband could do whatever they wanted, whenever they wanted. And if she wanted to fly a damn drone in her kitchen in the middle of the night, she would, and to hell with what anyone else thought. The noise of the drone's tiny engine was so loud that she still couldn't hear the TV in the living room. Phil had been watching an action movie of some kind, and he'd left it on with the volume too loud when he'd gone upstairs. He had trouble hearing these days, but the stubborn bastard refused to get his ears tested, claiming he heard everything *clear as a fucking bell.* Yeah, right.

Speaking of hearing, she realized something.

"I don't hear no more firetrucks!" she called out, yelling extra loud so Phil would hear her.

He didn't respond right away, so she piloted the drone into the living room and followed. A moment later she heard him come thumping down the stairs. He was a heavyset white man with only a few wisps of gray hair on his otherwise bald head. To compensate, he sported a full Santa Claus beard. He was sixty-five, a couple years older than her, but he thought he looked younger. He was wrong. He wore a plain white T-shirt and jeans so ratty that Sondra didn't see how the damn things still held together. And, oddly enough, he was wearing his CPAP mask over his nose and mouth. He suffered from sleep apnea, and if he didn't use his CPAP machine at night to help him breathe better, he snored—*bad*. It was like sleeping next to a chainsaw.

Phil stepped over to Sondra and eyed the drone, which she was now directing to fly in a circular pattern around the living room. When he spoke, his voice was slightly muffled by plastic.

"My goddamn sleep apnea mask smells like Lucky Strikes from when your mother borrowed it."

She kept her eyes on the drone as she answered.

"I smell it too. That stink ain't cigarettes. It's Laurie Strode's house on fire!"

On the TV, a presumably exciting car chase was happening, but Sondra didn't give a shit. Who watched action movies on Halloween? You were supposed to watch spooky movies then. But Phil didn't like horror movies, said they were too unrealistic for him. The forty-two-inch flatscreen TV was mounted on a brick wall opposite a sinfully comfortable leather sofa with built-in recliners that featured power recline *and* power headrest. The sofa was positioned to afford an excellent view of a bank of windows that looked out onto their front yard. Sondra loved to sit on the couch in the morning, gaze out at the trees, and watch the birds and squirrels cavort as she had her first coffee of the day. Before Phil retired, he was a supervisor at the water plant, and Sondra still worked as a cemetery caretaker. They weren't rich, but they'd splurged on this couch, which, as far as she was concerned, was the best damn purchase they'd ever made as a couple.

There was a small serving table in front of the sofa, upon which rested a bottle of wine and a pair of empty glasses. Phil—still wearing his CPAP mask—picked up the bottle and began to refill the glasses.

"From upstairs, it looks like they put it out," he said.

Sondra continued flying the drone in its circular pattern.

"I hope she's okay." She didn't know Laurie well—the woman wasn't exactly interested in becoming close friends—but they talked now and again. Sondra found her to be pleasant, if a bit distant. She certainly didn't bear the woman any ill will. The poor thing had been through enough in her life already, *more* than enough. She thought about those two British podcasters she'd shown around the cemetery yesterday, the ones doing a program on the Myers killings. People in town sometimes wondered why Laurie couldn't simply put the past behind her. But the world seemed determined to make her remember.

Phil finished pouring the wine. He sat the now empty bottle back on the table and picked up a glass. "Saw out the window when I was going number two. That'll teach her not to shoot off AKs and drop grenades all hours of the night. Fuckin' A. Preparin' for Armageddon is one thing, but that nutbag lives a highly flammable lifestyle."

He pulled off his CPAP mask, tossed it onto the table, and took a sip of wine.

Sondra sighed. Phil had never much cared for Laurie, and Sondra had to admit she *could* be a noisy neighbor, what with her private shooting range and all. And she practiced all the damn time, like she was expecting civil war to break out any day. Still, Sondra felt a need to come to Laurie's defense.

"Don't talk shit about that woman. She'll fuck you up."

Phil put his glass down on the table. "That's what they told Joe Frazier when he was challenged by Gwen Gemini." He punctuated his words with a pair of air punches.

Sondra looked at him. "I have no idea what in the hell you're talking about."

He grinned and picked up her glass and offered it to her. She ignored it. She was wondering how close she could get the drone to his bald head without actually hitting him.

Undeterred, Phil tried again. "How about you and I snack on some Cheez-Its and suck off this nipple of Beaujolais Nouveau for a while?"

Sondra decided she was going to buzz Phil, teach him a little lesson about running his mouth. She worked the remote's controls, and the drone obediently moved toward him like a large lazy insect. He continued sipping his wine while holding onto her glass as well, his attention now focused on the TV, where the damn car chase—which Sondra figured was a contender for the longest, dullest scene in movie history—was still going on. But at the last minute, she chickened out, afraid she was going to ram the drone right into Phil's head, and she jerked the controls. The drone veered away from him, but she'd moved too fast, and the machine buzzed out of the living room, down the hall, and through the open door of a bathroom. She frantically worked the controls, trying to make the drone come back....

She heard a noise in the bathroom, a kind of *thump*, and the drone's engine fell silent. If the goddamn thing had flown outside, she'd still be able to hear it buzzing. But there was no sound at all. The only explanation she could think of was that it had stopped working.

"Cheap piece of shit crash-landed," she said.

"You don't know how to fly that thing. Gimme the controller. My turn."

He put both of their glasses on the table and took the remote from her hands. She gave it up willingly. She'd had enough of playing drone-master for one evening.

Phil started toward the bathroom. Sondra figured he wanted to check out the drone before trying to get it back into the air. But when he was only halfway down the hall, the drone—its insect legs bent and broken—came flying out of the bathroom's darkness toward him. The damaged machine landed at his feet, whirring and grinding.

"The fuck was that?" Phil said. He looked over his shoulder at Sondra, and they exchanged worried glances. Something was wrong, she could *feel* it. She grabbed the empty wine bottle by the neck in case she needed a weapon. Gripping the bottle tight, she held her breath as Phil continued down the hall.

"Somebody in there?" Sondra called out.

No reply.

Phil wasn't by nature a fearful man. He believed that if you had a problem, you faced it and took care of it. As an interracial couple, Sondra and he had encountered their share of hostility and even outright hatred. Haddonfield was a good town filled with good people, but there were always a few shitheels in the mix, and it seemed like they'd been coming out of the woodwork more and more these last few years. So if someone had broken into his house, he wasn't going to slink away and call the cops. He was going to deal with it, right here, right now.

Phil stepped over the dead drone and continued walking toward the bathroom. There was a door in the middle of the hall that separated the downstairs bathroom and laundry room from the rest of the house. They usually left it open since it was just the two of them, but Phil now wondered at the wisdom of this practice. He passed the open door and crossed the rest of the way to the bathroom.

The bathroom door wasn't opened all the way, and the light from the hallway only illuminated so much of the inside. He couldn't see much from where he stood, so he stopped a moment and listened. The goddamn TV was so fucking loud, and despite what he told Sondra, he knew his hearing wasn't all that great these days. If someone *was* in the bathroom, he or she could be blasting away on a trumpet, and Phil probably wouldn't hear it. He did, however, *smell* something—a burnt, smoky odor, thick and harsh. Smoke from Laurie Strode's burning house? Probably, but the bathroom window was on the other side of the house and didn't face Laurie's property. *Guess the fire was worse than I'd thought.*

He crossed to the door, gently pressed his fingers to its surface, and then slowly pushed it open further. He reached inside—wondering for the first time why the fuck he hadn't thought to grab something he could use as a weapon—and fumbled for the light switch. He found it, flipped it, and bright light flooded the bathroom.

He saw a reflection in the mirror over the sink: a tall apparition with a smoke-smudged skull for a face. No, not a skull. A mask. The man—what else could he be?—wore wet, fire-damaged coveralls, and there was little doubt the thick smell of smoke came from him. They kept a first aid kit in the cupboard beneath the sink, and the man had placed it on the counter and pulled out the supplies. There was blood everywhere—in the sink, on the counter, on the floor... There was blood on the man's hands and his clothes, and Phil had a horrible sinking feeling that not all of the blood was his.

The man's head swiveled to look at Phil, and he punched upward, shattering the light fixture and returning the bathroom to darkness. Phil had seen more than enough. He pulled the door shut, turned, and hauled ass back down the hallway. He paused halfway to close and lock the extra door, then he ran to the living room.

Sondra wasn't there anymore. Phil felt an icicle of fear lodge in his chest.

"Sondra? Hey, *Sondra*!"

He spun around, searching for her, and was relieved when she poked her face through the kitchen doorway. She looked scared as hell, but she still held the empty wine bottle like a club, was still ready to fight if it came down to it. God, he loved that woman!

His pulse pounded like a jackhammer, but he forced himself to speak calmly. He didn't want to scare Sondra any more than she already was.

"There's a big fella in our bathroom wearing a monster mask."

Sondra looked at him incredulously. "What the hell does he want?"

His pretense of calm deserted him. "Who gives a shit? Call the police!"

He started toward Sondra, passing the front windows on the way. Something about this, about the *windows*, nagged at him, but he didn't— Wait. Not windows. *Window*. Singular. The bathroom window was still open, which meant the man in the monster mask could climb out, and—

Glass exploded, and he felt powerful hands grab onto his shoulders. Flying shards cut his face and neck, but before he could fully register the pain, he was yanked off his feet, pulled through the window, and thrown to the ground on the other side. He hit hard, and he thought he felt something inside him break. The man in the monster mask looked down at him, and Phil thought he was a goner for sure. But then the man climbed through the window and into the house—

—where Sondra was.

He tried to call out to his wife, to warn her, to tell her to get the hell out of there, but all that came out of his mouth was a moan of pain accompanied by a trickle of blood.

*

It happened so fast, Sondra didn't have time to scream. One instant Phil—her poor, sweet husband—

was walking toward her, and the next a window exploded and he was pulled through. He disappeared rapidly, the masked man lifting him as easily as if he was an oversized rag doll. She stood frozen, waiting to hear Phil's cries as the masked man killed him, but there was no sound. Was he already dead? Then the masked man was at the window and coming through.

The sight of the half-burned *thing* emerging from the darkness outside shocked her out of her paralysis, and she turned and ran toward the kitchen, still holding the wine bottle. She'd left her phone upstairs in her bedroom, and she sure as hell wasn't going to try to go get it now. There was a door in the kitchen that led to the outside. If she could reach it, get out, she could run to Laurie's. There were police there. They'd stop the masked man and save Phil, and everything would be okay. All she had to do—

She reached the door, saw that it was triple-locked, let out a harsh, "Fuck!" Every night she made sure all the doors to the outside were locked, more out of habit than because she feared intruders. But a precaution designed to keep people *out* was now keeping her *in*. *Home security, my ass,* she thought. Chain lock, deadbolt, lock on the doorknob. She reached a trembling hand toward the chain lock, tried to disengage it, but it was hard to get a grip on it, bad as her hand was shaking.

She heard the heavy tread of the masked man's boots on the kitchen floor behind her, and although she told herself not to look, knew that it would do her no good, she couldn't stop herself from shooting a glance over her shoulder. The man had walked over to the stove and now looked up at the ceiling. *Could it be Michael Myers?* she wondered. She didn't see how it was possible. The man should be as old as she was by now. Laurie had always thought the motherfucker would come back for her one day. *Looks like you were right, girl.*

At first she didn't know why Michael was staring at the ceiling, but then again, why the hell did a crazy person do anything? Above the stove was a three-foot-long fluorescent light tube. He reached up and pulled it from its socket. The light flickered out, and he held the tube, turning it one way then another, examining it. *What the fuck...* With a single fast motion, he slammed the tube against the edge of the stove, knocking six inches off of it and creating a jagged edge. *No, not an edge,* she thought. He'd made himself a glass knife.

She turned her attention back to the chain lock. Panic focused her and her hand stopped shaking. With rapid motions she undid the chain, flipped the deadbolt open, and was just about to disengage the lock on the doorknob when Michael jammed the broken end of the light tube into the side of her neck. She tried to gasp, but all that came out of her mouth was a gurgling sound, followed by a gout of blood. More blood fountained from the wound itself, and she felt the empty wine bottle— her useless weapon—slip from her fingers and fall to the floor. Michael pushed the tube in harder, twisting it, *grinding* it, and then her legs gave out and she joined the bottle on the floor. She slumped against the kitchen door, used it to support herself.

Her body had slipped off the light tube when she fell, and she looked up to see that the frosted fluorescent casing had filled with blood—*her* blood. The effect was strangely beautiful in its own way. Michael was also looking at the tube, his head cocked to the side, and she wondered if he saw the same beauty she did. She looked down at the floor then, saw the bottle lying there, crimson pooled in front of it, making it look as if she'd spilled a particularly rare vintage of wine.

Funny, she thought. *The things you notice... at the end...*

Then she was gone.

*

Get up, you old fucker. Get your ass back in there!

Phil's body didn't want to do anything except lie there and hurt. His back was on fire, and his head—which he'd hit hard when he'd landed—felt as if it were going to explode. But as long as he had a single breath left in him, he intended to fight. His Sondra was in there, alone with the man in the mask, and she needed him.

He pushed himself to his feet, gritting his teeth against the pain in his back, and climbed through the broken window. He was no fitness freak, but he was still in good shape for his age, and once he was inside, he raced toward the kitchen. As soon as he entered the room, he saw Sondra sitting on the floor, leaning against the kitchen door, her neck a ragged ruin, sweatshirt soaked with blood, eyes wide and staring. The man in the monster mask held a broken fluorescent light tube in his hand as he looked at Sondra, and Phil saw that the inside of the tube had been darkened with his wife's blood. He knew instantly what that sonofabitch had done to her, and without slowing he charged the motherfucker.

He grabbed the man by the back of the head— back of the *mask*—and slammed his face into a cabinet door next to the stove. The man dropped the broken light tube, and it burst when it hit the floor, the blood caught within flying outward in an explosion of red. He then turned to Phil, seemingly unfazed. Phil, features contorted in fury, punched the man in the face as hard as he could. The man's head snapped back, but otherwise, he seemed unaffected. That was okay. Phil had a lot more where that came from. He made to swing again, but this time the man caught his fist, twisted his arm back, spun him around, and pushed down, folding him at the waist. Phil struggled to free himself, but the man had too strong a hold on him. And then slowly, painfully, the man forced Phil's arm upward inch by inch, increasing the pressure, until Phil heard a loud *crack* and agony flooded his body. He cried out, then the man shoved him forward onto the kitchen table, flipping him around so he was on his back.

The man looked at him for a moment, as if contemplating what to do with him. Then he turned his head, and Phil saw that the man's gaze was drawn to a magnetic strip affixed to the wall—a strip with six kitchen knives mounted on it.

"Oh no," Phil said softly. "Please, no…"

The man stepped over to the strip, selected a knife, returned to the table, and without hesitation, slammed it into Phil's chest. The pain in his broken arm was eclipsed by this fresh agony, and he screamed. The man returned to the strip, selected a second knife, and repeated the process. By the time the man in the monster mask had finished, all six knives protruded from Phil's chest and abdomen, and Phil had joined his wife in darkness eternal.

9

Laurie floats somewhere between life and death. In its own way, this limbo is rather pleasant. Quiet. Peaceful. For the first time in a long time—since she was seventeen, really—she feels like she can truly rest and perhaps never wake again. *Sounds good to me*, she thinks.

She's dimly aware of voices. They seem to be coming from a great distance, and she has trouble making out what they say. She only catches a few words—*heart rate, blood pressure, suction, doing fine, strong as hell, tie off that vein, more gauze…* She has the impression that she's lying down, that there are people around her, doing things to her. She feels a spark of panic, but then she realizes what's happening. *You're hurt. You're at the hospital. You're being operated on. They're trying to help you.* She isn't sure she likes this idea, doesn't know if she wants to return to the world of the living, but at least no one is intent on harming her.

She opens her eyes.

She expects to see men and women in surgical garb surrounding her, faces obscured except for their eyes, each doing their part to repair her damaged body.

What she sees instead is Michael. Or more precisely, *Michaels*. A half-dozen of him stand at the operating table—three on one side, three on the other—backlit by a large fluorescent lamp hanging above. Their masks and coveralls are splattered with blood, and each holds a different surgical instrument: scalpel, scissors, pliers, bone saw, bone chisel, trocar… The instruments are old, rusted, blood-stained. The Michaels look at her for a long moment, eyes gleaming with anticipation. Then they begin their work.

And in her mind, Laurie screams.

*

Karen knew she should be sitting with Allyson, but she was too anxious about her mom's surgery to keep still. Plus, there was something she had to do, something she had to *see*.

The hospital's morgue was, stereotypically enough, located in the building's lowest level. Finding it wasn't difficult. Its location was clearly indicated on the YOU ARE HERE maps mounted in the hallways at periodic intervals. A little walking, an elevator ride, a little more walking, and Karen was there. She'd never been to a morgue before—she was a child therapist, not a medical doctor—and she was surprised to see how mundane the entrance looked: a plain white door, like any other in the hospital, with a small sign on the hallway wall that simply said MORGUE in black letters on a white background. In a way, it was depressing. The plain entrance, which looked no different than a storage closet, made death—which in many ways was the ultimate human experience—seem small and unimportant.

She expected there to be a warning on the door— AUTHORIZED PERSONNEL ONLY, something like that— but there wasn't. When she tried the door, she found it unlocked, so she entered.

Cold was the first word that came to her, followed by *sterile*. The walls, floor, and ceiling were all a stark, almost blinding white, as were the counters and cupboards. To the left, stainless-steel refrigerators— each only large enough for a single body—took up an entire wall. Cadaver gurneys, a dozen or so, filled much of the empty space in the room, and they were all occupied by bodies covered with white sheets. Rectangular fluorescent light panels in the ceiling hummed softly, washing the room with too-bright radiance. The air smelled of bleach and disinfectant, and breathing it in made her throat hurt.

She saw no one—no one living, that is—but there were doorways that branched off from this area leading to an autopsy room, maybe an MRI machine, and likely some office space as well. The staff on duty were probably in one of those other rooms right now, which suited her fine. She preferred to search on her own. She started walking among the cadaver gurneys, pausing at each to raise the sheet so she could view the toe tag identifying each body. She was certain some, if not all, of the bodies on the gurneys were victims of Michael Myers, killed by the maniac as he'd rampaged through Haddonfield for the third time in close to sixty years. First his sister Judith, then fifteen years later her mom's friends, and now... these poor people. And there were likely more bodies out there somewhere still waiting to be discovered. Each time Michael returned, the number of killings escalated. How many lives had he taken tonight? And did the final tally even matter? Losing one life was too many. Each was unique, irreplaceable...

Like Ray.

Michael had killed him at her mother's house. Ray hadn't been a fighter, certainly not like Laurie was. He'd been an accountant, and had never fired a gun in his life. He'd been a sweet, goofy guy, and the closest she'd ever seen him come to violence was when a ref made a bad call during a Super Bowl game. But he'd taken one of the guns Laurie had offered him, and he'd done what he could to protect the rest of them from Michael. Who knows? His death might've slowed Michael down, bought them enough time to take out the bastard. She liked to think so, anyway.

But when she, Laurie, and Allyson had fled her mother's burning home, there had been no time to look for Ray's body. But now that Michael was dead and with Laurie in surgery, Karen had plenty of time. She knew that Ray's body had most likely been cremated in the fire, but if there was a chance it had been recovered, she wanted to know. She wanted to give him a decent burial. It was the least he deserved. She wanted it for Allyson as well, to give their daughter a chance to say a final goodbye to her father. And she wanted the closure for herself as well. She was still having trouble believing Ray was gone. *She* hadn't seen his body. Only her mother had. And while she had no reason to doubt Laurie, she didn't think Ray's death would truly become real to her until she gazed upon his body.

She continued moving among the dead, reading the names on their tags. Even when a body clearly wasn't Ray's—it belonged to a woman, or a man of a different age or race—she read the name anyway. It seemed the respectful thing to do.

One of the interior doors opened, and a thin, brown-bearded man wearing a short-sleeved blue medical smock over a long-sleeved orange mock turtleneck came in. He carried a clipboard with some paperwork on it, and when he caught sight of Karen he did a doubletake, almost as if he thought one of the corpses had gotten off its gurney and started to wander around the joint.

"Excuse me," Karen said as she checked another tag. *Harold Castillo.* "I'm looking for someone."

Her voice came out flat and emotionless, and she wondered idly if she was in shock.

"Sorry, miss," the man said. "You can't be in here." She didn't answer, continued her search. The man raised his voice as he repeated, "*You can't be in here!*"

Karen nodded, as if acknowledging his words, but she made no move to stop searching.

She sensed the man looking at her for a moment, as if he wasn't quite sure what to do. She supposed he didn't have many problems with living people

110

down here. There was a phone on the wall next to the door. He went to it, picked up the receiver, spoke to someone for several seconds in a strained voice, then hung up. He turned to watch her after that, but he made no move toward her and said nothing further, both of which were fine with her.

She'd finished with the bodies on the gurneys and was about to start checking the refrigerators when the main door opened and a woman in surgical garb walked in. She gave Orange Sleeves a quick look before heading toward Karen. Karen watched her approach, puzzled why she would be dressed for surgery in a morgue. Then she understood. This was a nurse from her mother's surgical team.

"Karen?" the woman asked, then went on without waiting for Karen to confirm her identity. "Your mother is resting now. The surgery was a success."

Karen looked at the nurse blankly for a moment as she attempted to process her words. But then slowly, she smiled.

*

The OR nurse led Karen back to the ER waiting area. Karen saw Allyson still sitting in the same seat as when she'd left for the morgue, only now an older man in a security guard uniform sat beside her. It appeared they were talking. Karen didn't say anything, didn't wave to get her daughter's attention, but Allyson—as if alerted by some instinct—suddenly looked around. When she saw Karen, she stood and turned toward her,

her expression guarded and fearful.

Karen felt tears welling. Ray was gone, but her mother was alive and out of danger. Best of all, she still had Allyson. Smiling, tears rolling down her cheeks, she walked to Allyson and wrapped her arms tight around her daughter.

"She's going to be okay," Karen said.

At first Allyson smiled, but it didn't last.

"Dad's gone," she said, voice thick with emotion.

If Karen hadn't already been crying, she'd have started then.

"He'll always be here," Karen said. "Even when you can't see him."

She wasn't sure why she said this—she wasn't an especially spiritual person—but it seemed like the right thing to say. More, it *felt* like it.

She hugged Allyson tighter and the two women cried together for the husband and father they'd lost.

*

At that very moment, in the northwest section of Haddonfield—specifically within a two-story colonial house at 45 Lampkin Lane that once belonged to the infamous Myers family—a lean, handsome man in his early fifties stood in his kitchen, arranging a butcher board of charcuterie: bits of cheese and meat, veggies and dip, olives, a variety of crackers, fruit slices, and mixed nuts. He believed good food deserved good presentation, so he was taking his time with the arrangement. Music played loudly upstairs, a jazz tune called

"It's Halloween" by Pete Antell, and he hummed along as he worked.

John Massey—Little John to his friends—had short white hair, a full white beard, and wore round glasses that he thought made him look intelligent. His husband, however, said they made him resemble a hirsute owl, and Little John privately agreed, although he'd never admit it. He wore a pirate costume—white puffy-sleeved shirt, black vest, red sash, black pants, black boots, a gold earring (fake) in his right ear, and that accessory that no self-respecting buccaneer could do without: an eyepatch (even if he had to wear it under his glasses). Although he'd gotten tired of having half his vision blocked, and had flipped the eyepatch up so he could see. He had a toy cutlass around here somewhere too, but he wasn't sure where he'd left it.

When he'd finished with the charcuterie, he gave it one last look, pronounced it good, and carried it into the living room. He set the board down on the glass coffee table in front of the sofa, next to a basket that had been refilled with full-sized candy bars. The flat-screen TV was tuned to a Halloween horror movie marathon, although the sound was currently muted. He'd started a fire in the wall-mounted fireplace earlier, and with the living-room lights set low, it created a cozy, festive atmosphere. Perfect.

"Big John!" he called out.

He waited for a reply, but all he heard was Big John singing along with Pete Antell about cornstalks, old gray houses, and the cold white moon. He walked to the staircase and tried again, shouting more loudly this time.

"Big John!"

Still nothing.

Now he was getting irritated. He liked music as much as anybody, but he preferred it to be played at a decent volume so you didn't have to shout at the top of your lungs to get someone's attention. He started up the staircase, the music becoming increasingly louder as he went. When he reached the second floor, he walked to the study and opened the door. The room contained built-in bookshelves, a burnished walnut secretary desk, and an all-in-one turntable system. Big John—legal name John Soto—sat on the leather loveseat in the middle of the room, garbed in pumpkin-pattern pajamas, smoking a joint, and grooving to the music.

Little John watched his husband for a moment, smiling and shaking his head. He then tiptoed forward, slowly, stretched out his hand, and tapped Big John on the shoulder. Big John yelped and nearly dropped the joint. He turned and shot Little John an accusing look.

"Jesus, Little John! You scared me."

Big John was five years younger than Little John, slightly shorter, and stocky—hence the *Big*. He was bald and sported a salt-and-pepper goatee, although there was a good deal more salt than pepper in it these days. They'd been together twelve years, married for seven, and business partners for most of that time. When they'd first started dating, their friends had given them their nicknames because they'd gotten tired of trying to figure out which John they were referring to at any given moment. Little John was thin, Big John wasn't, and thus their new names were born. Although whenever someone asked Big John how he'd gotten his nickname, he claimed it was due to the extraordinary size of a certain portion of his anatomy.

"Would you turn the music down?" Little John asked. "I thought we were gonna watch a movie."

"Fuck that. It's Halloween. I got all these spooky records." He gestured to a stack of vinyl albums resting on the loveseat next to him then grinned at his husband. "Let's get high and dance."

"Tempting," Little John said.

Big John held out the joint, but before Little John could take it, the doorbell rang.

Big John frowned. "Isn't it a little late?" He picked up the sound-system remote and lowered the volume.

The two of them had decorated the entire house for Halloween, and Little John plucked a horrible-looking plastic black cat from one of the bookshelves. It had big red eyes and glowing fangs.

"Wanna freak them out a little?" Little John waggled the cat and made a hissing sound.

Big John rolled his eyes.

"No. We've been trick-or-treated to death tonight. I just want to dance!"

Little John sighed. He put the cat back on the shelf and walked out of the study. As he headed downstairs, he had to admit that Big John had a point. It *was* a bit late for trick-or-treaters. They'd had a steady stream of ghosts and goblins until eight o'clock, and then a few stragglers over the next half hour, but no one had rung their bell since. It was kind of weird when you thought about it.

Little John reached the ground floor, walked through the living room to the foyer, opened the front door, and stepped onto the porch. To the left of the door, attached to the front banister with loops of thick wire, was this year's Halloween display—a campy horror riff on the classic painting *American Gothic* (which had been Little John's idea). They'd erected two mannequins, one dressed to look like a decomposing colonial woman, the other made up to look like a devil farmer, complete with red skin, black goatee, pointed ears, horns, and a real pitchfork clasped in his clawed hand. And for the *pièce de résistance*, they'd impaled a jack-o'-lantern on the pitchfork's tines and placed a burning candle inside. Little John was extremely pleased with how it had turned out, and they'd been awarded second place in the neighborhood Halloween decoration contest. First place had gone to one of the houses down the street, which had a collection of gaudy inflatable ghosts and ghouls on their lawn. Store-bought decorations that displayed no imagination whatsoever. He thought the judges had been smoking one of Big John's extra-large joints—the kind he saved for special occasions—before making their decisions this year.

But the visitor on their porch showed no interest in their decorations. It was a girl, twelve, maybe thirteen years old, he guessed. She wore a black shirt and pants, had light brown hair, and held a flashlight in one hand and a Silver Shamrock witch mask in the other. Little John remembered those masks from when he'd been a kid. Back then, all the kids thought they were the coolest things ever. His mother had never let him get one, though. She'd claimed the damn things weren't safe.

The girl spoke rapidly, voice strained, volume increasing as she went on.

"Excuse me, mister. I was trick or treating with my sister and we got candy bars from your house, and when she bit into one, there was a rusty razor blade!"

When she finished, she drew in a gasping breath, and Little John thought she was on the verge of bursting into tears.

He couldn't believe what he'd just heard. He knelt so his face would be on the same level as the girl's.

"Calm down, calm down. Your sister got hurt from a candy bar at my house? Where is she?"

"She's right… *there!*"

The girl's eyes went wide, and she directed her flashlight beam onto the front walk to reveal a second girl—roughly the same age as her, round face, glasses, braces, curly brown hair—lying in a puddle of vomit and blood. The girl's mouth was open, revealing a bloody razor blade protruding from her tongue. On the ground beside her lay a Silver Shamrock jack-o'-lantern mask.

Little John jumped to his feet. The sight of that poor girl lying there—eyes closed, body still—was too much for him. He felt nauseated, dizzy, and he began shaking.

"Oh my god! Oh my god! *Big John!*"

He jumped off the porch and ran to the injured — *Please, please, please god, don't let her be dead* — girl. He knelt next to her, but now that he was here, he had no idea what to do.

"Big John!" he shouted again. "Come out here. *Now!*"

"Can you help her?" The girl on the porch gripped her mask tight and gazed at Little John with a mixture of hope and fear.

Little John didn't answer. From the look of her sister, he thought it might already be too late to do anything for her.

Big John came running out of the house then, his bare feet slapping on the porch. He gave the girl with the witch mask a quick glance before moving past her onto the walkway and joining Little John at the injured girl's side. He crouched down and gazed at her in horror.

"What's happening?" he asked.

Little John placed his hand close to the girl's mouth and said a quick silent prayer. He felt a soft gust of warm air on his flesh.

"She's breathing, but there's blood everywhere. She bit into a razor blade. Call 911."

Suddenly the front door slammed shut, and both men started at the sound. They rose to their feet and turned to look back at the house. The girl with the witch mask still stood on the porch, but the front door was indeed closed.

"The fuck was that?" Big John said.

"Did someone just—" Little John broke off, and he and his husband exchanged worried glances.

From the porch, Witch Girl said, "Shhh! Be quiet!"

"What?" Little John asked.

"Did you hear something?" she asked in a small voice. Then her gaze was drawn to Pumpkin Girl, and she said, "Oh my gosh!"

"What is it?" Big John said.

But instead of Witch Girl answering, Pumpkin Girl's eyes flew open, and she shouted, *"Boo! We scared you!"* Although since she still had a razor blade in her mouth, the words came out more like *"Oo! We sceh oo!"*

The front door opened then, and a boy wearing a Silver Shamrock skull mask stepped outside. He carried a pillowcase in one hand, and in the other, he had the basket of full-sized candy bars that had been sitting on the coffee table in the Johns' living room. He dumped the chocolate into his pillowcase, then dropped the empty basket onto the porch. Then all three of the kids shouted in unison.

"Trick or treat!"

Grinning, Pumpkin Girl jumped to her feet and removed the fake razor blade from her mouth.

Little John understood what had happened. While the girls had distracted them, their accomplice had snuck into the house to steal the candy. It was actually kind of clever, now that he thought about it. Big John, however, was in no mood for Halloween pranks.

"You scared the *shit* out of me," he said. "Are you Mr. Hoover's kids? He and I are gonna have words!"

Pumpkin Girl bent over to pick up her mask. Then she looked at Big John and said, "Who the fuck is Mr. Hoover?"

The boy on the porch pulled off his skull mask to reveal a grinning human face topped by a thatch of curly black hair. He then held up his pillowcase in victory.

"I got the whole goddamn bowl!" he crowed.

Witch Girl giggled. "We got you good!"

Big John looked at the three thieves, and a dark glint came into his eyes. "You don't know who you're messing with, do you?"

Little John wasn't certain where Big John was going with this, but he had an idea.

"Easy, Big John," he said, playing along. "They're too young to know."

Witch Girl glanced at Skull Boy and Pumpkin Girl before giving Little John a skeptical look.

"Too young to know what?"

Big John lowered his voice. "You know whose house this is? You ever heard of Michael fucking Myers?"

Little John picked up the story. "Do you know what happens to anyone that comes into the Myers house without an invitation?"

Pumpkin Girl looked suddenly uneasy. "You talking about the Boogeyman?"

Skull Boy snorted. "That's just a made-up legend. Phony baloney."

"We're not scared," Witch Girl said, but she didn't sound as confident as Skull Boy.

"Oh yeah?" Big John said. "He stabbed his sister in the tits in this house. Right upstairs."

He pointed, and despite themselves, all three kids looked upward.

"And sometimes," Little John said, using his best telling-creepy-stories-around-the-campfire voice, "when the wind blows just right, we can still hear her ghost calling his name."

"That's right," Big John said. "She says, *Michael… Michael… Get the fuck outta my room, you little pervert!*"

Little John cracked up at that, and Big John started laughing too. The three kids looked disturbed, likely more by the old men's bizarre antics than the story itself, Little John thought. They slipped their masks over their heads and headed down the walkway. Little John didn't bother trying to get the candy back from them. He figured they'd earned it.

"Yeah, go on home with that chocolate and rot your teeth out!" he called. "See ya next year with your trick-or-treats. We'll be waiting!"

Still laughing, the two Johns watched as the mischievous trio slunk sullenly down the street. When they were out of sight, Big John turned to Little John.

"*Now* can we dance?"

Little John smiled.

10

Tommy picked up his glass, intending to take another sip of champagne, only to see that it was empty. Scowling, he picked up the last bottle they'd gone through, hoping a little bit of bubbly still remained at the bottom, but it was dry as a fucking bone. He sat it back down on the table with a disgusted sigh. Some celebration this was turning out to be.

The talent show was at intermission, and people had mobbed the bar to get more drinks or lined up in front of the restrooms to take a piss. Tommy, Lindsey, Marion, Marcus, and Vanessa sat around the table, all quiet now. Marion had taken Marcus' stethoscope and was playing with it, absently rolling the rubber tubing between a thumb and forefinger. They'd run out of conversation topics a while ago, and although the silence between them was companionable enough, it was beginning to grate on Tommy's nerves. He *liked* talking. Talking meant he didn't have to think. Because when he thought, he remembered, and he didn't *want* to remember. Booze helped dull the memories, even more effectively than talking, and he was debating heading to the bar to fetch another bottle—or two—when he felt his phone buzz in his pocket. He'd gotten a text alert.

He quickly took his phone from his pants pocket and checked the screen, hoping it was a message from either Lonnie or Laurie. But it was neither. It was a news alert, and the headline hit him like a kick in the balls. *HALLOWEEN KILLINGS IN HADDONFIELD!*

He looked up and saw that he wasn't the only one getting a text alert. Patrons throughout the bar were checking their phones, eyes wide, mouths open, babbling excitedly to their table companions. Lindsey, Marcus, and Vanessa had their phones out too, but not Marion. She was staring at a wall-mounted flatscreen nearby.

"Tommy, look!" she said, and pointed to the TV.

Mick had switched the video feed from the horror movie marathon to a local news channel. A blond reporter in a gray suit and blue tie was stood on a street, houses and trees behind him, microphone gripped in his hand, grave expression on his face. At first there was no sound, but then Mick unmuted the video, and the man's voice issued forth from a dozen different TVs throughout the bar. Everyone in the place shut up and turned toward the screen closest to them to watch.

"Earlier this evening, four bodies were discovered in three houses along the same residential street. Residents of North Haddonfield are on high alert and officials are investigating."

The image changed to what Tommy presumed was pre-recorded footage. The reporter was crouched down in front of a small African-American boy. He held the microphone in front of the boy's face, and he spoke rapidly, voice quavering, eyes shining with tears.

"I was in my bedroom and he killed my babysitter with a— He stabbed her and it was nasty and she was my number-one main best babysitter."

Seeing the shock on the boy's face made Tommy feel sick. He remembered being that young, remembered running and screaming alongside Lindsey, Laurie telling them to hide, the dark silhouette of the Boogeyman moving through shadows in the house, silent as a shark gliding through black water. He began shaking, and he looked to Lindsey. She too was staring at the TV, eyes haunted, face pale, and he knew she was caught in the throes of memory, too. He reached out a trembling hand to take hers. At first, she jumped at his touch, but then she realized it was him. She gripped his hand tight and gave him a grateful smile.

The reporter and the boy disappeared. Now the screen displayed photos of two men, both middle-aged, both wearing the white uniforms of patients at Smith's Grove. The man on the left had a roundish face with puffy cheeks. He was bald on top, the gray hair on the back and sides of his head overlong, fine, and wispy. His eyes were narrowed in a near-squint, and his mouth was downturned, as if he went through life in a perpetual state of disapproval. A reflection of light hit the screen, making the second man's features difficult to discern. He seemed a bit older than the first man, but that was really all Tommy could tell about him.

Lonnie had been right when he'd introduced Tommy during the talent show. He *was* a talented bird whistler. He'd started developing the obscure skill not long after that Halloween in 1978, when he'd been sitting in a classroom at school and felt another panic attack coming on. One day he looked out the window and saw a male robin hopping about in the grass, and it occurred to him that the bird had it good. *He* didn't know anything about the Boogeyman. All he knew was flying and hunting for worms and singing. Then, without being conscious he was doing so, Tommy softly began to whistle. And the more he whistled, the calmer he felt.

Over the years it had become a hobby, if a neurotic one, with him continually learning new bird whistles. By this point, he knew hundreds, most of them so well they would fool real birds. He'd never done anything with this weird talent, beyond using it as self-therapy—which, as far as he was concerned, was all that he needed it for. Now, looking at the images of these men, one of whom might well be Michael Myers, he needed it now, and he began whistling, so softly that you would've had to have your ear right next to his mouth to hear. And the species of bird? A robin, of course.

The reporter spoke over the men's photos.

"Two patients of the local Smith's Grove state hospital are still unaccounted for after yesterday's bus escape. Authorities have not confirmed a connection between the escape and the recent murders, but police are encouraging all residents to stay inside until further information is released."

Old news footage replaced the photos, footage Tommy knew well. He'd seen it countless times over the last forty years. Halloween 1978. Police cruisers parked outside houses at night, lights flashing, people milling around—men, women, children— confused and afraid. Sheriff's deputies standing stiffly, looking lost and unsure what to do next. EMTs wheeling sheet-covered gurneys from Lindsey's house containing the bodies of Annie, Lynda, and Bob. Their high-school pictures flashed on the screen one by one, and Tommy marveled at how young they looked—how young they would *always* look, frozen in time as they were. And, of course, there was footage of Lindsey and him in the street, blankets around their shoulders as their parents arrived to get them, mothers weeping, fathers looking dazed.

Tommy still held Lindsey's hand, and he gave it a squeeze. She squeezed back but didn't take her eyes off the screen. She looked mesmerized.

The screen returned to a live image of a street in Haddonfield. Sheriff's cruisers, EMT vehicles, emergency lights flashing... *It might as well be 1978 all over again,* Tommy thought. No, not again. *Still.* For some of them—him, Lindsey, Marion, Lonnie, and above all Laurie—that Halloween night had never really ended.

The reporter, standing in the street and lit by the harsh glare of a camera operator's light, continued.

"Tonight's tragedy is an eerie reminder of an event in Haddonfield history that the local community has spent decades trying to forget."

Marcus suddenly sat up straight in his seat.

"That's the street where we live!" he said.

Vanessa looked at him, startled. "What?"

Marcus pointed at the screen. "The reporter. He's standing in front of Mrs. Dewbottom's house."

Vanessa stared at the screen in disbelief. "Right next door to our house!"

"What the hell is happening?" Lindsey asked.

More archival footage on the screen now: images of Smith's Grove and, wearing a trench coat along with an expression of intense desperation, Dr. Samuel Loomis.

Marion spoke in a somber tone as she answered Lindsey's question.

"Evil has returned to Haddonfield."

The reporter was back, and now he was interviewing one of the neighbors, an older woman wearing a thick pullover sweater. Tears ran down her cheeks as she spoke.

"Haddonfield used to be a safe place for families. But not anymore."

"It's Michael," Tommy said. "Gotta be."

No one at the table disagreed.

*

Vanessa hurried across the parking lot, Marcus at her side. Her high heels *clack-clack-clacked* loudly, and she cursed herself for being stupid enough to dress

127

as a sexy nurse tonight. Not only was she reinforcing a patriarchal stereotype about her profession—that nurses took care of *all* their patients' needs—but these goddamn shoes were *killing* her feet. It was pride that had convinced her to wear the outfit. She might be closing in on forty, but she worked hard to take care of herself, ate right, exercised, so why shouldn't she show off what she had? Nothing wrong with a woman owning her own sexuality, right? That shit was supposed to be empowering. But right now, out here in the dark, October chill caressing the exposed skin of her arms, legs, chest, and back, she felt defenseless. *Shoulda gone as a goddamn knight in armor*, she thought.

Seeing the news report about the murders had shaken her. She hadn't grown up in Haddonfield, but she knew about Michael Myers. He was almost a celebrity in this town, but she'd always thought of him as a mythic figure, not a flesh-and-blood man who could one day come back and start hacking people to pieces again. And he'd done it right next to their fucking *house*! It could have just as easily been them. If they'd been home tonight... She forced herself not to follow that line of thought. All she wanted to do right now was get someplace safe, and—although she knew it might seem crazy after what had happened tonight—for her that meant home. And actually, where else in town could be safer? The police were already there, searching the neighborhood. They'd catch Michael—or better yet, gun down the motherfucker—or he'd hightail it to

128

another part of town to try and escape them. Either way, he'd be gone, and she and Marcus could hole up in their own little fortress, safe and sound—and then she could get good and goddamn drunk.

The parking lot wasn't as full as it had been when they'd arrived. They weren't the only ones who'd decided they'd had enough of Mick's Hallowine after seeing the news report. They'd driven here tonight in their metallic-blue Ford Fiesta. Everyone thought physicians were rich, but between student loan payments and malpractice insurance, docs—at least general practitioners like her husband—often weren't rolling in dough. And nurses? Their salaries were even worse. Marcus had driven tonight, and he'd parked toward the back of the lot, in a space twenty feet from the nearest light pole. At night, she preferred parking as close to the entrance of a business as possible, and if she could, she always chose a spot directly beneath a light. These things were basic, common-sense security precautions to her, but Marcus never seemed to give a damn where he parked. As long as the car was in the parking lot when he wanted to leave, he was happy.

As they headed for their car, her eyes were drawn to every shadowy place where someone could be hiding—beneath, between, and behind vehicles, around the sides of the building, on top of the fucking roof… Michael Myers could be here right now, cloaked in darkness, watching, waiting, looking for just the right moment to strike…

Stop it, girl, she told herself. *What do you think the*

man did? Teleport himself from your neighborhood? No way in hell he's here.

Then again, their house wasn't all *that* far away from Mick's. And it wasn't like the murders had just taken place. As a matter of fact, she wasn't certain precisely when they'd occurred. Long enough ago for a lunatic in a creepy-ass mask to walk here? Maybe.

When they reached the Fiesta, Vanessa hurried to the driver's side and tried to open the door. It was locked. And of course she didn't have her keys. Where the hell would she keep them on this outfit?

"Oh my god oh my god oh my god..." she breathed. She felt dizzy, and she wondered if she was close to hyperventilating.

Marcus caught up to her and began rummaging around his pocket. But before he could pull out his keys, he slapped his other hand to his chest.

"Shit! Forgot my stethoscope."

Seriously? she thought.

"We gotta get home, baby," she said.

"Hang on. I think Marion still has it."

He tossed the keys to her, then turned and ran back to the bar. She wanted to shout at him—*Are you fucking kidding me?* But the stethoscope wasn't a prop; it was real, and it was a good one, costing close to three hundred dollars. She understood why he didn't want to leave it behind. But that didn't mean she was happy about it.

The Fiesta was equipped with keyless entry, and now that Vanessa had Marcus' keys, she had the remote. She thumbed the button to disengage the locks, then reached out to open the door.

Still locked.

"Fuck," she muttered. The battery on Marcus' remote had been going bad for the last couple weeks. She kept reminding him that he needed to get a new one, and he kept saying he would but so far he hadn't. Sometimes you needed to press the buttons a couple times before you could get it to work, and sometimes it wouldn't work at all, and they ended up having to use her remote. She supposed they were lucky the damn thing had worked when they got here, otherwise the car would've been unlocked this whole time.

She frowned. Now that she thought of it, she didn't remember hearing the *clicks* of the locks engaging when they'd left the car earlier. Maybe they *hadn't* engaged, in which case... No. No way. She'd just tried to open the door and had found it locked. That proved the remote had worked last time. Unless... someone had found their car unlocked, climbed in, closed the door, and locked it after them.

She let out a nervous laugh.

"Vanessa, you are *way* overthinking this!"

She tried the remote again, and this time was rewarded with the extremely satisfying sound of the locks disengaging. She opened the driver's side door, got in, then closed and locked it. She'd leave the car locked until Marcus got back with his oh-so-precious stethoscope. Key remote still in hand, she reached out to press the ignition button, intending to start the car so she could get the heater going. But she hesitated. She looked out the windshield to see if Marcus had come out of the bar yet, but the view was obscured by what looked like condensation. Frowning, she reached out an index finger, touched it to the glass, and then slid it slowly downward, drawing a clear trail in the condensation. The moisture wasn't on the outside of the glass.

It was on the *inside*.

She heard a soft rhythmic sound, like breathing, followed by another, the sound of fabric sliding on fabric, as if someone sitting in the backseat had just shifted their weight.

Her own breath caught in her throat, and her blood turned to ice water in her veins. She didn't want to turn around, didn't want to *see*, but her body began moving without any conscious choice on her part. Her head turned, shoulders coming with it, and slowly—so slowly it seemed to take an eternity—the back seat came into her view. It was dark in the car, damn dark, thanks to Marcus not parking underneath a light, and at first she couldn't tell if there was anything there in the shadows. But then her eyes adjusted, and she saw there was nothing. She almost burst out laughing with relief—

—and then someone sat up.

All Vanessa could make out was an outline of a human form, but she didn't need to see that to know that Michael Myers was inside her goddamn car.

She let out an ear-splitting scream, opened the door, and practically threw herself out of the vehicle. She kicked off her heels and then hauled ass toward the bar, bare feet slapping asphalt the whole way. She had almost reached the front door when it opened and Marcus stepped out, stethoscope in hand. Vanessa ran to him and he caught her, immediately wrapping his arms around her. Before he could speak, she leaned close to his ear and whispered, voice trembling:

"Marcus, he's *in* there!"

Marcus swept his gaze around the parking lot.

"What? Where?"

Keeping her voice low, Vanessa said, "Michael Myers is in our *car*!"

Marcus focused his attention on the Fiesta. The car just sat there, engine and lights off. From this distance, Vanessa couldn't tell if anyone was still in the vehicle, but she didn't need to see to know *he* was there.

"In the back seat," she said. "Go look."

He eyed her as if she were the lunatic, not Myers.

"Go look? *Hell* no!"

Vanessa wanted to yell at Marcus to man the fuck up, but in truth she couldn't blame him. This was too much for two people to deal with. But then, they didn't have to face Michael on their own, did they? There was a bar full of people only a few feet away, and some of them—such as the new friends they'd made tonight—had a personal grudge to settle with the fucker.

She pulled away from Marcus and ran inside the bar. She stopped just inside the entrance and yelled as loud as she could.

"Somebody help! He's here!"

Silence fell over the bar as everyone turned to look at her. Most people appeared to be simply curious, but not Tommy and the others. They sat up straight in their seats, attention riveted on her.

She continued, speaking closer to normal volume now.

"He's in the back seat of my car in the parking lot. I went to get inside, and I *saw* him. The guy on TV! Like he was talking about." She pointed to one of the TVs in the bar. "It's him! Somebody call the police!"

Tommy got a faraway look in his eyes then, and although she wasn't close enough to be sure, she thought he said, "He's come back for me."

Tommy sprung up from his seat then and ran toward the bar. A second later, Lindsey and Marion followed. Tommy ran behind the bar, surprising Mick, who just gawked at him. Tommy pulled the mounted baseball bat off the wall and gripped it in one hand. Vanessa could see two words burned into the wood on the side of the bat: *Old Huckleberry*.

"What'chu doing?" Mick said, angry. "My father gave me that when I won the championship!"

Tommy traced the burned-in letters with his index finger. He answered Mick without taking his eyes off the bat, his lips forming a cold smile.

"Oh yeah? Think about how proud he's gonna be when it's covered in Michael Myers' blood."

There was a donation display sitting on the bar counter with the words *Tips for Treatments* printed on it. As Vanessa watched, Tommy took a five-dollar bill from his wallet and shoved it into the donation slot. There was a caption on the display, and Tommy read it aloud.

"Love lives today, people."

Lindsey and Marion stood with Tommy, and Marion made a fist and raised it high in the air.

"But evil dies tonight!" she said.

Tommy's smile widened, turned a few degrees colder, and he gave her a nod.

Tommy led the way outside. Vanessa, Lindsey, and Marion followed, and behind them came Mick's patrons. The people flowed out into the parking lot, forming a half-circle behind Tommy and the others. Tommy walked up to Marcus, who pointed toward the Fiesta.

"He's in the car right there. He just got out of the back and moved behind the wheel. I saw him. Looked right at me. Oh my god."

Vanessa realized then that she didn't have the car keys in her hands. Had she dropped them when she ran from the car? Or had she dropped them *in* the car, *before* she got out?

"I think I left the keys in there," she said. "I got scared."

"Quiet!" Tommy said. He held the bat in one hand, like a club. "I got this."

And then he did something strange: he started whistling like a bird. There was an eerie beauty to the sound, an otherworldly quality than sent a shiver rippling down Vanessa's spine. Then Tommy began walking toward the Fiesta, moving with a determined stride.

The car's engine turned over then, and the lights came on. A second later, the radio began blaring, the volume so loud they could hear the music from across the parking lot, even with the Fiesta's windows still up. The driver flipped through several channels before finally settling on... opera? Vanessa wasn't sure, but she thought she recognized the music as being from *The Barber of Seville*.

Marion and Lindsey stood close to Vanessa, and she heard Marion ask, "Is it him?"

"He's watching us," Lindsey said in a hushed, frightened voice.

As Tommy drew closer to the car, he called out to the crowd.

"I'm not going to live another forty years wishing I'd stopped this asshole. Let's give him a beatdown right now."

He reached the car and stopped in front of the hood. He glared at the man behind the steering wheel and shouted, "Hey, Michael! Wake up!"

He took a two-handed grip on the bat, raised it high, and brought it down hard on the vehicle's hood with a loud *whump!* The bat bounced off the metal, leaving a large dent behind. People in the crowd cheered, clapped, shouted their approval.

Tommy raised the bat again in preparation for a second blow, but before he could take another swing, the man behind the wheel put the Fiesta into gear and stomped on the gas. The car lurched forward, and Tommy had to dive to the side to keep from getting run down. He hit the asphalt, rolled once, then came back up on his feet, bat still in hand. Everyone watched as Marcus and Vanessa's car surged toward them, and the crowd swiftly scattered to avoid being hit. The Fiesta raced out of the parking lot and took off down the street, engine roaring. The driver swerved into the path of an oncoming pickup, and the other driver had to whip fast to the left to avoid a collision. Vanessa watched as the killer that had stolen their car continued on as if nothing had happened. He swung the vehicle around the next corner, tires squealing in protest, and then the Fiesta was lost to view. An instant later a horn blasted, brakes squealed, and then the night was split by the sound of crashing metal. Michael Myers, it seemed, couldn't drive for shit.

"Get him!" Vanessa shouted.

11

Tommy ran to rejoin the group, and the mob of patrons ran around the side of Mick's bar, heading en masse in the direction of the accident. Behind Mick's was a large gray building that housed Guzman's Tool and Manufacturing. The Fiesta had plowed into the building's east wall, and smoke curled from its crumpled hood. The crowd continued running toward the car, Tommy, Lindsey, Marion, Marcus, and Vanessa in the lead. When they reached the vehicle, they gathered around it and watched cautiously as Tommy yanked the driver's side door open with one hand, bat held tight in the other, prepared to smash Michael Myers' skull.

But there was no one behind the wheel.

Tommy stuck his head inside, and Vanessa leaned closer so she could get a better look herself. She saw what looked like blood on the steering wheel, as if whoever had been driving had hit their head on it. And sitting on the passenger seat was, of all things, what looked like a white umbrella. Vanessa went around to the passenger side, opened the door, removed the object, held it above her head, and thumbed a catch on the handle. White fabric stretched over metal ribbing sprung outward to reveal that the object was an umbrella, all right. Weird.

Lindsey opened one of the rear passenger doors and looked inside.

"Pizza boxes," she said in a puzzled voice. "Two of them."

So Michael Myers likes pizza, Vanessa thought. *Who knew?*

Tommy turned away from the car, face red with anger and frustration. He spoke, voice low, almost a growl.

"He thinks he can come around here. Thinks he can scare us." He held the bat up to his face and turned it one way, then another, admiring it. "When I catch him, I'm gonna pull his mask off and look him in the eye, then I'm gonna swing old Huckleberry…" His lips stretched into a savage grin. "And say night-night."

For the second time that night, a chill went down Vanessa's back.

*

Fifty yards from the scene of the accident, a middle-aged man wearing the white uniform of a Smith's Grove patient huddled behind a trash can at the mouth of an alley. Anthony Tivoli's head throbbed from hitting the steering wheel, and his forehead felt wet and sticky. He thought he might be bleeding, but he didn't want to reach up and check. He *hated* seeing blood. *Especially* his own. He watched the crowd of people gathered around the broken car with fear. They'd wanted to hurt him—especially the mean man with the baseball bat. He didn't understand why. He hadn't done anything to them, hadn't done anything to *anybody* since the bus crash last night. Yes, he'd taken the umbrella—such a pretty thing—when he'd found it propped up against the side of a wall outside a secondhand clothing store that morning. And yes, there'd been a price tag on the umbrella, which meant *technically* he should've paid for it, but he hadn't had any money at the time, and he really, really, *really* loved that umbrella. It belonged with him. Surely anyone could see that. He had a similar umbrella at Smith's Grove, a special one he'd kept since he'd been there as an adolescent. But they wouldn't let him take it on the bus for the transfer, and he'd had to leave it behind. Doing so had made him very sad. So when the universe offered him a replacement, he took it. And when no one came running out of the store demanding he bring it back, he knew it was a sign that the umbrella was destined to be his, so he could keep it in good conscience.

And when he'd seen a delivery guy from White Horse Pizza pull up in front of a house several blocks from here where a loud Halloween party was going on and carry several boxes inside, he'd just *had* to take a peek inside the man's vehicle. Which he'd neglected to lock. Very negligent. Just asking for trouble, really. Tivoli hadn't had anything to eat since leaving Smith's Grove, and the pizza had smelled *sooooo* good that his tummy began gurgling and he'd started to feel dizzy. Half a dozen white pizza boxes were stacked on the back seat, each with a drawing of a rearing horse printed on top, but he wasn't a greedy-guts and only took two. He'd hurried down the street with his newly won dinner—and his umbrella, of course—hoping he wouldn't hear Pizza Guy yelling for him to *Stop! Come back here with those pizzas!* But he heard nothing, and a couple minutes later, the guy drove right by him and didn't so much as slow down. Once more, the universe had provided for Tivoli.

He'd wanted to find a place where he could sit down and eat. His feet were swollen and sore after walking all day, and the slippers they gave you at Smith's Grove didn't have much in the way of arch support. He'd continued wandering, hoping he'd come across somewhere suitable where he could have his dinner, until he reached Mick's Bar and Grill. The parking lot was filled with cars, and he figured that if Pizza Guy had been silly enough to leave his vehicle unlocked, surely *someone* who'd parked here tonight had done the same. So he went from car to car, trying to open each one, until he came to the metallic-blue Ford Fiesta. Blue had always been one of his favorite colors. He had three: blue (of course), aquamarine (he mostly just liked to say the word), and a super-secret color whose name he would never-ever divulge, even under torture (it was goldenrod). He'd climbed into the Fiesta's back seat, chowed down, and before he knew it, he was yawning, so he'd decided he'd lie down and rest his eyes—just for a minute!—and the next thing he knew, the nurse in the too-small clothes had opened the driver's side door and gotten behind the wheel. He'd woken, confused at first, unsure where he was. He wasn't in his room at Smith's Grove, that was for sure, but where… Then he'd remembered. He'd sat up and when he saw the nurse in the too-small clothes, he'd softly gasped. She wore pigtails. Tied with ribbons. Black ones. *Curly.* He'd stared. His mouth had gone instantly dry and his heart had begun to race.

Dr. Sartain had spoken to him during many sessions about what he called his *fixation.*

It's quite understandable, Tivoli, and you must see that it is not your fault. Your parents had… unorthodox ideas about child discipline. They abused you horribly. The ways they used rope on you… Well, let us just say that they were quite inventive in their sadism, and leave it at that. It's only natural that the sight of rope—any kind, even objects that merely remind *you of rope—should provoke a strong reaction. It's okay to experience this reaction, Tivoli. What is not okay is to act on it, not when those actions might hurt other people. Do you understand?*

He did. The sight of rope so terrified him that he went into what Dr. Sartain called a *defensive rage.* He would lash out at whoever was closest, screaming, hitting, kicking, biting until he was convinced the threat had been dealt with and he was safe again. He'd hurt people this way over the years—not intentionally—but it *had* happened, and that was why he had ended up in Smith's Grove. He was glad they'd

put him somewhere he couldn't hurt anyone. Well…
somewhere it had been less likely he'd hurt anyone.
And it wasn't as if there weren't *incidents* over the years
at the Grove. But thanks to Dr. Sartain, not to mention
a strict regimen of some very strong medicines, it had
been years since he'd harmed anyone.

But there he'd been, looking at those fucking
ribbons dangling from that woman's hair, and all
he'd been able to think about was wrapping his
hands around her throat and choking her as hard
as he could until she fell unconscious and was no
longer able to hurt him with those… those *things*.
He'd been off his meds for an entire day now, and
he knew the thoughts he was having were wrong,
that this woman hadn't come to hurt him, that she
had no idea who he was, that he had chosen her car
at random and had been dumb enough to fall asleep
in the backseat with a bellyful of pizza. But what if
he was wrong? What if she *had* come here to hurt
him? If he didn't do something, do it *fast*…

Still, he'd fought the impulse, just as Dr. Sartain
had taught him, and when the woman turned
around, saw him, and screamed, he realized she was
just as frightened of him as he was of her. She'd fled
the car, and he'd nearly cried with relief. He hadn't
hurt her, he *hadn't*! Dr. Sartain had said he would
never be cured, that there was no such thing as a
cure for what he had. *It's part of who you are, Tivoli. It
always will be. But it doesn't have to be* all *that you are.*

Tivoli understood that then, and for the first time
since he'd strangled his mother and father with the

very rope they'd used to torture him for years, he'd felt a sense of hope.

The woman had dropped the keys when she'd screamed, and Tivoli had got out of the back and into the driver's seat as fast as he could. The universe had provided a car for him, and it would have been rude not to accept this latest gift. He'd started the car and was trying to decide where to go, when everything went wrong. The woman with the ribbons had gone inside to get help, and people flooded out of the bar—including the angry man with the baseball bat. The man had scared Tivoli so bad when he'd smashed the bat on the truck. He'd called him *Michael*—which in other circumstances would've made Tivoli laugh. He didn't look a thing like Michael! He'd been so scared that he'd put the car in drive, stepped on the gas, and driven through the parking lot fast as he could, not even considering that he might actually *hit* some poor people on the way! Luckily, he didn't, but once he was on the road, he had trouble controlling the Fiesta. It had been decades since he'd driven a car, and while he still remembered the basics well enough, he was sorely out of practice. After he'd hit the building, he'd fled—forgetting his new umbrella *and* the leftover pizza—and hidden here in this alley.

Now what could he do? He hadn't hurt anybody (unless you counted the car), but those people sure wanted to hurt *him*. He had to get away from here, but where could he go? He needed to find someplace safe, but he was beginning to think that there was no such place in this whole town that… A drop of blood fell from the cut on his forehead onto his nose then, and he shuddered. He told himself not to look at his nose so he wouldn't see the blood, but the *thought* of the blood made him think about how much his head hurt. Which made sense because he'd been in an *accident*. And what did people who got hurt in accidents do? They went to the *hospital*. And where had he felt safest for the majority of his life? Smith's Grove, which was… that's right! A hospital! From what he'd seen over the last day, this was a fairly good-size town. Big enough, he hoped, to have its own hospital. He just needed to find it.

He gave the crowd across the street one last fearful look, and then quietly stood and hurried down the alley as fast as his swollen feet could take him.

*

Allyson—still holding onto the knife wrapped in Laurie's blood-stained shirt—paced outside the recovery room where they'd brought her grandmother after surgery. Inside, her mother stood next to Laurie's bed, holding her hand and looking at her with a concerned expression. The OR nurse had told them that while Laurie's injuries had been serious, she'd come through surgery like a champ and was going to be fine. *She's a strong woman*, the nurse had said.

You don't know the half of it, Allyson had thought.

Her mom still seemed worried about Laurie's condition, and Allyson couldn't blame her. On a night like tonight, where one awful thing happened after another, it was hard to believe that something good might occur. Her father wasn't coming back, so what guarantee did they have that her grandmother was going to recover? None, that's what. There *were* no guarantees in this life. If nothing else, this night had taught her that.

She was too full of nervous energy to remain in the room with her mother. She couldn't stand still, needed to walk, to bleed off some of the tension that had been building inside her since the moment she'd discovered Oscar impaled on that fence... the moment she'd first seen Michael Myers. Images kept flashing through her mind. Her mother standing at the bottom of the basement stairs, rifle shouldered, gaze sharp and determined. Her grandmother clutching her stomach, blood flowing past her fingers, face ashen. Flames flaring to life around her, growing bigger, brighter, and hotter with each passing second. And Michael's face... the impassive chalk-white features that somehow seemed more than a mask, but at the same time less. She imagined that if you tore that mask off, you'd find nothing underneath, because that's what Michael ultimately was—nothing, an absence of all thought and emotion, of anything even resembling humanity. He wasn't a person, he was a *thing*, and she was glad he was dead.

She found herself thinking of Cameron then, and wondered where he was, if he was safe. If she'd had her phone, she could've texted him, but the asshole had dropped it into a bowl of nacho cheese sauce, ruining it. She'd been so angry, so *hurt* when she'd seen him kissing Kim on the dance floor, but after everything that had happened since, it seemed like such a small thing. She supposed dealing with life-or-death situations tended to give a person perspective on what was really important. When this was all over, maybe she'd talk with Cam, see if they could work things out. Or maybe she wouldn't. In the grand scheme of things, did it really matter either way?

A doctor and two nurses wheeling a man on a gurney came rushing down the hall toward her. The man had thick white bandages wrapped around his neck, and blood was beginning to seep through the fabric. One of the nurses kept his hand on the bandage to maintain pressure on the wound as they hurried, presumably transporting the injured man to an operating room. As they drew near her, the doctor spoke rapidly to the nurses.

"Internal bleeding, lacerations, but he's going to make it."

Allyson quickly stepped out of their way, and as they passed, she recognized the patient. She remembered sitting in the back of his cruiser, watching Dr. Sartain, lit by the glow of headlights, jam some kind of knife into the side of this man's neck.

"Officer Hawkins!" she shouted.

But of course the man was unconscious and couldn't hear her. She watched the doctor and nurses wheel Hawkins around a corner, and then they were gone. She hoped the doctor was right and that Hawkins was going to survive. He was tough, like her grandmother, and she thought his chances were good.

"Allyson?"

She turned to see two men in suits approaching her. One wore a cowboy hat, and she found it an odd affectation. Haddonfield was hardly Texas. The men's serious demeanor told her they were police even before they identified themselves.

The man in the cowboy hat spoke first. "I'm Sheriff Barker, and this is Detective Graham. Can we speak with you and your mother? We need to ask a few questions."

Allyson didn't feel like talking to anyone, but she knew this couldn't be put off.

"I'll go get her," she said.

*

They were taken to adjoining conference rooms. Detective Graham spoke with Allyson.

"What do you want me to say?" Allyson was frustrated. "I was always told I couldn't talk about Michael. I couldn't acknowledge the tragedy. It was as if my mom's biggest fear was that my grandmother was right and the Boogeyman was real."

And that fear had been justified, hadn't it? The Boogeyman *was* real, and far deadlier than Allyson had ever imagined.

"You said Michael tracked down Laurie," Graham asked. "How is that possible?"

"It was his doctor. Michael's doctor. He knew where to go. When Officer Hawkins wakes up, you can ask him. It was the doctor that brought them together. Michael and my grandmother. It was the *doctor's* obsession. Not Michael's."

She'd watched in horror as Dr. Sartain had attempted to kill Officer Hawkins after Hawkins had struck Michael with his cruiser. In his own way, the psychiatrist had been a monster too. Maybe that's what had compelled him to work with Michael in the first place—evil calling to evil. Or maybe Sartain had begun their therapeutic relationship as a mentally healthy man, and over the years he'd become contaminated by Michael's insanity— *infected*, as if Michael was some sort of disease.

She wondered if she was now infected by that same disease, if they *all* were—her grandmother, her mother, and herself. It wasn't a comfortable thought.

*

In the next room, Barker spoke with Karen.

"I thought my mother was paranoid. I thought she was crazy. She was preparing us for this night, and I didn't believe her."

Laurie Strode had raised her daughter to believe the world was dark and dangerous, that threats lurked everywhere, that you needed to be prepared and on your guard at all times, and if you relaxed your vigilance, even if only for an instant, you were dead. Karen had wanted so much to please her mother, to be strong and fearless, to be the daughter she'd wanted—no, *needed*—her to be. But Karen had failed. Every night she'd had nightmares

149

that featureless, shadowy creatures were trying to break into their house, ebon-clawed hands slashing at doors, scratching at windows... She'd wake up screaming, and Laurie would rush into her room to comfort her. She'd say the dreams were *good*, that they showed Karen's subconscious mind was focused on dealing with the dangers of the outside world, and that one day they wouldn't be nightmares anymore but instead dreams of victory where she vanquished the shadow monsters. But Karen had never felt reassured, and she eventually came to view her mother as a monster filling her head with paranoia and delusions. She'd been relieved when social services had removed her from her mother's home, and she'd fought ever since to battle the darkness Laurie had put inside her, to rid herself of it, to see the world as place of light and joy.

What a fool she'd been.

"But she was right. For forty years, he was waiting to come back and kill her. To kill Laurie Strode. He came back for her. He found where she lives. He came to her house. She put us in his path... And he murdered my husband. That's what happened." Ray had never been comfortable around guns, had never fired one in his life. But he'd accepted one from Laurie at her house, had been ready to use it to defend his family from Michael Myers. If she'd taken her mother's warnings seriously, if she'd continued her training with weapons, she could've taught Ray how to handle a gun, how to never hesitate, how to shoot to kill. If she had, maybe he'd be here right now, sitting beside her, helping explain what had happened to Sheriff Barker. She almost started crying then, but she pushed her grief aside. She'd weep for her husband later, when she was alone.

"But we did it. Shot him in the face. Burned him alive. So he won't hurt anyone ever again."

And I hope the bastard rots in hell, she thought.

*

Barker had been jotting notes on a legal pad while Karen spoke. Now he stopped writing and looked up at her. He didn't want to tell her the news, not after everything she and her family had been through tonight, but he had to.

"I'm sorry, Karen. Has no one told you?"

"Told me what?"

Barker took a deep breath and said the words.

"Michael Myers is still alive."

12

Allyson burst out of the conference room, unable to believe what Detective Graham had just told her. How could Michael Myers have possibly survived? She'd seen him standing in the basement, trapped, flames spreading all around him. She'd looked back at the house when she and her mom were helping Laurie to the road. Fire had blazed out of the front windows, rising up to the roof— the whole goddamn place had been an inferno! No one could have escaped from that, not even *him*. And yet, according to Graham, that's exactly what had happened. All her grandmother's preparation, her father's *life*... it had all been a waste. Michael Myers still walked the streets of Haddonfield— and Halloween wasn't over yet.

She headed for the ER waiting area, wanting to go outside, get away from this place for a few minutes, stand in the cool and the quiet and try to come to terms with everything that had happened. But as she approached the exit, she was surprised to see Cameron walk in. He'd changed out of his Bonnie costume and into regular clothes—shirt, jeans, jacket, sneakers. He didn't see her at first, and she considered turning around and walking away, but then it was too late. He caught sight of her and hurried over to speak to her. He stopped several feet away, as if hesitant to come closer.

"Allyson? Are you okay? Is everyone okay?"

She looked at him, expressionless, struggling with conflicting emotions. He took a step toward her, not quite within touching range, but close. His tone was apologetic, almost pleading.

"Anything you need. I just want to help. I'm sorry for everything."

Anger flared bright inside her. *Everything?* He had no fucking idea of *everything* that had happened tonight!

"He killed Oscar."

Cameron's head jerked back, as if she had slapped him. Before he could respond, she went on, fighting back tears. "He killed Dave and Vicky and… and…"

"What?" Cameron said, taking another step toward her.

"He killed my father, too. He's still alive. Michael. He's not dead."

Cameron looked at her for a long moment, then, without speaking, he stepped forward and put his arms around her. She stiffened, not wanting him to touch her, but he held on, and eventually she raised her arms and hugged him back. After a moment they separated, as if by unspoken agreement, but they remained standing close. Cameron told her about finding Officer Hawkins injured as he was walking home from the dance, how he'd called 911, then his father.

"Dad picked me up then took me home so I could change. He brought me here so I could check on Officer Hawkins, see how he was doing. I didn't know you'd be here. I'm glad I found you, though."

Allyson glanced around the waiting area, but she didn't see Lonnie Elam.

"Where is your dad?"

"Still out in the car. He's on the phone to Tommy Doyle. They spotted Michael tonight over at Mick's Bar and Grill. They tried to catch him, but he got away. Tommy intends to track Michael down, and my dad's going to help him."

Allyson's grandmother had protected Tommy Doyle from Michael when he'd been a boy, and she knew Tommy hated that masked motherfucker as much as anyone, maybe even more than her grandmother did. She wasn't surprised to hear that he planned to take part in a little vigilante justice this evening, and given how the sheriff's department had failed to capture Michael so far, maybe the authorities could use some help tracking down the sonofabitch and taking him out for good.

"I want in," Allyson said.

"What? You mean, you want to join Tommy?"

"Yes. For our friends." She paused, fought back a sob, then continued. "And for my dad."

Cameron looked at her, and for a moment she thought he was going to try to talk her out of it, but then he smiled grimly and nodded.

She caught movement from the corner of her eye, and she turned to see her mother headed in their direction, accompanied by both Sheriff Barker and Detective Graham. Her mother was speaking to the men, and she did *not* sound happy.

"No, you need to get everybody here right *now*! If he's not dead, he's on his way—"

Both men interrupted her at the same time, talking over each other.

"Gonna ask you to wait for me by Administration, and I'll—" Barker said.

"We're doing everything we—" Graham said.

Karen paid no attention to either of them. "He's not going to stop killing until my mother is *dead*!"

Allyson had never seen her mom like this before. Usually she was the calm voice of reason. Sensible, logical, always in control of her emotions. But now she sounded frantic, as if she was on the verge of losing her shit entirely. Her eyes were wild, like those of a trapped animal desperately searching for a means of escape. Her gaze fell on Allyson then. She was already walking fast, but her panic took hold of her, and she ran the rest of the way.

"Mom!" Allyson stepped forward and caught her mother by the shoulders, as much to slow her down as to reassure her with her touch.

Karen began speaking rapidly, words tumbling from her mouth.

"You are going to go with the detective and stay with your grandmother until she wakes."

Allyson knew she could soothe her mother by

agreeing, and probably should, but she couldn't just stay here and do *nothing*.

"No."

Karen looked at her, confused, as if she hadn't understood the word.

Cameron stepped in then. "She's coming with us. My dad and me. We're joining Tommy Doyle."

Karen turned her gaze to Cameron and frowned, as if only just registering his presence.

"She's *what*?"

Cameron glanced at Allyson before going on. "The police are understaffed. I don't know if you heard, but—"

Karen cut him off. "Every police officer should be coming *here*. Right now. We're not dealing with a normal human. Michael Myers is a *monster*."

Allyson couldn't believe what she was hearing. Throughout Allyson's entire life, her mom had resisted buying into Laurie's "delusion" about Michael Myers, that he was somehow a living embodiment of evil, destined to one day hunt her down and attempt to finish what he'd started on Halloween night in 1978. Now Karen had gone completely in the opposite direction. It sounded as if she'd wholeheartedly adopted her grandmother's belief, to the point where it seemed that her own sanity was in question. Karen had fought to keep her mother at arm's length over the years, trying to prevent Laurie's craziness from infecting her and her family. She'd given up the struggle now, though, and was one hundred percent on Team Strode—for better or worse.

Barker and Graham were watching the three of them closely, but they weren't the only ones. Allyson became aware that the other people in the waiting area—patients, family members, staff—were listening as well, and a number of them were moving closer. *Looks like we've got an audience,* she thought.

Cameron continued his attempt at an explanation.

"Tommy's organizing groups," he said. "Groups of people. To find him. To find *Michael*."

Karen looked at him as if he'd just made a particularly unfunny joke. "Tommy Doyle? You've got to be kidding me. He's unstable... as bloodthirsty as Michael is!"

Cameron didn't reply to this, but he stood confident, his decision unchanged. Allyson couldn't help but admire him for this.

"I'm going with them," she said. "We're going to hunt him down and put an end to this."

"But he's coming *here*," Karen insisted. "I keep telling them. He's *stalking* her. We need to stay here and protect her!"

Allyson wanted to tell her mother that Michael Myers was doing no such thing. Dr. Sartain had been the one obsessed with the idea that there was some kind of spiritual link between Michael and her grandmother, a primal connection between predator and prey. She'd been in the cruiser when he'd spoken about it, had been forced to ride along as he drove the unconscious Michael to her grandmother's house in order to purposefully force the confrontation that he believed was inevitable. If

Sartain hadn't done this, Michael never would've found her grandmother. It hadn't been destiny at work, just the madness of a single man.

She knew her mother wouldn't listen, though, not as worked up as she was.

Cameron spoke to Karen again, calm and resolute. "Michael has infected your family and mine with fear and grief for forty years. He's gonna die tonight."

People—including Brackett, the security guard she'd spoken with earlier—had continued to gather around them as the conversation progressed. More than a few murmured agreement with Cameron's words, but Allyson did her best to ignore them as she tried to make her mother understand.

"Mom, I'm not going to wait *here* while he's out *there*. I don't want to see another person die. Live in fear… or don't. Whether it's a nut with a high-powered rifle, a white nationalist, some radical terrorist… or Michael Myers. Michael killed my father, and I'm not—"

Allyson was cut off as someone shouted, "Please clear the area!"

Everyone turned to see two orderlies, each pushing a gurney toward the crowd. On one gurney was an ashen-faced man, eyes terrified, breathing ragged. A woman, tears streaming down her cheeks, followed close behind him. No one followed the second gurney. The sheet had been pulled up over the occupant's face, a clear indication that whoever it was hadn't made it. There were bloodstains on both sheets.

The crowd was slow to disperse, and the crying woman shouted to make them move faster.

"Excuse me. *Excuse me!* It's my husband, and he's been hurt very badly!"

Everyone stepped aside quickly, and the orderlies wheeled the gurneys past them swiftly. The woman gave the crowd a dark look, as if she intended to blame them if her husband didn't survive the night, and they continued down the hallway, one gurney bound for an operating room, the other for the morgue. When they were lost to sight, Allyson spoke to her mother once more.

"I'm not going to pretend this didn't happen. It *is* happening. *Now.* I love Dad… and somebody loves whoever was lying under that sheet!"

Karen's expression softened. She gave Allyson a sad look and took hold of her hands.

"We failed, baby. We caught Michael in a trap, set the whole house on fire and he lived through it! Think about that. He's killed our friends, our families, and he will never stop until he finishes what he started. The police are looking for him. And you think *you're* the one that's going to find him? To *stop* him?" Her voice grew louder, angry. "You need to go in that room and sit with your grandmother. *Now!*"

Karen's voice shook as she spoke this last word, and Allyson understood that her mother wasn't forbidding her from helping Tommy Doyle because she didn't like the man or thought that what he wanted to do was crazy—even if she did. She was a woman grieving her dead husband, who feared for her wounded mother's life, and was terrified that her only child intended to put herself directly in Michael Myers' path out of some need for revenge. Karen had been through so much already tonight, and Allyson didn't want to make things worse for her.

She nodded once, then turned and exchanged a glance with Cameron. He stood there awkwardly, as if unsure what—if anything—he should say. He settled for giving her an understanding smile, which she very much appreciated. Then she turned and followed her mother down the hallway. She knew she was doing the right thing, so why did she feel so defeated?

*

Allyson sat in a chair at the side of her grandmother's hospital bed. Laurie was asleep, her breathing soft but regular, and while Allyson couldn't understand the readouts on the monitoring equipment her grandmother was hooked up to, no alarms were blaring, so she figured that was a good sign. The light in here was dim, the better for Laurie to rest, but Allyson found it ominous. She didn't like the way shadows collected in the corners of the room, would've preferred the light to be blazing bright. She wanted to be able to see all around her. That way, no one could sneak up on her.

She'd tucked Laurie's bloody shirt and the knife wrapped inside it between her hip and the arm of the chair. She knew the hospital staff would take it from her if they found it, though, so she had to be careful.

She reached out to take Laurie's hand and was surprised by how light and fragile it felt, like she might break the bones if she squeezed too hard. She looked at her grandmother's face, and for the first time was struck by how old she appeared. Despite her age, Laurie had always seemed ageless to Allyson—filled with life and fire, haunted by memories of what had happened to her when she was a teenager, yes, but not broken by them. But lying here, after having been almost killed by Michael Myers, she no longer looked larger than life, wasn't the badass warrior who'd spent decades preparing to battle a knife-wielding maniac. She looked like a woman in her sixties who badly needed to rest and recuperate.

She heard voices then, her mom speaking with Sheriff Barker out in the hallway.

"Sheriff, where's Security?" Karen said, sounding on the verge of hysteria. "You need to have someone posted outside my mother's door. Do you understand? Michael is *coming*!"

Barker kept his tone even. "I need you to calm down, Karen. If this town starts to panic, he wins. That's all there is to it. I want to help you, but I need you to help *me*."

Allyson thought her mother would argue further, but she sighed, and when she spoke again, her voice was softer.

"I know. I'm sorry. I just don't know what to do. I'm sorry."

"*Please*," Barker said. "Go to the waiting room.

Get some rest. I'll have someone get you when your mother wakes up."

The two were silent for a moment, then Allyson heard her mother's footsteps as she headed for the waiting area. Allyson was glad. In her mother's current state, if she tried to stay in the room with Laurie, she might become agitated and disturb her sleep. Her mother had likely thought of this too. She was a therapist, which meant taking care of other people emotionally was her thing.

Allyson thought Barker might enter the room then, maybe to check on Laurie or ask her a few questions that Detective Graham hadn't gotten around to. But a moment later, she heard him walk away. Michael was out there somewhere making more work for him, and he had more important matters to deal with than talking to her right now.

She thought of what her mother had said to her in the waiting area. *We failed, baby.* What would her grandmother do when she woke and learned that Michael still lived to stalk the streets of Haddonfield? How could Laurie rest, knowing he was out there somewhere, killing again?

Allyson had seen pictures of her grandmother from when she'd been a teenager. Not only did her mom have some photos, but Laurie Strode was famous in her way, and you could find images of her on the Internet, posted on sites dedicated to serial killers and their crimes. Allyson had never understood the fascination some people had with the darkest aspects of human nature, but she'd been glad to see those pictures. One of the things that had struck her was how happy her grandmother looked in the photographs taken before that Halloween. The way she smiled, big and slightly wry, as if she was in on a joke that no one else knew about. Allyson loved that smile. She had never once seen it on her grandmother's face in real life, and she knew it had died the night Michael Myers broke into the Doyles' house. When Allyson thought Michael had burned to death, she'd hoped that smile might return some day. But Michael wasn't dead, and now she feared Laurie's smile would remain dead forever.

She looked at her grandmother. She was out of it, probably would be for hours. Allyson wasn't doing her any good by sitting here and holding her hand. But there was somewhere she *could* be of use, somewhere she could help make sure that when her grandmother finally woke up, it would be to a world in which Michael Myers no longer existed. A world where Laurie Strode would finally be free.

She picked up the bloody shirt—and the knife— and stood. She didn't believe, as her mother did, that Michael would come to the hospital tonight seeking to kill her grandmother. But she remembered how no one, herself included, had believed her grandmother when she'd insisted Michael would return one day. She didn't intend to make the same mistake again. She placed the shirt on the bed next to Laurie.

"This is for you. Whenever you need it."

She gently touched her grandmother's cheek, and then she walked out of the room, in search of an exit.

13

Lonnie leaned against his silver Nissan Altima in the hospital parking lot, arms folded across his chest, gazing out at the road, waiting. The lot was busy with emergency vehicles and sheriff's cruisers coming and going, as well as scores of civilians rushing into the ER, many of them crying. It was sheer pandemonium, like the aftermath of some terrible town-wide disaster—a violent earthquake or devastating tornado. Despite the chaos, he felt calm, even relaxed. For years, he'd dreaded the prospect of Michael Myers returning to Haddonfield, but now that it had happened, he found himself looking forward to his reunion with the masked motherfucker. He had a score to settle with the Boogeyman, and he wasn't the only one.

A moment later, he saw a black SUV approach the hospital, engine rumbling. The parking lot was well lit, and when Lonnie waved, Tommy saw, pulled in, and drove directly to him. He parked next to the Altima and got out.

"We found her," Lonnie said. "Laurie's here. She's in recovery."

"Lucky she survived," Tommy said. "I just heard

from one of the officers at her compound. Eleven dead bodies of first responders."

Jesus Christ, Lonnie thought. How many more would die before they finally put that bastard down?

"Cameron's inside," he said. "Three of his friends have been killed. It's a madhouse."

Tommy's face darkened, and a cold glint came into his eyes that made Lonnie uncomfortable. He knew about Tommy's temper, what could happen when he lost control. He'd seen it, and it wasn't pretty.

Tommy, as if sensing his friend's sudden reluctance, put his hands on Lonnie's shoulders and squeezed firmly as he spoke.

"The only way we can stop this is if we're all in it together."

Slowly, Lonnie nodded. "Yeah. Line up your crowd, Tommy, but I want first crack at Michael. People have always seen me as a fuck-up and an outcast. I was a bully to some and bullied by others, but at the end of the day, I want to be remembered as the one that took down the bad guy."

Lonnie stepped away from Tommy and opened the trunk of his Altima to reveal a large tackle box and a long object covered by a dirty towel. Tommy opened the tackle box. Inside, amongst actual fishing tackle, were six handguns.

"You got a permit for these?" Tommy asked.

Lonnie grinned. "Some of them."

He pulled off the towel to reveal a sawed-off shotgun. Tommy whistled a couple notes in appreciation.

"Dad!"

Lonnie and Tommy looked up to see Cameron coming toward them.

"Where's your girlfriend?" Lonnie asked.

"She's okay," Cameron said. "She's staying with her family."

"Good for her," Lonnie said.

"It's where she should be," Tommy agreed.

A white Hyundai Elantra pulled into the parking lot. The driver drove up to them and parked on the other side of Tommy's SUV. Lindsey got out, along with Marion, Marcus, and Vanessa.

The gang's all here, Lonnie thought. He looked at Marcus and Vanessa.

"You guys coming too?" he asked.

"So many victims in our neighborhood," Marcus said.

"Close friends of ours," Vanessa added. "We just want to help. I'm a nurse. And Marcus is a doctor."

"Of *course* you are," Lonnie said skeptically.

"Seriously," Marcus insisted. "We'll do whatever we need to do."

Vanessa reached out, took her husband's hand, and nodded her agreement.

Lonnie, Tommy, Lindsey, and Marion exchanged glances. Should they let Vanessa and Marcus join them? It was going to be dangerous. Then again, if the two really *were* medical professionals, they might come in handy before the night was over. No one voiced any objections, and the decision was made.

"Lonnie, let's make sure these people have

protection," Tommy said. He then gestured at the trunk. "Share your shit, please."

Lonnie gave a large pistol to Marcus.

"Ever used a firearm before?" he asked.

Before Marcus or Vanessa could answer, Allyson said, "You squeeze the trigger and it goes bang, right?"

Everyone turned to see Allyson come toward them. Cameron looked surprised—and more than a little happy. When Allyson reached Lonnie's Altima, she reached into the trunk and picked up the sawed-off shotgun. Lonnie expected her to hold it awkwardly, as if she was afraid of it, but she didn't. She held it comfortably, and he wondered if her grandmother had ever given her shooting lessons on the sly, or if it simply came natural to her because she was a Strode.

"Michael Myers has haunted this town for forty years," Allyson said. "Tonight we hunt him down."

Lonnie smiled. Allyson was going to fit in with the rest of them just fine.

*

The group split up after that. Lonnie drove Cameron and Allyson, while Lindsey took Marion, Marcus, and Vanessa. The plan was for them to drive around Haddonfield and search for Michael. If they found him, they were to alert the others, and they'd regroup and proceed from there. As for Tommy, he had some recruiting to do.

Michael might've escaped them back at Mick's, but the experience had helped Tommy realize something important. Michael wasn't just *their*

Boogeyman—his, Lindsey's, Lonnie's, Marion's, and above all, Laurie's. He was *Haddonfield's* monster. Everyone who'd lived in this town, from the night Michael had killed his sister to now, had been affected by the evil bastard in one way or another. Haddonfield itself deserved justice. Michael—however dangerous he might be—was just one man. He couldn't stand against an entire town determined to hunt him down and end his miserable excuse of a life. Sure, there might be some casualties along the way, but as far as Tommy was concerned, they'd be acceptable losses. All that mattered was that Michael Myers died tonight.

He slowed as he approached a Grab-N-Go convenience store. A couple pickup trucks were parked in front, and a driver was refueling a Mustang at one of the pumps. People stood outside, smoking and shooting the shit, a few wearing half-assed Halloween costumes—a Dracula cape, an army helmet, sunglasses and a fake beard... This looked like as good a place as any to get started. He pulled into the lot, parked next to one of the pickups, and got out. In front of his car was a bench with an advertisement on it. Someone had spray-painted graffiti on it in black—a stylized image of a hand holding a knife— but the advertisement was still legible.

Big John and Little John Home Advantage Realty— From studios to single-family homes, there ain't no place too big or too little for Little John and Big John!

He approached the group of people, hard-looking men and women who glared at him suspiciously as he came toward them, bodies tensing in preparation to fight if necessary. He smiled. *Perfect*.

"Excuse me!" he said. "I need a few good people who aren't afraid to get their hands dirty. Everyone else, go home. There's a killer on the loose tonight."

The guy in the Dracula cape—stubbly beard, shaggy brown hair, beer gut—scowled at him.

"What's wrong with you, man? You high or something?"

His friends laughed at this, but Tommy just smiled.

"You guys ever hear the name Michael Myers?"

That shut them up. Tommy spent the next few minutes introducing himself and filling them in on what had happened over the last twenty-four hours or so: how a group of patients from Smith's Grove were being transported to a new hospital in Colorado; how there had been an accident; how Michael Myers had escaped, returned to Haddonfield, and picked up where he'd left off forty years ago.

"I actually had an altercation with Myers myself about an hour ago, but he escaped."

While he'd been talking, more people had gathered around—the driver of the Mustang, and a group of twentysomethings who'd come to the Grab-N-Go to pick up beer for a party they were headed to. All of them listened to Tommy's story with rapt attention.

When he'd finished, Tommy wrapped up his sales pitch.

"So what do you say? Want to go hunting with me and my friends tonight?"

The man in the Dracula cape exchanged grins with his companions.

"Fuck, yeah! This Myers prick is going *down*!"

Now it was Tommy's turn to grin.

"Excellent!"

He told everyone his number, and they quickly programmed it into their phones.

"There is strength in numbers, guys," he said. "You all cover Spring Creek to the bypass and let me know if you see anything. Myers is a threat, and we need to stop him tonight. The only way to catch him is to play his own game. Use the element of surprise. He thinks you're going one place and you pop up someplace else. Keep your eyes open."

They hurried off to their respective vehicles, got in, and roared out of the parking lot. The hunt was on.

Tommy headed back to his SUV. His first recruiting stop had gone well. By the time he was done, he'd have the whole goddamn town on Myers' ass.

"Trick or treat, motherfucker," he said.

Whistling a blue jay's call, he climbed into his SUV, started the engine, and headed off to gather more recruits for his makeshift army.

*

Lonnie drove his Altima down a neighborhood street on the north side of town, a few blocks from Marcus and Vanessa's home. He had no reason to think that Michael would return here, but it was a place to start. Cameron and Allyson sat in the front seat with him.

The windows were down, and the cool night air felt good on his face. He sipped periodically from a coffee mug as he drove. It didn't *contain* coffee, of course, and he was sure that Cameron and Allyson could ell that by the smell, but neither of them said anything. He didn't intend to drink very much, just enough to keep the edge off. He couldn't afford to let his nerves get the better of him tonight.

Lonnie carried one of the handguns in his jacket pocket, and Allyson kept the sawed-off shotgun propped against the side of the passenger door. Cameron had taken one of Lonnie's guns, and he kept it on the seat next to him, one hand resting on it as if he was afraid it might slip and fall onto the floor if he wasn't careful. The other guns had been claimed by Tommy, Lindsey, Marion, and Marcus. Vanessa hadn't been interested in taking a weapon, which worked out well since there weren't enough for everyone. He'd originally planned on one gun apiece for him and his friends, with a spare, and the shotgun as extra backup.

Next time I go out hunting a serial killer, I'll make sure to bring more firepower, he thought.

As he drove slowly up and down the streets, they watched for any sign of Michael, listening for any screams or police sirens that might indicate his presence. So far they hadn't had any luck, but the night was still young.

They drew near a group of men and women standing on the sidewalk, neighbors who'd left their houses to gather together and talk about what was happening in their town, Lonnie surmised, to share their worries and offer one another support. Understandable, if foolish, given the circumstances.

Allyson leaned out the window and called to them.

"Go home. Go inside and lock your doors. It's not safe to be out. Protect yourself!"

They stared at her as the Altima passed, but they made no move to leave.

Idiots, Lonnie thought, and took another sip of his "coffee."

"Dad?" Cameron said.

Lonnie turned to his son. The boy had been quiet for the most part since they'd left the hospital. Cameron didn't talk much—not to him, at any rate—so whenever he chose to speak, Lonnie made it a point to listen.

"I didn't always believe you about Michael Myers, about your meeting him when you were a kid, I mean. I thought maybe you'd made it up to help you sell your book, you know? But after tonight… well, I just want to say I'm sorry. I didn't take you seriously, and I should have."

Lonnie smiled at his son. "I love you too, kiddo."

He faced forward once more and brought his mug to his lips. He hesitated, then stuck the mug out the window and dumped its contents onto the street. He then placed the empty mug in the cupholder.

Feeling better about himself than he had in a long time, Lonnie drove on.

*

Lindsey and her passengers were conducting their part of the search several blocks to the east of Lonnie, Cameron, and Allyson. Marion rode shotgun in the Elantra, while Marcus and Vanessa sat in the back. The couple seemed nervous—shooting glances at each other and fidgeting in their seats—and Marion wondered if they were having second thoughts about their decision to join the hunt for Michael Myers. If so, she didn't blame them. It was all she could do to keep from freaking out herself. She had a fucking *gun* sitting on the seat next to her. Would she be able to fire the damn thing at another human being if it came down to it? Even if that human being was a maniac who had killed god knew how many people? She didn't know, and she hoped she wouldn't have to find out.

Lindsey had lowered the windows so they could hear anyone who might yell for help, and Marion took advantage of the opportunity to smoke without bothering anyone else in the car. She held her lit cigarette out the window, bringing it in only to take a drag on it, and then blowing the smoke to the side so the breeze would take it away. Lindsey could still smell the smoke, but it wasn't *too* bad, and she figured she could tolerate it for one night. Everyone had their own ways of coping with stress. Lindsey relied on anti-anxiety meds. She'd popped a couple Lorazepam in the hospital parking lot before they left, but so far the pills hadn't done much good. Her nerves still jangled like her body was constantly shrieking an alarm.

Marion blew a stream of smoke out the window, then said, "No one ever took him seriously."

"Who?" Marcus asked.

"Sam Loomis," Marion said. "Michael's first doctor. That man knew a killer when he saw one."

"I wish we'd all listened," Lindsey said. She thought of all the lives that might've been saved if they had.

They approached a neighborhood park. Husker Park, she thought it was called. There were soccer fields, trees, and, of course, a playground—climbing equipment, a slide, a merry-go-round, several swings, cedar chips on the ground to cushion falls, trash receptacle encased in red brick. As the Elantra's headlights illuminated the area, Lindsey saw a couple girls sitting on the swings, eating candy bars. One was dressed in orange, the other in black, and there were Halloween masks lying on the cedar chips near their feet—a pumpkin and a witch. A pillowcase lay on the ground as well, presumably where they'd gotten the candy bars from. There were no adults in sight.

Lindsey frowned. "What's happening over there?"

She pointed at the playground, and Marion, Marcus, and Vanessa looked.

"Better check it out," Marion said.

Lindsey pulled over to the curb next to the playground. She remembered this place, had brought her son here when he was little. Those had been happy times, and she felt a sharp pang of loss at the knowledge that they were gone forever. Time was a monster too, in its own way, its hunger without end. There were no lights here. It was the kind of playground that people weren't supposed to use after dark, but kids did all the time, especially teenagers. The moon was full tonight, though, and Lindsey needed no lights to see the girls. She activated the car's hazard lights, honked her horn to get the girls' attention, then took a flashlight from her glovebox and shined a beam out the window. The kids *seemed* like they were all right.

"What's going on?" she called out. "You guys okay?"

The girls looked at her, but neither answered. Concerned now, Lindsey got out and started walking toward them, shining her flashlight beam ahead of her. She'd left the Elantra running, its headlights on. The girls watched her warily, but they made no move to run. The playground equipment was more rundown than it had looked from the car. The chains of the swings were rusty, and one side of the merry-go-round was higher than the other. It didn't look like the damn thing could rotate properly. Worst of all was the trash receptacle. The actual container was housed inside a rectangular brick casing, probably to disguise it as well as prevent kids from knocking it over. But the brick was old, the cement that held it together crumbling. Several bricks had fallen onto the ground, and it looked like the remainder of the structure was barely holding together. Not exactly a safe thing to have around in a place where children played.

When Lindsey reached the girls, she addressed them in her Mother-Means-Business voice. It had worked with her son, at least when he was young.

"You guys should not be out right now. It's not safe out here. Have you seen a man wearing a white mask?"

The girls exchanged glances, and then one of them—the girl in black with shoulder-length light brown hair—looked at Lindsey.

"As a matter of fact, yes," she said, sounding far more adult than she looked. "We're playing hide and seek with him."

Lindsey couldn't believe what she'd just heard. What was wrong with these girls? They sounded too calm, almost eerily so.

"You're *what*?" Lindsey asked.

The other girl—the one in orange, with shorter, darker brown hair—pointed toward Lindsey's car.

"Oh, look! There he is!"

Lindsey spun around and shined her flashlight at the Elantra. Michael Myers stood at the back of the car, knife gripped at his side. In his other hand he held a skull mask, blood dripping from the inside.

Michael turned to look at her, and she felt cold, as if the temperature had suddenly plunged well below zero. In her mind, she was a little girl again, running alongside a child version of Tommy through his house, both of them screaming, Laurie telling them to hush, that it was going to be all right. Now here he was again, the monster that had chased her through her nightmares for the last forty years. Laurie wasn't going to be able to save her now. She was going to have to save herself.

14

Marcus watched as Lindsey approached the two girls. Marion tossed her half-smoked cigarette outside, then hit the switch to raise the windows. She picked up the handgun Lonnie had given her and checked to ensure it was loaded, her movements calm, practiced. She was getting ready. Just in case.

Marcus glanced at the gun sitting on the seat between him and Vanessa. Lonnie had told him it was a semi-automatic called a Desert Eagle, and the damn thing looked to him like it could stop a charging rhino. At the time, he'd taken it more to humor Lonnie than out of any real expectation that he might have to use it. But now the reality of it hit him in the face like a splash of cold water. Vanessa noticed him looking at the thing.

"That's a big gun," she said. "Think you can handle it?"

It wasn't a question of *could* he handle it. It was a question of *should* he. He was a physician, for Christ's sake. He had taken an oath to do no harm. And that oath applied to everyone, regardless of who they were or what they might've done—or what they might do in the future. It was his job to provide medical care to those in need, not to decide who deserved to live and who deserved to die. When he'd chosen to join Tommy and his group of vigilantes, he hadn't fully thought through the consequences. He'd been so horrified by what Michael had done that he'd wanted to do what he could to stop the sonofabitch. He hadn't considered what would happen if they actually found him. He supposed he'd expected they would act in a civilized manner, hold Michael prisoner until sheriff's deputies arrived to take him into custody. He was beginning to realize how naïve he'd been. The rule for this night was simple: kill or be killed. Did he have enough killer in him to do what needed to be done? He didn't know.

Vanessa must've sensed his internal struggle, for she picked up the Desert Eagle and examined it. "Heavier than it looks," she said, but she didn't put it back down, and Marcus didn't ask her to hand it to him. He didn't know how she and Marion—who were both nurses—could be comfortable with the prospect of shooting someone. Nurses didn't have to take the Hippocratic oath when they graduated, but they were expected to adhere to the same basic principles. How could they contemplate killing someone?

Maybe, he thought, *because they're both stronger than I am*.

Marion glanced up at the rearview mirror and let out a strangled gasp. Marcus turned and peered through the rear window. He immediately wished he hadn't. A tall man wearing dark clothes and a white mask stood behind the Elantra. In one hand, he held another mask—a skull—and in the other he held a very large, very scary-looking knife. Blood dripped from the mask, and Marcus saw more blood smeared on the blade.

Michael Myers. In the fucking flesh.

Before Marcus could say anything, Michael stepped up onto the Elantra's trunk, and from there onto the car's roof. He took a couple steps, and then an instant later a white shape smacked onto the windshield: the bloody skull mask. When Marion saw it, she let out a shriek, raised her gun, and fired. The explosion was deafening in the confined space of the car, and the round punched a large hole in the windshield. The bullet struck the mask and flung it onto the hood. There was no sign of Michael, though.

An instant later there was a loud *crump*, and a portion of the ceiling above Marion's head was dented in. Marcus imagined Michael stomping on the roof to create the dent. It was almost as if the bastard was taunting Marion, letting her know precisely where he was because there was nothing she could do to stop him. Marion pointed her gun barrel toward the ceiling, as if she intended to shoot at Michael through the roof.

Vanessa screamed, and Marcus was concerned that any delay in acting might get them all killed.

"Fuck this bullshit!" he said. "We need to get out of here!"

Lindsey had left the Elantra running when she'd

gotten out. All they needed to do was put the engine in drive, floor the gas pedal, and they could leave Michael Myers' latex-covered ass in the dust. Marion didn't scoot over behind the wheel, though. She just kept staring up at the ceiling, eyes wide with terror, paralyzed by fear. Fine—if Marion wasn't going to get them out of here, he would.

Marcus started to climb into the front seat, but as he did, a hand struck the front passenger window with such force that the glass cracked. Marion screamed, pointed her gun at the window, and fired. Thunder boomed again inside the Elantra, and the window shattered. Michael's hand was no longer visible, and Marcus couldn't tell whether or not Marion had managed to hit him.

Panicking, Marion stabbed a finger onto the control that locked the Elantra's doors—all four of them.

Vanessa tried to open one of the rear passenger doors, but it refused to open. Marcus slipped back down into the backseat and tried the other passenger door with the same results. He realized then what had happened. In her panic, Marion had accidently activated the child locks on the back doors. Vanessa must've figured it out too, for she yelled, "Unlock the doors!"

Marion didn't listen. She whirled her gun around, aimed at the driver's side window, and fired. Glass exploded, and once more Marcus couldn't tell if Marion had succeeded in hitting Michael. He hadn't seen the man reaching toward the window, and he wondered if Marion was so jumpy that she'd fired without confirming a target. If she continued firing wildly like this, there was a good chance she'd end up hitting him or Vanessa, and that was a risk he didn't want to take.

A hand reached through the front passenger window and grabbed a fistful of Marion's hair. She moved to the side just as Michael pulled, and his hand came away with a clump of hair, leaving her with a blood-smeared patch of skin on her scalp.

Marcus had seen enough. He took the Desert Eagle from Vanessa, pointed it at the driver's side passenger window, and fired two shots. The weapon bucked in his hand like a thing alive, taking out most of the glass. He shoved the gun back in his wife's hand.

"Vanessa, go! I love you, baby!"

It took her a second to understand what he wanted her to do. Then she crawled over his lap and began wriggling through the broken window. She was slender and would have no problem getting through. She might cut herself on the remnants of window glass protruding from the door frame, but with any luck she wouldn't be injured too badly. Besides, a few cuts beat the hell out of getting accidently shot by a hysterical nurse with a bleeding scalp wound. Vanessa pushed her bare feet against the car seat to give herself a final shove forward, and then she was through the window and onto the ground outside.

His turn.

He started for the window, but just as he reached toward it, Michael dropped down off the roof in front of him, knife in one hand, a fistful of Marion's hair in the other.

*

Lindsey watched in horror as Michael attacked her friends. She winced at the sound of multiple gunshots, but Michael didn't fall. She wasn't surprised. Tommy might believe that Michael could be killed, and logically, Lindsey knew that he could. But the little girl inside her, the one that had sat next to Tommy on his couch watching the Dr. Dementia horror movie marathon while Laurie made popcorn in 1978, knew better. Michael was a monster, and true monsters never died.

The girls on the swings were watching Michael with wide-eyed disbelief, holding onto the chains of their swings with death grips, as if doing so would activate some kind of magic charm that might protect them. But Lindsey knew there was only one way to ensure their safety. She turned and gave them a command in the sternest mom voice she could muster.

"Run! *Now!* Go home!"

The girls looked at her, startled, and then they jumped off the swings and ran like hell across the park in the opposite direction.

Thank god, Lindsey thought. Two fewer victims for Michael to claim. Now she had to see what she could do to prevent Michael from killing her friends. She hadn't brought her gun with her when she left the car—hadn't wanted to scare the girls—but now she wished to hell she had. She would just have to improvise. She looked around to see what she might be able to work with. The girls had left their masks behind when they'd fled, but those wouldn't be of any use. They'd also left the pillowcase filled with candy, but unless Michael had a sweet tooth, she didn't see what they... Her gaze fell upon the crumbling brick of the trash receptacle then, and a plan came to her.

She snatched the pillowcase off the ground, ran over, and emptied the remaining candy into the receptacle. She then kicked at its brick housing, once, twice, three times. There had already been a couple bricks lying on the ground, but she wanted more, as many as she could get. She managed to dislodge several additional bricks and she crouched down and quickly filled the pillowcase with them. She stood, hefted the pillowcase, liked the feel of its weight. *This'll do*, she thought.

She started running toward the car.

*

When Marcus saw Michael standing before the broken passenger window, he scuttled to the other side of the car and tried to open the door, but it remained locked. Marion opened the front passenger side door and tried to get out, but suddenly Michael was there, and he attacked. Marion fell back onto the seat, and Michael reached in for her. She still had hold of her gun, but in her fear, it seemed she'd forgotten all about the weapon.

"Marion! Shoot him!" Marcus yelled.

She screamed and kicked, but Michael managed to grab hold of one of her feet and began pulling her toward him. She remembered her gun then and struggled to aim it at Michael, but she squeezed the trigger too soon, firing off two rounds, both of which struck the ceiling, missing him entirely. And then Marcus watched as Michael leaned in over Marion and slammed his knife into her chest. The strike was surgical in its precision, the blade slipping through the intercostal space between the fourth and fifth ribs to the left of the sternum.

Marion's eyes closed and she fell still.

As a doctor, Marcus was no stranger to death. He'd dissected cadavers in medical school, had patients with conditions that, despite his best efforts, had ultimately killed them. You learned to deal with death when you were a physician, to make your peace with it, or else you couldn't do the job. But he had never seen someone die like this before, her life snuffed out so easily, like someone blowing out a candle flame; one breath, then gone. And he could never have imagined the monstrous indifference toward human life demonstrated by Michael Myers. He was no different than a disease, a cancerous rot masquerading as a human being, a mindless thing that killed simply because it could. Well, Marcus was a doctor, goddammit, and it was his duty to combat disease, wherever he found it.

He'd given the Desert Eagle to Vanessa, but he had another tool to fight with, one much more appropriate for his profession. He reached into the pocket of his lab coat and pulled out his stethoscope. Michael had yet to remove the knife from Marion. He held it inside her body, his masked face mere inches from her own, and Marcus wondered what, if anything, he saw in the woman's lifeless eyes. Perhaps only his own emotionless reflection.

Marcus lunged over the seat toward Michael, wrapped the stethoscope around his neck and pulled it tight. Michael let go of the knife and reached upward with both hands, attempting to pull the black rubber tubing loose. But Marcus kept up the pressure, now twisting the tubing, making it tighter, his hands shaking from the effort. It shouldn't take long for the motherfucker to slip into unconsciousness. Most people could be choked out in five seconds or less, and even if they knew how to tense their neck muscles to slow the process, it still wouldn't take more than fifteen seconds, max. Once Michael was out, it would only take a few more minutes of pressure to kill him. Or maybe he'd speed things up by removing the knife from poor Marion and cutting Michael's throat, give the bastard a taste of his own medicine.

Michael's hands fell away from the tubing then, and Marcus thought that this was beddy-byes for the Boogeyman. But then Michael raised his left arm and rammed his elbow into Marcus' jaw. White light flashed behind his eyes, and he fell back, releasing his hold on the stethoscope. His ears rang, and he felt dizzy, but his vision cleared in time for Michael to yank the knife out of Marion, turn, and slam the blade up into Marcus' head just below his left eye. The metal penetrated his brain, killing him instantly.

*

When Vanessa climbed out of the Elantra's window, she fell onto the sidewalk next to the street. She didn't fall far, but she landed awkwardly on the concrete, and the impact stunned her for a second. She rolled onto her back and tried to catch her breath, then looked up and saw Michael Myers standing on the roof of Lindsey's car. He turned—his attention no doubt drawn by the sound of her falling—and when she saw that ivory face, when she felt the monster *looking* at her, *contemplating* her, as if trying to decide if he'd rather kill her now or save her for later, she freaked the fuck out. She jumped to her feet and ran into the park, propelled by blind unreasoning terror.

It felt like she ran forever, but when she glanced back to see if Michael had followed her—she imagined him right behind her, knife raised, ready to ram it into her flesh—she saw that she'd only run a dozen yards or so from the car. More than that, she saw that Michael had decided to ignore her for now. He'd jumped down from the Elantra and stood on the vehicle's passenger side, trying to get at Marion. A gun went off, firing twice, and Vanessa jumped at the sound. Then she grinned and felt like pumping her fist in the air. Marion had got the bastard!

But her sense of victory was short-lived. She couldn't make out specific details of what was happening in the car, but she could tell that a struggle was going on inside. She saw silhouettes moving, the car shaking in response to their exertions. It could only mean one thing: either Marion had only wounded Michael or she'd missed him altogether. Vanessa waited a second to see if Marion would fire the gun again, but no third shot came. Maybe Marion couldn't shoot again. Maybe she was dead. And if that was the case, only two people remained in the car: Michael Myers and Marcus. She felt like such an absolute shit for abandoning Marion and her husband. She'd fled from Michael out of pure instinct, without a single thought for anything but her own survival. She hadn't done it on purpose, but she *had* done it. What kind of person did that make her? If someone else had done the same thing, she would've told them that they were simply being human. But she still felt like a selfish bitch. Maybe if she hadn't dropped the Desert Eagle when she'd fallen out of the Elantra's window, she might've been able to do something, but as it was…

She realized something then. Her right hand wasn't empty. There was something in it, something *heavy*. She looked down and saw she still gripped the Desert Eagle. She *hadn't* dropped it when she'd hit the sidewalk. Without realizing it, she'd held onto the gun and carried it with her when she'd panicked. She'd been so terrified of Michael Myers that she'd completely forgotten she had a weapon which could fill him full of holes. *Big* ones. If she hadn't panicked, hadn't run, if she'd simply gotten up, aimed the Desert Eagle at Michael, and fired, he'd be dead now, and her Marcus wouldn't be in that car fighting for his life. She started running again, only this time she ran toward the Elantra.

I'm coming, baby, she thought. *Hold on…*

When she drew near the car, she started firing one-handed, but the gun's recoil was so strong, she nearly dropped the weapon. She got lucky, though, and her rounds stitched the side of Lindsey's car. Still, she doubted any of the bullets penetrated far enough to strike Michael. She needed to get closer.

She hurried around the front of the car to the passenger side. The door hung partially open, and she saw Michael was in the front seat, facing the back—facing *Marcus*. Marion lay on the front seat too, Michael's knife protruding from her chest, a widening bloodstain on the front of her blouse. Marcus was using his stethoscope to strangle Michael—*Hell, yeah!*—but she didn't know if he'd be able to choke Michael out. A stethoscope was hardly a garotte. She needed to get a little closer, then she could fire through the window and send Michael Myers straight to hell, where he belonged.

Hold on, baby, she thought. *Just a few seconds more…*

She saw Michael suddenly elbow Marcus in the face, watched Marcus recoil from the blow, saw Michael yank the knife out of Marion's chest and bury it her husband's brain, the blade sliding in just below the left eye.

"Marcus!" she screamed.

Michael spun around as she raised the Desert Eagle. He kicked the passenger side door hard, and it flew all the way open, striking Vanessa's gun hand. The impact caused her arm to fold at the elbow, bringing the Desert Eagle up so that the barrel pointed toward her face. Her finger tightened reflexively on the trigger, and for a fraction of a fraction of a second, she heard the sound of the gun going off, saw the bright muzzle flash.

And then she was as dead as her husband.

15

The Shape steps out of the car, knife in hand. He feels no exhilaration at having killed the vehicle's occupants, nor does he feel any amazement at the absurdly lucky way he managed to dispatch the woman with the gun. He observes the scene with clinical detachment, looking over the three bodies before turning his cold gaze to the playground, checking to see if the other prey—the woman with the long black hair, the two girls who aren't wearing their masks—are still there. If so, he will kill them next. But the playground is empty. The prey has escaped.

This does not dismay him. Perhaps he will run across them again, but if not, it doesn't matter. The world is filled with prey, and one is the same as another to him. They bleed, they die, and that's all he requires of them.

He starts to walk away from the car when he hears something behind him, a soft scuffing sound, like a shoe sliding on asphalt. Curious, he begins to turn...

*

Lindsey came around the back of the car, holding the pillowcase of bricks by one end, gripping it tight with both hands. Michael's back was to her.

He'd finished with Marion, Marcus, and Vanessa, and was preparing to move on in search of someone else to kill. She didn't intend to let that happen. Moving as quietly as she could, she stepped up behind him, lifting the pillowcase…

Michael started to turn around, and Lindsey swung the pillowcase hard and slammed the bricks against the back of his head. She put everything she had into the strike, and the blow caused Michael to grunt in pain and stagger forward. Encouraged, she moved toward him, stepped to his side, and this time swung the pillowcase directly at his face. He grunted again, louder this time, and when he staggered backward, he stumbled and fell onto his hands and knees. Lindsey didn't let up. She swung the pillowcase one more time, smashing it against the side of his head. The impact knocked him against the car, and he bounced off and slumped to the ground. He was still moving, although he was clearly dazed, and Lindsey made ready to hit him one more time with what she hoped would be the killing blow.

But this time when she raised the pillowcase, the fabric ripped and the bricks spilled onto the asphalt. Feeling weak and shaky, Lindsey dropped the useless pillowcase and walked toward the front of the car. She had to pass Vanessa's body on the way, and while she tried not to look too closely at the poor woman, she caught a glimpse of the bloody ruin that used to be her face, and she thought she would throw up that instant. The only thing that stopped her was the fear that she'd vomit *on* Vanessa's body, and that thought slammed a lid on her nausea. She didn't want to leave the woman here, lying in the street like some piece of unwanted refuse, but there were already two dead bodies in the car. Vanessa would just have to stay here for a bit until the police arrived.

Lindsey hurried around the front of the car, opened the driver's door, and started to climb in, but then she stopped. Marion lay on the front seat, taking up most of the room. Lindsey had left the engine running when she'd gotten out to check on those girls, and all she needed was enough space to squeeze in, then she could put the car in gear and get the hell out of here.

"Sorry, Marion."

She reached inside and, grimacing, awkwardly tried to push Marion's body to the side. It took some effort, but Lindsey made the room she needed. She got in, pulled the door shut, and reached for the gear shift. Next stop: the sheriff's department.

Lindsey had made a fatal mistake, though. She'd failed to lock the door behind her.

The door flew open, and Michael grabbed hold of Lindsey's arm and yanked her out of the car. He slammed her against the side of the vehicle, wrapped his hands around her neck, and began to squeeze. She grabbed hold of his wrists, tried to pull his hands away from her throat, but he was too strong. Then, as if to prove how truly strong he was, he lifted her off her feet with ease, as though she weighed nothing to him. The bastard was in his sixties! How could he *do* this?

Lindsey thrashed and kicked, but all her exertions did was use up the remaining oxygen in her lungs that much faster. She heard a roaring in her ears, saw bright speckles of light in her eyes, and she knew that she was going to die. She told herself that she'd managed to live an additional forty years after Michael had failed to kill her the first time, which was a damn good run, all things considered. But the thought did little to comfort her as darkness gathered on the edges of her vision, like storm clouds rolling in.

Suddenly, the horn blared, one long blast followed by several shorter ones.

Lindsey had no idea who could be doing it, but then she heard Marion—voice raspy, barely audible—say, "Let her go, Michael! And take what's coming to you! The killing must stop!"

Michael tossed Lindsey aside, and she fell to the ground and hungrily gulped for air. She was too weak to move. Her throat felt as if it was on fire, her lungs burned, and all she could do for the moment was lie there gasping for breath, and listen to what Marion said next.

"This is for you, Dr. Loomis…"

Then Lindsey heard a soft *click*.

She realized with horror what had happened. Marion, severely wounded, maybe even dying, had managed to aim her gun at Michael and pull the trigger. Unfortunately, she was out of ammunition. That, or the gun had misfired. Either way, she was fucked.

Lindsey saw Michael reach into the car. She heard

rustling, as if he'd grabbed hold of Marion and she fought him with what little strength remained to her. Then there was a *thud* and the horn blared again. Another *thud*, another horn blast. A third, a fourth… Lindsey felt a sick twist in her gut as she realized that Michael was slamming Marion's head against the steering wheel, over and over, each blow setting off the horn.

No… She tried to speak, but no sound escaped her swollen throat.

Another *thud*, another horn blast, only this time the horn continued blaring. It took Lindsey a second to understand what was happening. Michael had shoved Marion's head against the steering wheel, and this time he was holding it there, pushing, pushing, exerting more pressure with each passing second…

There was a sickening *crunch*, and Lindsey knew she had just heard the sound of Marion's skull being crushed. Her friend was dead.

Fear propelled Lindsey to her feet, and she staggered away from the car, coughing. Her head swam with vertigo, and she had to fight to maintain her balance, but she knew if she couldn't put distance between her and Michael—*fast*—she was a goner. She continued on, struggling to draw in air, and with each step she took it got easier. But then her right ankle rolled under her on the uneven ground, and she fell to the grass. The pain was sharp, and she cried out, reflexively wrapping a hand around her injury. She sat up, turned to look behind her, saw Michael walking across the grass, moving with the smooth, mechanical stride that she remembered so well from her childhood. How many times had she lived through scenarios like this in her nightmares? A hundred? A thousand? Now here she was, living the nightmare for real.

Then, as if she really was in a dream, she heard Laurie's voice speak to her. Not the voice of today's Laurie, one roughened by age and years of drinking. This was the voice of a young girl, a teenager, and it said three words.

Run, Lindsey! Hide!

Just like she had forty years ago, Lindsey listened to that voice. She forced herself to get on her feet and start moving again, half-running, half-limping, ignoring the screaming protests of her injured ankle. She didn't look back to see if Michael followed. She didn't have to. Michael *always* followed.

As she ran, she tried to remember what she knew about this park from when she'd brought her son here years ago. She remembered pushing Evan on the swings, playing tag with him on the grass, kicking a soccer ball back and forth… What else? At the back of the park was a stream — really a drainage ditch that sometimes filled with enough water to mimic a stream. The parks department had erected a small bridge over it so people could cross more easily, and Evan had liked to stand on the bridge, look down at the water, and pretend there were little fish in it, so small that only kids could see them.

She headed in the direction of the bridge — at least, she *hoped* it was the right direction. She hadn't been here for almost fifteen years. Her ankle throbbed, her leg felt like so much dead weight, and she was still having trouble getting full breaths. She was beginning to slow down, and she knew she couldn't keep running much longer. If she didn't find the bridge soon, Michael would catch up to her, and she would die.

But then she saw it—a short wooden bridge with rails on both sides—stretching across a sloping ditch, trees all around, houses in the distance. She risked a backward glance and saw Michael, a silhouette against the night sky, coming toward her, single-minded, relentless. He was several hundred feet behind her, she judged, but gaining. She didn't have much time. She reached the ditch and intended to climb down into it, but her injured ankle betrayed her, and she slipped and fell. The last time it had rained had been several days ago, and while the ground at the bottom of the ditch was moist, there was little actual water. She crawled toward the bridge, hoping to hide beneath it, but it was smaller than she'd remembered, and she wasn't sure it would provide sufficient cover, especially with the light from the full moon. Her hands and knees slid on mud, slowing her progress, and she had a flash of memory—Evan, jumping down into the ditch when it was like this, muddy after a recent rain, laughing as he rolled around, getting mud all over him. God, what a *mess* he'd made! She did the same now, rolling in the mud, scooping up handfuls and smearing it onto her face and neck. Then she moved beneath the bridge, pressed herself low to the ground, and waited.

Moments later, she heard heavy footfalls on the wooden planks above her. They stopped in the middle of the bridge, and then all she heard was Michael's breathing inside that mask of his, a labored, beast-like sound. Lindsey held her own breath. Her swollen throat was irritated, and she had to fight the urge to cough. If she made a noise—any noise—it would all be over for her.

There were small spaces between the bridge's floorboards, and she glanced upward. She once more saw Michael's silhouette—his *shape*—against the sky, saw the metal of his blade gleaming in the moonlight. Seconds passed, and then Michael started moving again, his boots clomping across the bridge. He'd turned around and was headed back the way he had come. Then he was on the grass, and she heard him continue on. She allowed herself to breathe then, and tears began to flow down her mud-stained cheeks. She'd listened to Laurie, or rather to her *memory* of Laurie: she'd run, she'd hid, and she was still alive. The babysitter was still taking care of her after all these years.

"Thanks," she whispered.

A wave of dizziness hit her then, and she felt herself losing consciousness She fought it, but she was too weak, her energy spent, and she had no choice but to surrender and let the darkness carry her away.

16

Karen stood at the bottom of the basement steps. Allyson, Ray, and Laurie lay on the floor around her, dead, their bodies mutilated, covered in blood. Bars stretched across the opening in the kitchen floor above, and Michael Myers stood on the other side, looking down at her, silent, impassive.

"What are you waiting for, you bastard?" she shouted, tears streaming down her face. "Aren't you going to kill me too?"

Michael just stood there, still and quiet as death itself. Then flames *whooshed* into life around Karen, quickly spreading to the wooden shelves on the walls, catching on the stairs. The flames rose higher, burned hotter, and smoke began to fill the basement. She tried to scream, but smoke rushed into her lungs, and she began to cough violently. But when the flames reached her flesh, she screamed then, loud and long. The fire took its time devouring her, and Michael watched every moment of it.

*

Karen jumped. Disoriented, she looked around wildly, expecting to see Michael Myers standing above her, bringing his knife down to strike. But he wasn't there. She was sitting in the ER's waiting area, people all around her, not one of them holding a weapon. She recognized the woman standing in front of her as the person she'd spoken to at the reception desk when they'd brought her mother in. She realized the woman must've woken her, had probably reached out and gently shaken her shoulder.

"I'm sorry, ma'am," the woman said. "I was told to get you. Your mother is awake."

"Thank you."

Karen rose from her seat, still groggy, and headed for her mother's room. God, she could use some coffee. After she'd spent some time with Laurie, maybe she'd run to the cafeteria and get some. It had already been a long night, and it looked like it was only going to get longer. She needed to stay alert, for when *he* came.

The lights were on in her mother's room, but Karen still hesitated in the doorway, not wishing to disturb Laurie in case she'd slipped back into sleep. But her mother sat propped up in the hospital bed, looking a little shaky but wide awake.

"Mom? Oh god, thank you." Karen hurried to her mother's side. "Just take it easy now."

Laurie gave her a loving, if exasperated, smile. "Karen, I'm fine."

Now it was Karen's turn to be exasperated. "You're *not* fine. You had a knife in your fucking stomach."

"Paper cut. Don't worry about it. Where's Allyson?"

Karen had been so happy to see her mother awake that she had momentarily forgotten about Allyson. She looked around, didn't see her anywhere. Had she stepped out to go to the restroom?

"She was supposed to be here," Karen said. "With you. You haven't seen her?"

"I've been geeked out on pain meds, kiddo, so… no."

Karen looked to the empty seat at Laurie's bedside and saw a greeting card sitting there. She picked it up and examined it. It was a get-well-soon card, a cutesy one with a cartoon doctor on the front holding an old-fashioned glass thermometer in the mouth of a fluffy cloud that had thin arms and legs. Karen opened the card. Inside, the cloud had turned black and bolts of electricity were shooting off of it. One had struck the doctor, making his hair frizz out. The caption read: *Hope you get well lightning-fast!* There were words written below in blue ink. Karen recognized Allyson's handwriting.

Evil can't win. I love you. I love Dad. I love Grandmother.

No, Karen thought. *No, no, no…*

"Is everything okay?" Laurie asked.

Karen closed the card and forced a smile.

"She went out with Cameron. Probably just needed to get some fresh air."

No way was she going to tell her mother the truth. The woman had just had major surgery, and the last thing she needed was to be worrying about her granddaughter.

Karen noticed something on the bed next to her mother, a wadded-up bundle of cloth with reddish-brown stains on it. Was that her shirt, the one she'd been wearing when Michael had stabbed her? What the hell was it doing here? One of the staff should've gotten rid of it when Laurie had arrived. Things *were* chaotic tonight, though—to say the least—and she supposed the shirt had just been overlooked. She put Allyson's card back on the chair, facedown so Laurie wouldn't be tempted to look at it, then picked up the bloody shirt and dropped it in a plastic waste receptacle next to her mother's bed.

When she'd finished, Laurie said, "I'm so proud of you, honey. We finally killed Michael. We *got* him."

Karen realized then that her mother didn't know the truth: that Michael Myers still lived.

There would be time to tell Laurie later, once she'd had a chance to recover a bit. If she knew Michael was still out there, she'd probably yank out her IV, hop out of bed, and head for the door, determined to go back out and hunt him down and finish the job she'd started. And in the process, she'd reopen her wound and likely bleed to death. Karen had to make sure that didn't happen.

"That's right," she said. "We got him."

"Burnt him to the goddamn ground. Wish I had a drink to toast you." She mimed raising a glass. "To victory."

Karen couldn't share her mother's celebratory mood. There had been no victory tonight, not for any of them. Laurie must have sensed something was wrong because she reached out and took one of Karen's hands.

"Now we can be a proper family like—" Laurie broke off, as if realizing something. "Oh god, honey. I'm so sorry about Ray. I can't imagine… But he died for a reason. Michael is gone."

Karen almost told her then. *Ray died for nothing. Michael is still alive, still killing…* But before she could say anything, an orderly wheeled a gurney into the room. A man lay on it, his throat wrapped in gauze, blanket pulled up to his chest. A nurse entered then and gave Laurie an apologetic smile.

"We're running short on rooms tonight. I'm afraid I'm going to have to ask you to share."

Laurie didn't respond to the nurse, though. She was looking at her new roommate.

"Frank?" she said.

It was Sheriff Hawkins.

*

Lonnie, Cameron, and Allyson continued their patrol of Haddonfield's streets. They hadn't seen anyone for a while now, nor had they gotten any word from Tommy or Lindsey. No calls, no texts. Lonnie told himself not to worry. They'd set out on their half-assed quest to track down Michael Myers themselves with every expectation they'd find the motherfucker, but really, what were the odds that any of them would? Haddonfield was a big town, and it wasn't like Michael would make things easy for them by walking down the middle of the goddamn street.

Most likely they'd drive around all night without seeing a single sign of the man, and in the morning they'd gather in a diner, drink bad coffee, and talk about how stupid they'd been to think they could do what the sheriff's department couldn't.

After a while, Allyson broke the silence. "You knew my father?"

"Ray? He used to sell me peyote. One time we were out on Lake Cherokee in a canoe with a shaman from Little Rock, and your dad got freaked out by his own reflection. He took off his pants and jumped in. So I stopped doing drugs with him, but I'll miss him."

"Dad?" Cameron said.

"What? It's true."

"No. Dad, what's that?"

Cameron pointed out the windshield. Lonnie looked and saw Tommy's SUV coming toward them. On their right was a small neighborhood park, and sitting next to the curb in front of it was a Hyundai Elantra—Lindsey's car. Headlights on, blinkers flashing, engine running.

"Oh shit," Lonnie breathed. "It's Tommy."

Tommy pulled up behind the Elantra, and Lonnie did a quick U-turn and parked behind him. He got out of his Altima, followed by Cameron and Allyson. Lonnie and Cameron carried their pistols, and Allyson held the sawed-off shotgun.

"You ready to use that, son?" Lonnie asked Cameron.

"Yes, sir," he said.

Tommy had gotten out of his SUV, gun in one hand, flashlight in the other. He exchanged a worried glance with Lonnie, but neither of them said anything as they stepped forward together to examine Lindsey's car, Allyson and Cameron close behind them.

Right away, it was clear some serious shit had gone down here. Bullet damage on the driver's side of the car, broken windows, bullet hole in the windshield, a ripped pillowcase on the ground near a bunch of scattered bricks... and inside the car, blood. *Lots* of it. No people, though.

Tommy turned away from the Elantra and shined his flashlight into the park.

"Lindsey?" he called.

"Marion?" Lonnie shouted.

No response. Tommy yelled again, louder this time.

"Lindsey!"

Still nothing.

Not good, Lonnie thought.

By unspoken agreement, the four entered the park to start searching for their missing friends. Both Lonnie and Tommy called out their names again, with increasing desperation, but still no one answered. There were trees and bushes all around, lots of places to hide. Even with the moonlight to aid them, they could search here for hours and not—

Tommy had moved away from the others, toward the playground area, and now he cried out.

"Oh no, oh *no*—Lonnie!"

Lonnie ran toward Tommy, gun extended, ready to fire, Cameron and Allyson hot on his heels. Tommy was shining his flashlight on the play equipment, and when Lonnie saw what the light revealed, he recoiled in shock.

Marion hung by her neck from one of the swing-set chains, head covered by a witch mask. Marcus sat on a slowly spinning merry-go-round, slumped against one of the bars, wearing a jack-o'-lantern mask. Vanessa had been arranged upside down on the slide, a skull mask on her head.

Lonnie had researched Michael Myers' previous murders for his book on the Boogeyman, and he was well familiar with Michael's predilection for staging macabre tableaus like this one. He'd done the same thing at Lindsey's house with Annie, Bob, and Lynda in '78, a deeply disturbed, homicidal child playing with life-sized dolls.

Lindsey, he realized. She wasn't here! Was she still alive, or had Michael killed her and staged her body elsewhere?

The four of them moved on, walking away from the slaughterhouse Michael Myers had made of the playground and heading deeper into the park. Tommy swung his flashlight beam back and forth as they went, but they saw nothing until they came upon a drainage ditch spanned by a small footbridge. Tommy played his flashlight beam over the bridge, revealing it to be empty. Allyson stepped closer to the ditch and shined her flashlight into it. At first, it seemed like nothing was there but a mound of mud, but the longer Lonnie looked at it, the more he realized it was a human form *covered* in mud.

He heard Allyson call out. "Over here!"

"Lindsey?" he said.

Tommy scrambled down into the ditch, and Lonnie, Cameron, and Allyson followed, slipping and sliding in the mud. Tommy knelt beside Lindsey and brushed mud from her face. Her eyes were closed, and Lonnie feared that Michael had killed her too, but then her eyes flew open and she drew in a rattling gasp of air. Her sudden movement caused everyone to jump back, as if they'd just seen a corpse return to life. Lindsey coughed several times and spit up a bit of blood. She struggled to sit up, and Tommy helped her. She looked at him blankly at first, without any sign of recognition. Her eyes were wide, terrified, and Lonnie thought she might scream. But then Tommy put a hand on her shoulder, and that seemed to calm her somewhat. She began speaking then, her voice a harsh whisper.

"I saw him," she said. "I saw *everything*. He's out there."

None of them had to ask who *he* was.

"I believe you, Lindsey." Tommy turned to the others. "I'll take her to the hospital. You guys go on without us."

Lonnie wanted them all to go, to ensure that Lindsey reached the hospital safely. But she was right. Michael *was* still out there, and likely not all that far from here. The rest of them had to keep searching in order to prevent him from killing again, no matter the cost.

Allyson took Lindsey's hand and gave it a reassuring squeeze.

"You're gonna be okay," she said.

Lindsey gave her a weak but grateful smile, and Lonnie marveled at the symmetry of the moment. Once, Laurie had reassured Lindsey that she was going to be all right, and now here was Laurie's granddaughter, doing the same. Lonnie's grandfather, long deceased, had had a weird folk saying that he liked to pass on: *Life sure is a funny old possum, ain't she?*

She sure is, Grandad, Lonnie thought.

Lindsey turned to Tommy and Lonnie then. "Who would've thought he'd bring us all back together like this? When we were kids, we used to dare each other to sneak into the old Myers house. Lonnie was the only one brave enough to do it."

Lonnie grinned. "I lied. I never made it inside."

Tommy and Lindsey laughed at this, but that set Lindsey off on another coughing fit. Together, Lonnie and Tommy helped her out of the drainage ditch, and the five of them—all now muddy to one degree or another—trudged back toward their vehicles.

*

The staff foot traffic was heavy outside Laurie's room. She could feel excitement building in the hospital, but she wasn't sure what was happening. Maybe news that Michael was dead was getting around, which meant that reporters would be

207

showing up soon, if they weren't already here. She hoped the hospital staff would keep them away from her. She'd spoken to far too many journalists over the years, and she'd long ago had her fill of them. The only writer she wanted to have anything to do with these days was Lonnie. She'd reluctantly let him interview her for his book on Michael, and she'd only allowed it because he was a friend. But he'd actually done a pretty decent job. Sure, his book was sensationalistic in places. Given the subject matter and reader expectation, how could it not be? But overall, she thought it was a respectable piece of journalism, and he'd treated her very fairly, like a person instead of some kind of fortunate freak who'd managed to escape Michael's knife.

She wondered if Lonnie would write a follow-up to his book, this one covering Michael's new murder spree in Haddonfield. If so, she'd be glad to help him out again. Because this time would be the *last* time. No coming back for Michael. He was nothing but blackened bone and ash now, and good fucking riddance. Maybe now she could get on with her life, pick up where she'd left off. Back in high school, she'd wanted to be a teacher. She wasn't so old that she couldn't finally fulfill that dream if she wished.

Frank had been sleeping ever since he'd been brought in, and she didn't know where Karen was. She'd left a bit ago—taking that greeting card with her for some reason—saying only that she'd be back soon. But soon had come and gone without any sign of her. Maybe she needed some time alone to deal with her grief over Ray's death. Neither of Laurie's two marriages had lasted all that long, so she had no idea what it would be like to be married to someone for almost twenty years, and then suddenly they were gone, their life cut short by a madman's knife. Ray had been kind of a flake, certainly not the sort of partner she would've chosen for her daughter. But he'd loved Karen, and together they had made a stable home for their child. That was a hell of a lot more than Laurie had been able to do, and she had to respect Ray for that, if for no other reason. She thought of the pain Karen must be enduring right now, and while she understood the desire, the *need*, for solitude better than almost anyone, she wished her baby was here so she could comfort her.

She also wished she had stronger pain meds. A *lot* stronger. She'd told Karen that she hadn't been hurt that bad, had called her injury a paper cut, but that had been bullshit. Getting stabbed in the gut hurt like a *bitch*. Still, it wasn't the first time she'd felt Michael's blade. She'd recovered in 1978, she'd recover now. Although she imagined it might take her a little longer this time. She wasn't a teenager anymore.

She looked over at Frank, studied his sleeping face. When he'd first been brought in, she thought he'd been another victim of Michael's, but Karen told her that in reality it was Michael's doctor—the man she'd called the new Loomis—who'd stabbed him in the neck. Further proof, as if she needed any, that Michael's evil was like a disease. Anyone who spent too much time around him had to be careful not to become infected. The real Dr. Loomis had managed it, but Sartain, it seemed, had been a far weaker man.

Frank stirred then, only a little, but she decided to see if he was awake.

"Frank?" she whispered. "Frank?"

His eyes remained closed, but she began talking softly anyway.

"Remember the time… a long time ago? I never told you—because I couldn't be sure… There are a number of guys it could have been, but… I always liked you. I liked to hope she was yours."

"You're crazy."

Hawkins opened his eyes, turned to look at her, smiled.

"You're awake."

His voice was weak as he spoke. "I kissed you that night. You held my hand. That was it. I was hoping for more. I always kind of liked you, Laurie. But I knew you were sweet on that Ben Tramer."

It was a warm moment between two old friends. They had history together, and they'd have even more after this night.

"We got him, Frank," Laurie said. "Michael's dead."

He smiled. "It's about time."

The nurse that had brought him in earlier returned now, carrying a plastic tray with several individually wrapped syringes and small vials of medicine on it, along with a thin laptop tucked beneath one arm. When she saw Hawkins, she smiled.

"Oh good, Officer, you're awake. The doctor has requested that I administer another round of lidocaine for your pain."

She placed the laptop on the rolling bedside table, then put the tray next to it. She then began to fill a syringe from a vial while Hawkins watched her work.

"I'm scared, Laurie," he said.

"No reason to be afraid anymore."

"No," he said. "That goddamn needle. Size of a chopstick."

Laurie smiled. She reached out her hand, and Hawkins took it. His grip was weak, but his hand felt good in hers.

"Help out my friend here, will ya?" she said to the nurse. "Make it a double. And while you're at it, see if you can rustle up some for me."

17

It had been one hell of a night so far, and it looked like it was only going to get worse.

Barker had lost track of the exact number of people Michael Myers had killed since escaping that transport bus. He had every deputy in the department out scouring the goddamn streets, and so far no one had so much as caught a glimpse of the spooky bastard. Sheriff was an elected position in Haddonfield, and Barker had been a longtime member of the department when he'd stood for election. He'd been well aware of the legend of Michael Myers, the indestructible murderer who stalked the night like some wrathful demon from hell. He'd never bought into that bullshit, of course. He didn't believe in the supernatural, only in what he could see, touch, and shoot. Myers was just a man—a seriously *fucked-up* man, but still human in the end. If the fucker had any kind of special powers, they never would've been able to capture him in the first place, *and* he wouldn't have had to wait forty years until a transfer to another hospital to escape. He'd have just walked through the goddamn walls of Smith's Grove like a serial-killing Houdini.

But the thing with legends was that people *wanted* to believe them. They made life more colorful, gave shape to people's hopes—and to their fears. Legends had power. They could inspire or they could frighten, and the more power people invested in them, the more they *believed*, the stronger the legends became and the greater their impact. This was what he'd been seeing since Myers had gotten free and started killing again. People all over town had begun losing their shit. They began seeing Michael Myers hiding in every shadow, lurking behind every tree, coming personally for them and their loved ones, like he was the fucking Grim Reaper or something. People were working themselves into a frenzy. He could *feel* it happening, right here in the hospital, and he was sure it was happening out there in the streets as well. Frightened people were *dangerous* people, especially when they gathered in groups and started feeding one another's fear. And if the situation reached critical mass, people became a singular unit—a mob—and that was its own kind of monster. As bad as things were now, and make no mistake, they were deep in the shitter at the moment, it would get infinitely worse if the good people of Haddonfield went crazy.

Case in point, former Sheriff Brackett. The man had retired from the department years ago, and now worked at the hospital as a security guard—a fact Barker had not been aware of until tonight. Barker had been on his way to speak to one of the clerks at the reception desk. He wanted to talk to a hospital supervisor, get them to do something, maybe post extra security, to keep a lid on what was slowly but surely escalating into an unstable situation. But when he saw Brackett and recognized him, he thought maybe the man would be able to help him, so he went over to talk to him. Big mistake. Michael had killed Brackett's daughter Annie in '78, and the former sheriff wasn't able to discuss the matter of her killer rationally.

"When they arrested Michael that night, I was telling my wife that our daughter had been killed," Brackett said. "So I wasn't there to put a bullet in his brain *like we should have*. Trust me, this is no time for prudence. Next time, maybe it's *your* daughter he takes."

There were at least twenty people milling around in the ER waiting area, all of them agitated, and Brackett—loud, angry, voiced filled with pain—had drawn most of their attention. They stopped what they were doing and turned to listen to him. *Like animals catching a scent*, Barton thought, *checking to make sure what they've detected isn't a threat.*

He wanted to say something that might calm Brackett, but no words came to him. Barker had children, two boys and a girl, all of them around the same age Annie had been when she'd died. He couldn't bear the thought of losing any of them, couldn't imagine the pain.

He still hadn't thought of a reply when a man standing at the reception desk started shouting at the clerk on duty, his face red with anger.

"How will I know if my brother is alive or not? I've been waiting for an *hour*. Who's in charge here?"

The clerk struggled to maintain her professional demeanor, but Barker could tell that she was frightened by the man's intensity.

"I need you to calm down, sir," she said, her voice shaking slightly.

The ER's entrance doors opened, and a middle-aged woman with a riot of red hair rushed in, ten people coming along behind her. Barker had no idea if they were all together or separate, and right then he didn't care. His attention was fixed on the woman. Her eyes were wild, and her head kept darting around, as if she was looking for something but wasn't sure what. The woman stopped just inside the doors and then yelled in a high-pitched hysterical voice:

"He's gonna kill everybody!"

Everyone in the area, staff and civilian alike, whipped their heads around to look at her.

"Jesus Christ," Barker breathed. He exchanged a look with Brackett, then stepped forward and spoke in his best crowd-control voice.

"We need to clear this entry point of civilians. Authorized medical and security personnel *only*. There is not enough security or medical help."

The red-haired woman fixed her wild-eyed gaze on Barker.

"Where are the police?" she demanded. *"Where are they?"*

Detective Graham walked into the waiting area then, with two doctors and another five people behind him. *More goddamn people*, Barker thought. *Just what we need.*

Graham had heard the woman's question, and he answered.

"We've requested backup officers and medical staff from Russellville and Eaton County for support but no confirmation. We can't account for this scope of crime scene and—"

Graham was cut off as another woman ran into the ER. Another five people entered behind her.

Too many, Barker thought. *Too fucking many...*

This woman had curly brown hair, and her eyes were red from crying. She rushed to the reception desk and pushed aside the angry man, who glared at her poisonously.

"My son Oscar," she said. "Is he here? I got a call. I'm his mother. Is he alive?"

Brackett walked away from Barker and headed toward several security officers standing in the back of the waiting area. Good. Maybe he could get them to do something to help with this crowd before the situation blew up in all their faces.

A loud despairing wail came from one of the hallways, and Barker knew someone had just received horrific news. He heard movement from that direction, as if a second crowd was gathering back there. Two smaller mobs equaled one *big* mob. He needed to shut this down now, but he didn't know how. He could feel the situation getting away from him, like a snowball rolling down a hill, gathering more snow as it goes, mass increasing, picking up speed, rolling faster and faster until there's nothing anyone can do to stop it.

The ER doors opened once more, and the blare of sirens came from the parking lot, heralding the arrival of more ambulances. A man burst into the waiting area, supporting a woman whose clothes were slathered with mud. Behind him, ten more people struggled to fit through the entrance, pushing and shoving in their need to beat the others inside.

"Help!" the man called out. "This woman needs help!"

The two doctors who'd entered the waiting area with Graham rushed over to assist the man. Barker heard the desk clerk speaking to the crying mother.

"Triage expansion has just opened up. I'm gonna have you sign in here."

She handed the woman a clipboard and a pen. The woman took them, but her hands were shaking so badly she couldn't write, and she handed them back to the clerk.

"I can't use this pen. The last name is spelled B-E-R-L-U-C-C-H-I..."

An orderly had brought a gurney for the mud-covered woman, and the doctors got her on it and pushed her into a hallway. The nurse's station was located down that hall, and now ten people fought their way past the doctors and the gurney to surge into the waiting area.

Brackett had finished speaking with the other

guards and was heading back in Barker's direction. The man who had brought in the mud-covered woman spotted the former sheriff, and made a beeline for him.

"Tommy!" Brackett said.

"Brackett! I had a run-in with Myers and then witnessed the aftermath of a slaughter at Husker Park."

That caught Barker's attention. Christ, was it ever going to end?

Karen entered the waiting area from the hallway then, and Barker actually groaned. What the fuck did *she* want? But as it turned out, she didn't want anything from him. She went straight to Tommy. He hurried to meet her.

"Karen! How's your mom? How's Laurie? Is she okay?"

Karen did not look pleased to see the man. In fact, she looked downright pissed. "Where's Allyson? I want my daughter back!"

Tommy retreated a step, raised his hands in a Don't-Worry-Everything's-Cool gesture. "She's okay. She's with Lonnie and Cameron."

Karen did not look reassured. If anything, Tommy's words seemed to upset her even more. "But he's coming *here*! She's not supposed to be with them. She's supposed to be with *me*!"

Tommy frowned. "He's coming here? How do you know?"

Barker knew who *he* was—Michael Myers. This had to be hysteria on Karen's part, a result of the trauma she'd experienced when Myers had attacked her, Allyson, and Laurie earlier that evening. There was no way she could know what the freak would do next, no way anyone could. As near as Barker could tell, Myers didn't select his victims according to any predictable pattern. Anyone unlucky enough to get in the bastard's way became his victim. Still, he wasn't about to take any chances tonight, especially not here, where the emotional atmosphere was like a ticking bomb ready to go off any minute.

He turned to Graham and nodded. "Secure a perimeter," Graham said to the other officers present. "Hospital on lockdown."

Barker turned to look at Tommy and Karen, and he saw a crowd had gathered around them, some people in street clothes, some in Halloween costumes.

Tommy raised his voice so he could be heard by them all.

"The Boogeyman is at large. He has no choice but to emerge. He's an apex predator."

People in the crowd looked at each other, confused, frightened. Karen spoke next.

"He killed our loved ones. Our husbands, our friends. And now his prey is here at this hospital."

Some in the crowd gasped in surprise and shock, while others looked angry, as if they'd be happy to tear Michael apart with their bare hands if they could get hold of him.

Tommy looked at Karen. "If you're right, Karen, I'm right beside you. When he surfaces, there will be no pause, no empathy. This ends when Michael is dead!"

A number of people in the crowd shouted their agreement, and more than a few cheered. Most took out phones and began texting, and it was in that moment that Barker realized the whole situation was about to go to shit. People were contacting friends and relatives, telling them what Karen had said, that Michael Myers was coming to the hospital. Some would stay away, but more would come, maybe most of them, come to help stop the monster that had haunted their town since 1963. It would be a madhouse.

Encouraged by the crowd's response, Tommy went on, sounding more confident now.

"Michael Myers will be executed on sight, and it will not go without witness. We need all of you! *Evil dies tonight!*"

The crowd roared with one voice, a fusion of fear and hate. It was the sound of a pack of animals, thirsty for fresh meat and hot, sweet blood. Barker felt a sinking sensation in the pit of his stomach, and he knew he had only seconds to defuse the situation—if it wasn't already too late.

He shouldered his way through the crowd and joined Tommy and Karen at its center.

"Everyone calm down!" he shouted. "The sheriff's department has—"

Tommy cut him off. "We will not calm down! We've seen your department fail tonight. This is *Haddonfield*. This is *our* town!"

Brackett stood at the forefront of the crowd, and now he spoke.

"He killed my daughter forty years ago and desecrated her body. This has to end. Evil dies tonight!"

Shit, they have a rallying cry now.

"Goddammit, Brackett!" Barker shouted. "I'm the law—not you!"

The crowd roared again, took several steps closer. Fury twisted their features into inhuman masks, and Barker knew there was no law in this place, not anymore.

*

Tommy hurried down the hallway in the direction he'd seen Karen come from. Laurie's room had to be this way. All he had to do was find it. Karen caught up to him, grabbed his elbow to try and stop him, but he shrugged her off and kept going.

He knew he'd reached the right room when Karen said, "Tommy, you can't go in there!"

The door was open, and Tommy ignored Karen and walked straight in.

For a moment, he thought he was in the wrong room. There were *two* patients in this one, their beds divided by a curtain. A nurse stood by the bed of a man with a bandaged throat. His eyes were closed, and from his heavy breathing, Tommy assumed he was sleeping. The nurse was typing something on a laptop resting on the rolling bedside table. *Probably recording the man's latest stats*, he thought. Blood pressure, heart rate, that kind of shit. The man looked familiar, but Tommy didn't... And then it hit him. Officer Hawkins! What the hell had happened to him?

But before he could follow this line of thought any farther, he realized he *did* have the right room. The patient in the bed on the other side of the curtain was...

"Laurie!" he said.

She looked as if she might have been on the verge of dozing off herself, but when she heard his voice her eyes flew open.

"Tommy?"

He hurried to the side of her bed. Karen came into the room then, but Tommy kept his gaze fixed on Laurie.

Words spilled out of his mouth in a rush. "He killed Marion and others. He attacked Lindsey."

Laurie's eyes widened in disbelief. *"What?"*

Tommy went on. "I just want you to know that when he comes here, he's a dead man. You protected me forty years ago. Tonight, I'm protecting you!"

Karen stood on the other side of Laurie's bed now, and Laurie turned to her daughter, confused.

"Mom... I'm sorry," she said. "We didn't know for sure."

Laurie looked at Karen, then at Tommy, her face clouding with a storm of emotion. She grabbed hold of the curtain between her bed and Hawkins and yanked it back.

"Excuse me, nurse," she said, voice tight. "I appreciate you, but would you please get the fuck out of here and excuse us for one second?"

The nurse held up a finger. "I just need to enter one more—"

"*Now!*" Laurie shouted.

Startled, the nurse snapped the laptop shut, picked it up, and hurried out of the room, leaving so abruptly that she forgot the tray with the syringes and vials of lidocaine. When she was gone, Laurie gave Karen an accusing look.

"I didn't know what to tell you," Karen said, voice soft, eyes downcast. "I just want you to be okay."

Laurie's face softened, and she lay back against her bed, wincing, as if moving pained her. A faraway look came into her eyes, and when she spoke, her voice held a tone of bemusement.

"He's followed me all these years," she said. "We had him. We *had* him, Karen. It's impossible." She turned to her daughter. "How did he escape that fire?"

"I don't know," Karen said.

Tommy knew the basics of what had happened to Laurie tonight. Karen had quickly filled him in back in the ER's waiting area.

"What can we do?" he said. "The police don't have the support."

Laurie's features hardened into a mask of determination. Tommy had seen that expression before, forty years ago, when Laurie had risked her own life to protect him and Lindsey.

"We fight," she said. "We never stop fighting." She grabbed hold of his hand and held it tightly as her gaze bore into him. "Find him, Tommy!"

She gave his hand a last squeeze and then let it go. Tommy looked at her a moment, and an understanding passed between them, something that only he, Laurie, and Lindsey shared. He nodded, then turned and ran out of the room.

He had work to do.

*

As soon as Tommy was gone, Laurie started to get out of bed. She wouldn't let him fight alone. She tried to sit up, but the movement strained her stitches, and fiery pain erupted in her abdomen. She grimaced and drew in a hissing breath. Fuck, that *hurt*! She continued trying to sit up, but Karen took hold of her shoulders and held her still.

"Don't, Mom. *You* need to listen to *me*. All the preparation in the world—and for what? Ray is dead. So many people are dead because we are not equipped. Allyson has run off with Lonnie and everyone is losing their minds. There are authorities trained to help with exactly this kind of…" She shook her head, unable to think of the words. Finally, she said, "There's a system!"

"Fuck the system," Laurie said.

She gently pushed Karen's hands away, then she yanked the IV out of her arm. Blood welled from the wound, but she ignored it. She pulled off the leads attaching her to the monitoring equipment, then—gritting her teeth against the pain—she sat up, gingerly swung her legs over the side of the bed, grabbed hold of Karen's arm to brace herself, and put her feet on the tiled floor. One of her ankles had been fractured during her battle with Michael and had a molded cast on it, with an Ace bandage to keep it in place. It hurt when she tried to put weight on it, but the pain was nothing compared to that in her abdomen, and she could deal with it. She let go of Karen and, moving with slow shuffling steps, walked over to the rolling table next to Frank's bed. She tore open one of the syringe packets his nurse had left behind, took out the syringe, then picked up one of the lidocaine bottles.

"No!" Karen said. "What are you doing? Stop it. You're being a crazy person!"

Laurie inserted the needle through the vial's rubber stopper and began to draw the medicine into the syringe.

"What are you doing?" Karen said, frantic now. "Do you even know what that stuff *is*?"

"It makes the pain go away."

With her free hand, Laurie lifted her gown to expose her belly. Her wound had been covered with packing gauze, pressed against her body by a bandage secured with medical tape, and holding all that together was an abdominal wrap, which looked to her like another big Ace bandage. *At least my guts won't spill out*, she thought.

She jammed the needle into her belly, then fought to hold back a scream as she injected the medicine. When the syringe was empty, she removed it and took several deep breaths. The pain was already beginning to lessen. She looked at Karen.

"Let him come," she said. "Let him take my head as I take his. Maybe the only way he can die is if I die too. Let's get this nightmare over with. You and Allyson shouldn't spend your lives running from the darkness I created."

"Stop it, Mom!" Karen sounded close to tears. "I'm not going to let anything happen to you."

"We can't stop until this is over."

Laurie put the used syringe on the tray, then started toward the trash container next to her bed. Her fractured ankle protested, but she told it to shut the hell up. She reached inside, removed the bloodstained shirt, unwrapped it, and withdrew the knife that Allyson had left for her. She straightened, and then turned to face her daughter.

"Michael will not stop killing until he finds me. He's after me, but I can kill him. I *will* kill him." She held up the knife, tilted her head to the side, examined the way light shone on the metal. Then softly, she said, "He breathes, he kills, he dies."

18

Anthony Tivoli limped into the parking lot of Haddonfield Memorial Hospital. Since wrecking that car back at Mick's Bar and Grill, he'd been walking all over town, and his feet were *killing* him. Damn slippers. It had only been a day since he'd left Smith's Grove, and the cheap things were falling apart. It made him sad. He wondered if feet could get sad. If so, his surely were.

Finding the hospital had taken longer than he'd thought. It didn't help that he'd kept having to hide whenever a police car drove by—and there were a lot of them out tonight! When he'd first seen a police cruiser after the accident, he'd almost walked into the street to flag it down, hoping the officer would give him a ride to the hospital. But then he thought about how he'd left the bus last night, after Michael had caused it to run off the road when he'd escaped his restraints and attacked the driver. Tivoli hadn't done anything wrong, hadn't hurt anyone, but he hadn't remained behind to help, either. He'd left as fast as he could, mostly because he'd been scared and hadn't known what else to do. But he had fled the scene of an accident, and he knew that was wrong. And he'd done it again tonight, after driving that Ford Fiesta into a wall. What if the police knew what he'd done and were out looking for him? They would take him to jail, lock him up, and throw away the key, and he would never reach the hospital then, would never be *safe*. So he'd hid instead of trying to catch the officer's attention, and he'd hid every time another cruiser drove past.

But he was here now, and soon he'd be inside and there would be doctors to take care of him, bandage the cut on his forehead, give him medicine to make him feel calmer, take him to a room with a soft bed so he could lie down and rest. And they'd give him brand-new slippers too! An orderly would bring him something to eat. Maybe a piece of chocolate cake and some milk. He really liked chocolate cake. His mouth watered just thinking about it.

The hospital parking lot was very busy tonight, cars coming and going, people rushing inside, more people standing outside talking. There were ambulances in the lot, police cruisers too, and Tivoli knew he would have to be careful going inside so the police didn't see him. He would have to be *sneaky*. Once he'd spoken to a doctor, he thought he'd be okay. The doctors would make sure the police wouldn't take him away. But he had to make sure to avoid the police until then. It wouldn't be easy. Police could read your mind when they stood close to you. Their badges contained tiny mind-reading machines given to them when they graduated police school. It was how they identified bad guys. He decided that if a policeman came too near him, he'd concentrate on the Queen of the Night's aria from Mozart's *The Magic Flute*. Not only was it a favorite of his, it was one of the most difficult arias ever composed. *That* would be sure to block any police officer's telepathic powers!

As he approached the hospital's emergency room entrance, Tivoli became aware that the people standing outside were watching him. He wasn't worried about them reading his mind—they weren't wearing badges—but their scrutiny made him uncomfortable nevertheless.

They're looking at you because you're ugly. His mother's voice.

And because you're fat. His father.

You're disgusting.

Filthy.

They can smell the crazy on you.

They hate you.

Tivoli rarely heard his parents' voices anymore, but he'd been without his medicine for over twenty-four hours, and they'd begun speaking to him again. He balled his hands into fists and ground them against his ears.

"Shut up, shut up, *shut up*!"

The crowd outside the ER entrance looked at him with a mixture of concern and wariness. He heard several of them speak.

"Check it out. Who is that?"

"Mister? Hey, mister? Are you okay?"

He ignored them. Everything would be all right once he was inside. He'd be *safe*. He kept his head down to avoid meeting anyone's eyes as he hurried through the ER doors.

*

The two Johns sat on the leather couch in their living room, nibbling on the last of the goodies from their charcuterie board. The fire was still going, and a horror movie was playing on the TV, the original version of *Black Christmas*. They'd seen both of the remakes, and they agreed that the original was still the best.

Little John held a joint in his hand, and he took a hit now, drawing the smoke deep into his lungs. He held it as long as he could, and then slowly released it. He felt satisfyingly mellow, so much so that he was no longer irritated at the little snots who'd stolen their candy bars. They had chutzpah, those three. He'd have never attempted anything so bold when he'd been a kid. He figured they'd probably take their thievery pro one day, become lawyers or maybe go into politics.

Big John leaned forward on the couch, slowly twirling a wooden dipper inside a jar of manuka honey resting on the coffee table. Out of nowhere, he began talking.

"The waggle dance is how bees actually communicate. It's how they share the information of where the flower is to the colony of bees."

Little John frowned. "A colony of bees? What?"

Big John lifted the honey dipper from the jar, held it over his mouth, and allowed a stream of the thick, delicious stuff to fall onto his tongue. He swallowed, made a *mmmmm* sound, then looked at Little John.

"They communicate the precise location by shaking their butts."

Little John laughed. "You're high."

"They still shake those furry little tushies."

Little John grew quiet then.

"My mother used to keep bees before she died," he said.

"No shit?" Big John said. "You never told me that."

Little John and his mother hadn't gotten along all that well. She'd desperately wanted grandkids, and when she learned her son was gay, she believed that dream had died. Little John had tried to explain to her that he could still adopt, but that wasn't good enough for her. She wanted *real* grandchildren, she'd said—as if adopted kids weren't real. Jesus fucking Christ.

There was a loud knock on their back door.

He groaned. "Not again. Halloween is over!"

Big John put the honey dipper back in the jar, picked up the remote, and turned off the TV. Little John placed the joint in an ashtray.

Another knock, just one, louder than the last. It sounded to Little John like someone was trying to batter the door down.

The Johns exchanged a look, then they rose from the couch and walked into the kitchen. Big John flipped on the light, and then—keeping close to one another—they crossed to the back door. It was shut, and when Little John tried the knob, he found it locked. Big John turned on the back porchlight and peered through the window. No one was there. He unlocked the door, opened it, and stepped outside.

"Knock it off, kids!" he shouted.

Silence, and then they heard another loud knock—only this time it came from the front door.

Little John shivered. He was *not* enjoying this. Halloween pranks were one thing, but this was just fucking creepy.

Big John stepped inside and closed the door behind him.

"Goddamn kids," he muttered. He headed back toward the living room, and Little John followed, automatically turning off the kitchen light as they went.

Big John stopped at the hall closet, opened it, and rummaged around for a moment. He withdrew a nine iron from a golf bag and gripped it tight in his hands. He closed the closet door and headed for the front door, Little John right behind him. When he reached the door, he held up the club, ready to swing, then opened the door quickly and stepped out onto the porch. Little John followed, worried. Their horror versions of the *American Gothic* couple stared out at the yard, candle flame still flickering inside the jack-o'-lantern impaled on the devil farmer's pitchfork.

"Don't do anything stupid," Little John said. "We don't want to get sued. It's just those kids trying to scare us."

Big John ignored him as he scanned the yard. A breeze blew, making one of the bushes rustle softly.

"One of those little bitches is out there," Little John said. "I hear 'em."

A thought occurred to Big John then. "Did you lock the back door?"

Big John looked at him for a moment, unsure. Little John re-entered the house to go check. *It's the kids,* he told himself. *That's all. Playing one last prank before Halloween night is over.*

When he entered the kitchen, he flipped on the light—and froze. The back door was slightly ajar, the kitchen trash can had been overturned, and there was a bloody handprint on the countertop. If this was a prank, it was a damn sadistic one.

"John?" he called out.

From the front porch, Big John called back.

"Yes?"

"Someone's in our house," Little John said.

A moment later Big John entered the kitchen. He'd discarded the nine iron and was now holding a small paring knife he'd grabbed from the charcuterie board along the way. *A weapon,* Little John thought. *That's an excellent idea.* He reached for the butcher block on the counter and pulled out a large carving knife.

Ready—or at least as ready as they were going to be—they stepped out of the kitchen.

*

Laurie, dressed once again in the bloody, tattered clothes she'd been wearing when she got here, walked into the ER waiting area. Karen hovered at her side, as if she expected her mother to pass out at any moment and was determined to catch her when she did. The lidocaine she'd injected into her abdomen was keeping the worst of the pain at bay, if not all of it. She had no idea how long the medicine's effect would last, so she'd taken the remaining vials and syringes with her when she'd left the room. She carried them in the front pocket of her jeans, ready for when she needed them. She'd brought the knife, too, had it hidden beneath her shirt, tucked into the abdominal wrap. The cold metal felt reassuring against her skin.

She was looking for Tommy, hoped he hadn't left yet. She wanted to go with him, to join the hunt for Michael. She knew Karen would do whatever she could to stop her, and while she didn't want to upset her daughter any further, she wasn't about to lie in a fucking hospital bed while the sonofabitch was still killing people. Plus, if Michael really *was* coming for her, she needed to get out of the hospital before he arrived. Ray had died tonight at Michael's hands, all because he'd been in *her* house when the bastard had attacked. She wouldn't endanger anyone else.

The waiting area was *insane*, packed wall to wall with people, many of them in costume, all of them talking animatedly. It seemed like the entire population of Haddonfield had crammed themselves into the hospital. A lot of them looked scared, but more looked angry. The atmosphere felt charged, like the moment before a violent thunderstorm broke loose. It felt wild, dangerous, like anything could happen. From where she stood, Laurie had only a partial view of the ER entrance, but she saw the doors slide open and caught a glimpse of a man walking in. He had some kind of wound on his forehead, and was dressed in a white T-shirt and white pants. Something about his outfit seemed familiar to her, but she wasn't sure what. She tried to get a better look at his face, but there were too many people in the way.

Others noticed the man and began talking about him, but Laurie only caught a few snippets of their conversations.

"Is that *him*?"

"There he is! I saw his face on TV."

She saw Tommy then. He was watching the man, same as everyone else in the crowd, although it looked as if his view was just as obscured as hers. Holding onto her stomach for support, Laurie headed toward him, Karen following. When she reached him, she said, "What's going on, Tommy?"

He didn't turn to her, just stood on his tiptoes, straining to see overtop the crowd.

"I don't know," he said.

Karen tried standing on her tiptoes as well.

"Who *is* it?" she asked.

Then someone in the crowd, as if hearing Karen's question, shouted, "It's Michael Myers!"

Laurie felt a cold sensation deep in her gut that had nothing to do with her wound.

He's here. He's come for me. I didn't get out in time...

Tommy started shoving his way through the crowd, desperate to get at Michael. Laurie was too weak to follow him, so all she could do was mentally urge him on.

Go, Tommy, go!

*

"Help me."

Tivoli held out his hands to the person nearest him—a woman wearing clown makeup and a frizzy red wig—but she recoiled from him and turned away. He knew she wasn't a doctor or a nurse. Clowns lived in circuses and made people laugh. They didn't work in hospitals. But there were so *many* people in here, more, he thought, than he'd ever seen in one place in his entire life, and there were no doctors or nurses *anywhere*. None that he could see, anyway. He hoped someone in the crowd might help him, or at least tell him where the doctors were, but many of them shied away from him, like Clown Lady had done, while others looked at him with scary eyes, like they *hated* him, like they wanted to *hurt* him.

Maybe, he realized, he'd made a mistake coming here.

He saw a man pushing through the crowd, fighting to reach him, and he allowed himself to hope that it was a doctor coming to his rescue. But the man wasn't wearing doctor clothes, and his eyes burned with a hatred so strong, Tivoli wouldn't have been surprised if laser beams blasted out of them and melted his face on the spot. Maybe he really *could* shoot laser beams, and if that was so, Tivoli had to get out of here before the man could get a clear shot at him.

He shoved aside an old man with a cane, and started to run. He heard people cry out, heard someone shout, *Did you see him stab that old guy?* Tivoli fought his way through the crowd, hitting, kicking, clawing, doing whatever was necessary to make progress. He didn't *want* to hurt anyone, but he didn't want to die, either, he really, really didn't. He saw a hallway ahead of him. It wasn't as crowded, and he thought if he could reach it, he'd be able to run, even in these goddamn falling-apart slippers, and then maybe he'd be able to find a doctor or nurse who would protect him from the man with the laser eyes.

Seeing him escape, the man shouted, "Michael! Stop!"

Tivoli didn't understand. Was Michael here too? Had he also come to Haddonfield Memorial in search of someone to help him? That didn't seem right. Michael would be more likely to put people *in* the hospital than come here himself.

"He's getting away!" Laser Eyes yelled. "Stop him!"

Tivoli wished he had his umbrella with him. He could use its comfort now.

Then Laser Eyes shouted three words that chilled Tivoli to the core of his being.

"Evil dies tonight!"

Several people in the crowd repeated those words, then several more. Soon the entire crowd was chanting in unison. *Evil dies tonight! Evil dies tonight!*

They're coming for you, his mother said.

They're going to give you what you deserve, his father said.

Then together they said, *They're going to punish you!*

Tivoli sobbed as he reached the hallway and began running. Behind him, led by Laser Eyes, the crowd surged after him.

*

Laurie kept trying to get a look at the man's face, but not only were there too many goddamn people, they were in constant movement, so every time she *did* catch a glimpse of him, her view was instantly blocked again. Still, she saw enough to make her doubt the man was Michael. His body shape was different for one thing. He was shorter and stockier than Michael. But more than that, he didn't *move* like Michael. Michael moved with precise, economical motions, not a single iota of energy wasted. He was like a machine that way. But *this* man… he was awkward, clumsy, moving more like a frightened animal than a cold, emotionless killer.

"It's him!" someone shouted.

"Wait!" Laurie shouted. "That's not him!"

"It *is* him!" someone else insisted.

"I've seen his face!" she called, but no one paid any attention, and no one slowed down, let alone stopped.

Karen gave Laurie a confused look. "It's not him?"

Laurie grabbed Karen's hand.

"C'mon! We have to stop them!"

Karen still looked confused, but she allowed Laurie to pull her forward. Together, they joined the crowd that was pursing "Michael" down the hallway. *No, not crowd*, Laurie thought. *Mob.*

19

The man made it into the hallway, but when the medical staff saw Tommy and the others coming, they rushed to hold the swinging entry doors at the end of the hallway shut. The crowd slammed into the doors and pushed with all their combined strength. The pressure was too much for the staff, and the doors flew open, sending them stumbling backward. The sudden release of the doors allowed the crowd to surge through, and Tommy—in the forefront—was almost knocked down by the people behind him. But someone grabbed hold of his arm to steady him, and then he was moving forward again, once more leading the chant.

"Evil dies tonight!"

The crowd echoed him in a voice like thunder.

The exhilaration Tommy felt was an electric current running through his veins. He'd never experienced a sense of *power* like this before. It was beyond any sensation; sex, drugs, booze—nothing could compare. This was what it felt like to be strong, unstoppable, *unafraid*… He'd spent the better part of his life being scared one way or another, but he felt no fear now. He had the strength of the pack behind him, and together, they could accomplish anything—including ending Michael Myers' life once and for all.

This is for all the victims, he thought. *We kill tonight in your names*.

The pack continued running.

*

Once the mob flooded into the hallway, it began breaking up. Some people inspected offices and rooms, while others ran down branching hallways. Still others entered the stairwell, intending to search the upper and lower floors. In one way, Laurie found this encouraging. Smaller groups were less dangerous overall. But they came with their own problems. Spread out, they would be even harder to control, and they could cause mischief all over the hospital, not just in one location. Speaking of control, where the *fuck* were Barker and Graham? The situation was on the verge of becoming a full-scale riot—if it hadn't already reached that point—and it needed to be shut down immediately.

Laurie and Karen stood off to the side as men and women ran back and forth down the hallway, shouting encouragement to each other and chanting Tommy's mantra. *Evil dies tonight!* From somewhere farther down the hall came the sounds of glass shattering and equipment hitting the floor. Laurie's frustration boiled over.

"It's not him, you fucking sheep!" she shouted. "It's the wrong person!"

Everyone ignored her.

A doctor came running toward her, a scalpel in his hand, and Laurie knew he'd gotten caught up in the mob's frenzy. As he drew near, his shoulder smacked into Karen's, the impact almost knocking her down. Without thinking, Laurie grabbed hold of the asshole and slammed him against the wall.

"Watch it, lady!" the doctor growled. "Don't you know there's a killer on the loose?"

He pulled away from her and continued running down the hall, scalpel gripped tight.

Laurie watched him go, feeling helpless. She was only one person. What could she hope to— She felt a sharp pain in her stomach, and she lifted her shirt to reveal a bloodstain spreading on the abdominal wrap. She'd pulled a stitch or two when she'd stopped that asshole doctor. *Fuck!*

Karen saw the blood before Laurie could lower her shirt again. She took hold of Laurie's elbow, as much to keep her from running, Laurie thought, as from concern.

"Mom, let's get you out of here!"

Laurie didn't answer. She looked around and saw a nurse—the one who'd been taking care of Frank—halfway down the hall. She looked lost, as if she didn't know what to do or where to go. Laurie shrugged off Karen and started walking toward the woman.

"Nurse!" she said. "I need bandages!"

The blood had begun to soak through Laurie's shirt, and the nurse noticed it immediately.

"You *need* to get back to that bed!" the woman said.

Laurie stepped close to her, leaned forward, got in her face. "Do you know who I am?"

"I don't give a shit!" the nurse said.

Laurie was about to unload on the woman, but a wave of vertigo hit her, and she collapsed to the floor. Karen swiftly knelt down in front of her, as if to shield Laurie from the people still running up and down the hallway.

Laurie waved Karen off as she struggled to sit up. "I'm okay, I'm okay."

Karen wasn't having any of it. "Mom, you're *bleeding*. We've gotta get you out of here."

She looked for the nurse, but the woman had run off. She was almost at the other end of the hallway, but when Karen shouted for her to stop, she just kept going. Karen looked around, searching for someone else. "Somebody help me!" she cried out.

But no one did. Haddonfield Memorial Hospital had become a war zone, and it was every person for themselves.

*

Karen managed to get Laurie to her feet, and she held onto her mother as they made their way in the direction of her hospital room. The going was slow, primarily because Karen didn't want to risk tearing her mother's wound open any further, but also because so many people were running around like lunatics.

The situation had started out as chaos but had degenerated into pure pandemonium. As a therapist, she understood the basic dynamics at work. Fear combined with a herd mentality was a volatile cocktail, and people who otherwise would never dream of harming someone could commit all manner of atrocities, believing they were acting for the greater good. She wasn't immune to the effect herself. Back in the ER waiting area, when she'd first heard someone call out Michael's name, she'd been afraid that he'd come for her mother, and she'd been prepared—even eager—to join the crowd in hunting down the bastard that had killed her husband. And she might have gone with them too, if Laurie hadn't stopped her. She believed her mother when she said that the man whose blood the crowd was howling for wasn't Michael Myers. Who outside of Smith's Grove would know better than Laurie Strode? When Karen had been growing up, her mother had told the story of that night in 1978 so many times that she could practically recite it word for word. During her struggle with Michael, Laurie had pulled off his mask, revealing the face of a perfectly ordinary twenty-one-year-old man. Ordinary physically, at least.

I saw him only for a couple seconds, Laurie had told her. *What struck me was how* empty *his face looked. It was like a doll's face, or a mannequin's. It had a semblance of humanity. The pieces were there—eyes, mouth, nose, ears—but they might as well have been carved out of stone for all the expression they had.*

Whoever the man was that the crowd was searching for, Karen knew he'd be in serious trouble if they found him. At the very least, they'd injure him severely, and given how frenzied they were, there was a good chance they would kill him. She wished to god there was something she could do to help him, but she had to take care of her mother first. She—

They rounded a corner and came in sight of the nurse's station near her mother's room. Standing there, talking on their phones while people ran by, were Sheriff Barker and Detective Graham. Karen almost laughed with relief. When Graham saw them, he quickly put away his phone, and hurried over to help.

"We need to get her back to her room," Karen said.

Graham nodded. He took up a position on Laurie's other side, and together he and Karen were able to usher Laurie down the hallway easily. Barker finished on his phone, tucked it away in his suit jacket, then came over to join them.

"God*damn*, this whole situation has turned into a ten-mile-long shit sandwich! We've been calling surrounding towns for backup, but so far—"

Laurie interrupted him. "That man, the one the crowd's chasing… it's not who they think it is. Please! Stop them!"

Horrified realization dawned on Barker's face. He gave Laurie a grim-faced nod.

"Graham, help this lady back to her room. I got a riot to try to contain."

He ran off down the corridor. "People, *stop*!" he bellowed.

Karen didn't think the sheriff had much chance on his own, but she admired the man's bravery. She almost wished she'd voted for him in the last election.

It took Karen and Graham only a couple more minutes to get Laurie in her room and settled. Hawkins lay in his bed, eyes closed. Karen couldn't believe that he was able to sleep through the bedlam the hospital had become. He was lucky to be missing the whole shitshow.

Once Laurie was lying down, Karen said, "Mom, I can take care of this. You're not well. You have to *stay* here. Guards are outside."

Graham had a small handheld radio clipped to his belt. A voice spoke over it, and he raised the device to his ear to listen. The noise from the hallway was too loud, and Karen couldn't make out what the person on the other end was saying.

"What is it?" Laurie asked.

Graham put his radio back on his belt. "Staff sightings on the second floor. He's on the move."

Karen looked at her mother. "I can stop them."

Laurie looked as if she wanted to protest, but instead she sighed and nodded.

"Be careful, Karen."

She wanted to reassure her mother, tell her she was going to be fine. But Laurie had a finely honed bullshit detector and could spot a lie a mile off. Instead, Karen smiled one last time, then turned and hurried out of the room, accompanied by Detective Graham.

*

Big John ascended the stairs, paring knife gripped tight in his right hand. Now that he was heading to the second floor of his home to search for an intruder, he wished he hadn't been stupid enough to exchange the nine iron for such a little knife. He supposed he hadn't been thinking straight. If Little John could've read his mind right now, he might've quipped *Since when have you ever thought straight?* Big John had been so worked up by the idea that those asshole kids had returned to harass them that when he'd been standing on the porch and Little John had said *Someone's in our house*, he'd freaked. He'd run inside and into the living room, and when the charcuterie board had caught his eye, he'd seen the paring knife, and its pointy blade had seemed a more suitably dangerous weapon than a golf club. So he'd ditched the nine iron, grabbed the knife, and joined Little John in the kitchen. If the intruder turned out to be a giant plate of fruits and vegetables that needed slicing and dicing, Big John was ready, but if it was a human being, he'd rather be able to whack them upside the head with the nine iron. Too late now.

As he reached the top of the stairs, he called out, "Little John?"

It was their version of Marco Polo, something the two of them did when they were separated and wanted to make sure the other was okay. Little John had stayed downstairs to check the first floor, and as nervous as Big John was going upstairs, he was just as nervous not being able to see Little John and know he was all right. But a second later, he heard his husband call out.

"Big John!"

Relieved, he started walking down the upstairs hallway. First he checked the study, and when he found it empty, he moved on to their bedroom. He opened the door carefully, then reached in and flipped on the light. He saw their handcrafted brass bed with the burgundy duvet, their five-piece French provincial bedroom set, the antique vanity sitting by the window, and on the wall above the bed, their ridiculous painting of a cat wearing Elizabethan clothing enclosed in a far-too-expensive mahogany gallery frame. Everything *looked* good. Now to check the master bathroom.

Big John entered the room, and out of the corner of his eye, he saw a blur of motion as something came at him. He felt a sharp pain in his right armpit, and he realized with a mixture of horror and surprise that he'd been stabbed. He reflexively drew away from his attacker, the blade slid out from under his arm, and he felt a gush of hot blood pour down his side.

He turned and saw a tall man in a fire-singed white Halloween mask and dark coveralls looking at him. The man held a knife—one way bigger than Big John's dinky paring knife—in his right hand. Big John's blood dripped from the blade.

Big John's first thought was that he was looking at Michael goddamn Myers in the flesh. The Boogeyman had come home, to what had once been his sister Judith's room. Big John's second thought was that he and Little John shouldn't have split up.

People did that in horror movies all the time, and they always regretted it in the end.

I can't believe I was killed by a cliché, he thought.

He still had hold of the paring knife, and although he knew it was futile, he intended to go down fighting. But before he could raise the blade, Michael dropped his own weapon, stepped forward, and grabbed Big John's head with both hands. He jammed his thumbs into the man's eyes and kept pushing until they popped and his thumbs slid into soft brain meat. Big John felt blood mixed with aqueous fluid splatter onto his cheeks as pain beyond anything he'd ever imagined possible screamed through his nervous system. It happened so fast, he wasn't able to make a sound, but in his mind he whispered, *Little John…*

And then Michael gave one last hard push, digging even deeper into his brain, and Big John died.

*

"Big John?"

Little John stood in the dining room, close to the upright piano, and listened for his husband's reply. He heard movement upstairs—their bedroom was directly above him—but Big John didn't say anything.

"Big John? No more pranks!"

Still nothing.

Could Big John be playing a Halloween prank on him? Maybe while they'd been watching the movie, he'd texted one of their friends—Manuel, most likely—and had him come over and pound on both the front and the back door. Then when he and Big John went onto the front porch to investigate, Manuel had snuck in the back, made that fake bloody handprint on the counter, then headed upstairs. He was probably in the bedroom with Big John right now, both of them fighting to keep from laughing their asses off.

"Big John?" he repeated, louder this time. "*Please!*"

Silence.

Maybe it's not a prank, he thought. *Maybe…* He told himself to stop it. There was no use in working himself up like this. If it was a joke, the faster he got it over with, the better. And oh, how he'd make Big John and Manuel pay for it! And if it wasn't a joke… He didn't want to think about that.

He exited the dining room and started toward the stairs. On his way up, he tried one more time.

"Big John?"

No reply.

When he reached the top of the stairs, he saw that the bedroom door was open and the light was on. He trembled as he approached the room, and he prayed that this *was* a joke, and he promised God that he wouldn't be angry with Big John, just please let him be okay.

When he stepped into the room, he let out a sigh of relief. Big John was sitting at the antique vanity, gazing into the mirror. He had no idea why Big John was there, but he *could* be a bit theatrical at times. Maybe it was part of the joke.

He walked over to his husband, grinning.

"Mirror, mirror, on the wall," he said. "Who's the most beautiful man…"

He trailed off when he caught sight of Big John's reflection in the glass. His hands lay limp on the vanity's surface, and his head was tilted slightly to the left. There were streaks of blood on his face, more blood on the front of his pajamas, and his eyes… Sweet Jesus, he *had* no eyes, only a pair of gore-rimmed sockets staring sightlessly at nothing.

A scream tore free from Little John's throat, and then an apparition appeared in the mirror behind his own reflection—a white-faced thing in dark clothing, a large blood-stained knife held in his right hand, and in his left, Big John's paring blade. Little John tried to scream a second time, but he never got the chance.

20

Karen and Graham found a stairwell, entered, and began climbing. Graham insisted on taking the lead, and since he was the one with a gun, Karen was happy to let him. As they ascended, Karen heard distant sounds—footfalls, a lot of them, coming closer—and a second later a scared group of patients came pounding down the stairs. Karen and Graham moved to the side to let them pass, but there were so many of them that they couldn't all squeeze through at once. A pair stumbled and fell, an older man and woman, but the others kept on going, either not noticing or not caring.

Karen helped the man to stand, and Graham helped the woman.

"Ma'am, are you okay?" he asked.

The woman had bumped her head when she'd fallen, but she seemed more scared than hurt.

"He's upstairs!" Karen said.

Then the man added, "Michael Myers!"

"It's not Michael," Karen said. "You don't know what he looks like!"

"I know enough to run from the sonofabitch!"

the woman said, and she continued hurrying down the stairs, the man following close behind.

Barker burst through the stairwell door, and when he saw the terrified patients rushing toward him, he shouted, "Stay calm! It's not him!"

"Bullshit it ain't!" the older man said, and he and the woman shoved past Barker, nearly knocking the sheriff down in the process. As they exited the stairwell, Karen heard the woman shouting, "He's up there, he's up there!"

Barker climbed up to join Karen and Graham.

"Reinforcements from Russellville finally showed up," he said. "I've got 'em downstairs helping our guys, but we still don't have enough officers to get this fucking asylum under control!"

The stairwell door flew open once more then, and a mass of angry, shouting people poured through. At the front of the pack was Tommy, who was clearly their leader. His features were contorted with rage, his teeth bared, as if he were a predator ready to take down a kill. Karen recognized some of the people following him, had seen them in the waiting area: the woman in clown makeup, the woman with wild red hair and half-crazed eyes, and the security guard she'd seen Allyson speaking with earlier. The expression of fury on this man's face rivaled Tommy's.

Tommy charged up the stairs toward them, his crew close behind. Barker stepped forward to block their path, and Tommy practically growled at him.

"Out of the way!"

Karen stepped next to Barker, and Graham joined

him. Neither man had drawn his gun yet, but their hands rested on their weapons. She had to defuse this situation fast before someone got hurt.

"Tommy, stop!" she said. "It's not Michael you're chasing. You've got the wrong man!"

Tommy *did* stop, which meant the others behind him did too. He frowned at her, as if he were having trouble processing what she'd said. This was her chance. If she could just get him to see reason...

The radio on Graham's belt activated, and a tinny voice emerged, clearly audible in the stairwell's silence.

"All available personnel on the scene at HMH, be advised, suspect has been sighted ascending the northeast staircase on the fifth floor at Ward 273. Possibly armed. Fifth floor, Ward 273."

Those words broke the momentary peace that had descended upon the stairwell. Tommy lunged forward, shoved Barker and Graham aside, and pushed his way past them. The pack followed, almost knocking Karen down as they raced up the stairs after their leader.

"No!" Karen shouted. *"Stop!"*

But of course they didn't. She feared nothing would stop them now until they got their hands on the poor bastard they'd mistaken for Michael Myers and tore him limb from limb. But she had to try.

She started running up the stairs, Barker and Graham following in her wake, both men now with guns drawn.

Laurie's gut throbbed like hell, but she didn't want to give herself another injection of lidocaine just yet. She wanted to save the medicine. She had a feeling she would need it before this night was finally over. She'd slipped the knife out of the back of the abdominal wrap and had it concealed under the sheet next to her leg. She had a feeling she'd be needing that too.

She listened to the noise and chaos out in the halls, the madness raging like ocean waves lashed by hurricane-force winds. She prayed that Karen was safe out there, and she wished she had some way to contact her to make sure.

She's a tough girl, Laurie thought. *I trained her well. She'll do good.*

Still, she couldn't help being afraid for her daughter.

So far, Frank had managed to sleep through all the tumult, and Laurie envied the hell out of him. But now his eyes opened and he drew in a gasping breath, as if he was waking from a nightmare. *More like waking* to *a nightmare,* she thought.

He blinked in confusion for several seconds, and then he turned to look at her, wincing as his neck gave him a twinge of pain.

"Laurie," he said. "What's going on? It sounds… bad."

She stared straight ahead as she answered him.

"It's all happening. Michael's masterpiece. This chaos is what he created, but I brought it all upon Haddonfield."

Frank turned his head back and settled onto his pillow. He didn't speak for several moments, and then in a low, quiet voice, he said, "I could've stopped it."

Laurie turned to Frank, eyebrows raised in surprise. He didn't look at her as he went on.

"All of this. I could have killed him. I could have let the others take him down. I could have made all of this go away. It's not your fault." He turned to look at her again, his eyes haunted. "It's *mine*." He took a deep breath. "It was the night you were attacked…"

*

Haddonfield, Illinois
Halloween Night 1978

Hawkins stood on the porch of the Myers house, Dr. Loomis next to him. They watched as Michael—unarmed—stepped into the street, lit by the flashing lights of half a dozen sheriff's cruisers. Deputies got out of their vehicles, guns drawn, and closed in with a tactical formation to apprehend the madman.

Loomis grabbed hold of Hawkins' arm and shook it to get his attention.

"Did Michael kill again?" the doctor demanded.

Hawkins held his revolver at his side, and he looked down at his weapon now. In a small voice, he said, "There was an accident."

Deputy Tobias was the first to approach Michael. He drew his nightstick from his belt, gritted his teeth, and struck Michael a vicious blow on the head. Michael staggered, went down on his knees, but he didn't make a sound. As if goaded by the man's silence, Tobias struck Michael on the head again, slamming him to the asphalt. Once more, Michael made no sound.

Loomis let go of Hawkins' arm. He rushed down the porch steps and ran into the street toward Michael. The doctor joined the deputies surrounding Michael, his own gun gripped tight in his hand.

Michael lay face down on the ground. Tobias knelt, grabbed hold of his mask and yanked it off his head. He stood, held the mask high, and his fellow deputies cheered.

In his mind, Hawkins relived the moment he tried to shoot Michael but hit McCabe in the throat instead. He saw the shock in the man's eyes, saw the blood gush from his wound…

What they wanted was more. More death. I couldn't take it. All I could think about in that moment was that somewhere in that monster was someone's baby boy.

Loomis stepped close to Michael, aimed his gun at the back of his patient's head, and cocked the hammer. He spoke then, his voice thick with regret.

"I'm sorry, Michael. This is the only way I can help you now."

"No! Wait! Don't shoot!" Hawkins shouted.

He jumped off the porch, ran past his fellow deputies toward Loomis. When he reached the man, he grabbed his gun hand and pulled his arm to the sky. The gun went off with a sound like thunder—a sound that would echo throughout Hawkins' life for the next four decades.

Haddonfield, Illinois
Halloween Night 2018

Frank sighed. "But now I know there's nothing inside that man but pure evil."

Laurie tried to imagine the guilt Frank must have been carrying inside himself all these years. And when Michael escaped the transport bus yesterday and the killings resumed, Frank must've blamed himself for every life that Michael had taken since.

"It's not only Michael," she said. "It's what he's done to the town. These people…" She nodded toward the hallway, where the sounds of running and yelling indicated the riot was still going strong. "You're a good man, Frank. You did your job."

She reached out her hand to him, and he took it gratefully. They looked into each other's eyes for a moment before Laurie continued speaking.

"But now it needs to die. Every time someone is afraid, the Boogeyman wins. This town can't bring Michael down."

"It needs to die," Frank agreed.

Her voice was cold as steel when she spoke next. "I'm the one that needs to kill him."

*

Karen raced up the last flight of stairs to the fifth floor. Her heart was pounding and she could barely catch her breath, and from the way Graham and Barker were gulping air, they sounded just as exhausted as she was.

Barker shoved the stairwell door open, and the three of them rushed into the hallway. There was no sign of Tommy or his followers, and Karen assumed they must have dispersed to search for "Michael." Evidently, Barker thought the same, for he said, "Graham and I will try to find them. Stay here. If you see anyone, don't engage."

Karen hadn't come here to stand by while others risked their lives, but she knew there was no point in arguing, so she nodded. Barker looked at her one more moment, as if attempting to gauge her sincerity. Then he and Graham turned and hurried off down the hallway. When they reached the far end of the hall, they split up, Barker heading down the right corridor, Graham the left. Karen heard sounds in the distance—people shouting, supplies being thrown to the floor—and she guessed that Tommy and his mob were searching individual rooms in pursuit of their quarry.

Not knowing what else to do, she started walking forward. According to the report that had come across Graham's radio, the man everyone was looking for was somewhere on this floor—assuming he hadn't gone back into the stairwell since then and moved to a different level. Haddonfield Memorial Hospital was big, and there were so many places one man could hide, but this encouraged her. Dozens of people could search all night, and they might still never find—

Halfway down the hall, a door opened, and a man

tentatively stuck his head out of an office. He looked both ways, as if to make sure the coast was clear, and when he saw Karen, he froze. He had a large gash on his forehead, his lower lip trembled, and his eyes were filled with absolute terror. If she'd had any lingering suspicions that he actually might be Michael Myers, they were dispelled at once by the sight of him. This wasn't an inhuman, cold-blooded killer. This was an ordinary man, and an extremely frightened one.

Before he could retreat back into the room, she said, "It's not you. I know it's not you."

He hesitated. He looked doubtful, but he didn't slam the door shut and try to lock her out, and she took that as a good sign.

"You've got to get out of here," she said. "They're going to kill you. Run!"

The man continued to look at her, but he didn't move. He was trembling all over now, and Karen realized he was too gripped by fear to do anything other than stand there. Slowly, so as not to spook him, she walked toward him and held out her hand.

"Come on," she said, and gave him a smile.

After a moment, the man returned the smile and then stepped into the hallway. His slippers were falling apart, and she could see blisters on his feet.

"Can you help me?" he said.

As a therapist, Karen knew the vast majority of people suffering from mental illness were no threat to anyone. Most were passive, and if they did cause harm, it was usually to themselves. But this man had been a patient at Smith's Grove, just like Michael, and he'd been on the same transport bus. That meant he wasn't a typical mental patient, had most likely committed some violent offense in the past to warrant being put into a group with someone like Michael. Just because he appeared harmless at the moment didn't mean that he was.

Don't let fear rule you, she told herself. *Don't be like Tommy and the others.*

She worked with children, and to be good at her job, she needed to be able to read their facial expressions and body language, be able to glean information from the tone of their voice, the stories they told, the jokes they made, the drawings they created, the way they played... Children often couldn't verbalize their emotions, especially difficult ones, which meant she had to act like a psychological detective much of the time. And the thing that struck her most about this man was how childlike he seemed. Despite his age, he was acting like a scared little boy, and her heart went out to him. Whatever he may or may not have done in the past, he was here now, and he needed her help.

She stepped forward and took his hand. The man let her, and when she gently pulled him into the hallway, he came without resistance.

"Let's go," she said.

He nodded and, still holding onto his hand, Karen began to lead him down the corridor. When they reached the end, she looked both ways, and saw no one. She could *hear* them, though, continuing to ransack rooms, and she hoped they'd stay busy long enough for her to hide this man somewhere. Once he was safe, she'd find Barker and Graham, and hopefully they would be able to protect him from the mob. They might even be able to get him out of the hospital without anyone seeing. Better he was in custody at the sheriff's department than wandering the halls here, where he would surely get killed.

She took the corridor's right-hand branch and led the man past various rooms, searching for the right one. She needed a place where he could lock the door behind him, and where there would be enough items inside—furniture, medical equipment, filing cabinets, anything—that he could hide behind. Halfway down the corridor, they came across an office suite for Patel and Associates, Orthopedic Surgeons. Karen recognized it. She and Ray had brought Allyson here when she was in fifth grade. She'd broken her elbow during a collision with another player at a soccer game, and had needed some minor surgery to repair it. The suite had an outer reception area, along with examination rooms and doctors' offices in the back. Lots of places to hide.

The door was glass, and she peered inside. The lights were off, but she could tell the reception room was empty, which of course it would be, given the late hour. She tried the door and was surprised to find it unlocked. Was the door to the reception area always left unlocked or had the cleaning staff forgotten to lock it when they'd finished up tonight? It didn't matter. All that mattered was she'd found a place where her new friend could hide.

She opened the door all the way.

"Go inside. Lock the door behind you, then try to get into one of the rooms in the back. Once you're inside there, lock that door and find a place inside the room to hide. I'll be back with help as soon as I can."

The man looked doubtful, but he let go of Karen's hand and shuffled into the reception area. She closed the glass door and watched as he engaged the bolt lock. She gave him what she hoped was a reassuring smile, and then she turned and headed back down the corridor the way she'd come. She needed to find Barker and Graham. The two officers were the only chance that poor man had of making it out of this place alive.

But she only made it half a dozen yards before a pair of doors at the far end of the corridor burst open, and Tommy Doyle appeared, a mass of people flowing into the corridor behind him. Tommy saw her and started running toward her, and the others raced after him.

"Oh, fuck," Karen said and braced herself for what was to come.

21

Tivoli liked that lady. She was the first person who'd been nice to him since he'd gotten on the transport bus at Smith's Grove yesterday. She was pretty, too. She reminded him of one of the nurses on his ward. She had blond hair as well, and she always smiled when she brought him his morning pills. He thought of her as Nurse Sunshine because she got his day off to a pleasant start, and he decided he'd call this new lady Mrs. Sunshine.

He hoped Mrs. Sunshine would keep her promise and come back soon. He was really scared, and his feet hurt so bad now that he didn't know how much longer he could walk on them. He wished he'd never come to this hospital in the first place. Hospitals were supposed to be places where people who were sick or hurt got taken care of. Not here. This was a place where people wanted to *hurt* you. It was like a bad dream, except one that you couldn't wake up from. He knew it wasn't a dream, though. Earlier, he'd pinched himself really hard to check, but he hadn't woken up. That meant this was real, which was very disappointing.

Mrs. Sunshine had told him to go into the back and look for a place to hide. He thought this was an extremely good idea. The office he'd been hiding in when Mrs. Sunshine found him had been small, and he'd known that if the loud people broke in, they'd get him. There had been only a desk to hide under, and unless he suddenly gained the magic power to make himself invisible—and even he wasn't crazy enough to believe *that* would happen—they would've seen him the moment they entered. But here, there would be *lots* of places to hide, so many that even if the loud people searched here, they would probably get tired and eventually give up and leave. Yes, this was the perfect place, and he was so grateful to Mrs. Sunshine for bringing him here.

There was a wooden door next to the receptionist's counter, and since it was the only one in the outer suite, Tivoli assumed it led to the back. He walked over, put his hand on the knob, tried to turn it, and discovered it was locked. *No,* he thought as sudden panic gripped him. *No-no-no-no-no-NO!* He tried again, shaking the knob hard this time, hoping that by doing so he might jiggle it open. But it didn't work. He turned to look at the suite's entrance. It was locked too, but the door was made of glass. Anyone in the hallway could look in and see him.

Mrs. Sunshine had made a mistake.

He stood there, paralyzed with indecision. Mrs. Sunshine had told him to stay here while she went to find help, so if he left to go in search of a better hiding place, he wouldn't be here when she came back. What if she couldn't find him again? Or worse, what if the loud people found him first? But if he stayed here, the loud people might get here before Mrs. Sunshine could return, and then he'd be in trouble, big, *big* trouble. He wished he had his umbrella. He always thought more clearly with an umbrella in his hand.

He heard yelling then, and his first thought was that it was too late—the loud people had found him. But this yelling wasn't very loud at all, and it seemed to come from far away. There was a window on the far wall that opened onto the outside, and the yelling seemed to be coming from that direction. Curious, Tivoli walked over to the window and peered down at the parking lot below. He saw police cars and ambulances and regular cars, too. And he saw people—a *lot* of them. They were gathered in a large crowd in front of the emergency-room entrance, and they were shouting, some of them screaming, and even all the way up here Tivoli could hear some of what they were saying.

"You can't hide him from us!"

"Kill him for the families of his victims!"

He drew back in alarm, suddenly afraid that these angry people had magic telescope eyes and they would see him if he remained too close to the window. If they knew he was up here, they'd come for him, running up the stairs, howling for his blood.

No, not my blood, he thought. *Michael's.* Except... they thought he *was* Michael. But he was Tivoli... wasn't he?

They don't give a fuck what your name is, his father said.

They only care about what you are, his mother said.

You're a monster, his father said.

And monsters deserve to die, his mother said.

"No," Tivoli whispered.

But he feared they were right.

*

Karen stood in the middle of the hallway and spread her arms wide to block the oncoming mass of people.

"No, no, no!" she said. "It's not him!"

The mob slowed then stopped, unsure what to do. Tommy stepped forward to confront Karen.

"It *is* him, for god's sake!" he said.

She looked into Tommy's eyes, and what she saw there frightened her. She knew there could be no reasoning with him, with any of them. Emboldened by Tommy's words, the crowd began to advance once more, animalistic hunger on their faces. Karen could sense the situation teetering on the precipice, and she knew if she couldn't find a way to counter the mob's lust for vengeance, things were going to go very bad very quickly.

"Stop this! You don't understand!"

A doctor—the same one who'd almost knocked her down in the hallway earlier—stepped forward and pointed at her. "Get out of the way, bitch!" he snarled.

Karen had officially had enough. Her husband was dead, his body burned to a crisp, her daughter was out with a vigilante posse hunting Michael Myers, and her mother was lying in her hospital bed, bleeding from a hole in her gut. She grabbed the doctor's finger and broke it with a single savage motion. When he cried out in pain, she let go of the finger, and then kicked him in the crotch. He made an *oof* sound and doubled over. She instantly regretted her actions. She'd allowed the crowd's anger to infect her, and she'd been the first to resort to violence. No way could she hope to calm the mob now.

As if to illustrate her point, the security guard Allyson had spoken to—*Brackett*, his nametag said—stepped forward and aimed his gun at her head. When he spoke, his voice was coiled tight with tension, and she had no doubt he'd shoot her if he thought it necessary.

"Stand down. I'm gonna kill the man that killed Annie!"

Still, Karen held her ground. "This man is not who you think he is!"

Tommy's gaze bore into her, and she saw no sign of sanity in his eyes.

"Evil dies tonight," he said, his voice eerily calm.

The crowd picked up the refrain, voices growing louder with each repetition.

"Evil dies tonight! Evil dies tonight! Evil dies tonight!"

She'd helped instigate this mob. Along with Tommy, she'd stirred them up in the ER's waiting area, convinced them that Michael was in the hospital, and it was up to them to finally bring him to justice.

We make our own monsters, she thought.

Tommy started forward then, and that was the signal for the dam to burst. His followers surged toward her, and—knowing it was futile—instead of getting out of their way, Karen still tried to slow their advance. The leading edge of the crowd slammed into her and shoved her backward. She struggled to maintain her balance, but there were too many of them, and they were pushing too hard. She went down and the mob kept going, trampling her in their mad need to unleash their fury on the object of their hatred. She covered her head with her hands, curled into a fetal position, and tried to protect herself.

*

Tivoli heard them coming.

They sounded like a mass of stampeding cattle as they ran down the hall, chanting *Evil dies tonight! Evil dies tonight!* He felt the vibrations of their pounding footfalls in the floor beneath his feet, heard the suite's glass door rattle. It was like an earthquake, which he'd always thought was a funny word. *Earth quake*, like the planet was shivering because it was cold... or scared.

He jumped when the first bodies slammed into the door, and even though he didn't want to, he turned to look at them. The things he saw pressed against the glass didn't look human to him. They were wild, savage creatures, teeth bared, eyes gleaming with a lust to kill. Acting as one, they shoved against the door, and Tivoli heard it strain. He doubted a heavy oak door could keep those animals out, and this door was nothing but a thin layer of glass. They would break through in seconds, and then they would be on him and the pain would begin.

There is *a way to avoid it,* his father said.

It'll be faster, his mother said.

And it'll only hurt for a moment.

Be over in a flash.

And then you'll be gone, you miserable thing.

And good riddance.

Tivoli turned to look at the window. It was glass too. Thicker than the door, maybe, but not much. The suite's reception area contained furniture for patients to sit on while they waited to be seen by a doctor. A couple couches, a coffee table with old magazines spread out on the surface, and a number of chairs. Sturdy-looking wooden chairs. Heavy, solid.

The animals slammed into the door again, and Tivoli heard the glass crack, the sound loud as a shotgun blast.

There was a fire extinguisher on the wall. He hurried to it, grabbed it, and then ran back to the window. As he drew close, he used his momentum to help him hurl the extinguisher forward. He expected this action to fail, expected the extinguisher to hit the glass, bounce off, and fall to the floor. But it didn't. The extinguisher struck the window and kept on going. Glass exploded outward, the extinguisher soared into space, and then it plummeted to the parking lot below. He heard people shout. *Holy shit, look out! What the fuck?*

The animals smacked into the door again, and this time it gave way, its own glass shattered, metal frame bending and twisting half off its hinges. Tivoli heard the people pour into the suite, but he didn't turn to look at them. Instead, he took hold of the window frame's sides with his hands, lifted one leg over the bottom edge, then the second, and then he let go.

As he fell, he heard his mother and father speak in unison.

At least you did something right for once.

The asphalt came rushing up at him, so much faster than he could've imagined, and a split second later, his troubles were over.

Forever.

*

Karen rose painfully to her feet. She hurt all over, had a fresh crop of scrapes and cuts, but she didn't think anything was broken. She saw Tommy and the others massed in front of the orthopedic surgeons' office, and she knew that the man they'd mistaken for Michael Myers hadn't managed to hide himself from them. They roared with fury as they shoved against the glass door once, twice... It broke beneath their combined force, and they rushed into the suite. She limped forward, hoping she could reach the suite before they hurt the man, knowing she would be too late. But then there was a second crash of breaking glass, and an instant later she heard the crowd cheer.

She slumped against a wall and let the tears come.

22

HADDONFIELD, ILLINOIS

Halloween 1978

Hawkins sat on the front porch of the Myers house, head in his hands. Inside the house, a forensics team was going over the scene in Judith Myers' bedroom. He knew what the evidence would show—that he'd tried to stop Michael Myers and ended up killing McCabe. Soon, everyone in the department would know what the rookie had done, but he didn't care much about that. He couldn't stop thinking about McCabe, about his wife, his kids. God, his *kids*…

The street outside the house was empty now. Michael was in custody, and the deputies who'd arrived en masse to take him down had departed. Dr. Loomis was gone too. A sheriff's cruiser was taking Michael back to Smith's Grove as fast as the officer could drive, and Loomis was riding along, determined not to leave his patient's side. Loomis rode up front with the officer while Michael sat in the back, arms handcuffed behind him. Two additional cruisers followed, serving as both escort and backup. No way would Myers escape. This time when they put him in Smith's Grove, Hawkins hoped Loomis would shoot him so full of drugs that he could barely sit straight, and that the hospital staff would keep him that way until the bastard died of old age sometime in the next century.

Tobias had been upstairs with the forensics people, but now he came out onto the porch and sat next to Hawkins.

"I thought I was doing the right thing," Hawkins said, voice hollow.

"It was an accident," Tobias said. "It's hard to know for sure, but…"

The young deputy refused to meet the other man's eyes.

"Hey," Tobias said, tone gentle, understanding. "Look at me."

Hawkins raised his head and turned to look at his fellow officer. Tobias continued.

"From the looks of things, you didn't shoot McCabe. He accidentally shot himself. It was an accident. He shot *himself*."

Hawkins frowned, not understanding.

"My guess is the killer was choking him," Tobias said. "Pete went for his gun, and as he brought it up, it went off. Accidentally. McCabe shot *himself*. Got it?"

Hawkins didn't know what to say. He just looked at Tobias as the man reached out, slipped Hawkins' gun from his holster, and handed him a different one. It was McCabe's weapon, Hawkins realized. Tobias—with the cooperation of the forensics

273

team—intended to switch the guns. Hawkins would have McCabe's weapon, and McCabe would have the one that had fired the bullet that killed him, providing "proof" for Tobias' story.

Tobias gazed out into the street, and it was several moments before he spoke again.

"Just because you're determined to do good, to fight for justice… doesn't mean it always works out."

"I stood in the way," Hawkins said. "It was me."

"You're young, got a lot of years ahead of you, lot of chances to make a difference in this town. You shouldn't throw that away. Haddonfield needs people like you."

Hawkins almost laughed. People like *him*… In the end, was he really so different from Michael Myers? He had innocent blood on his hands too. The only difference was no one outside the men and women here tonight would ever know it. Tobias was taking a big risk to help him out, and although Hawkins felt he didn't deserve a second chance, he would do everything in his power to make it count. For Tobias, and especially for McCabe. His law-enforcement career would be a testament to both men.

He'd make sure of it.

*

Haddonfield, Illinois
Halloween, 2018

Tommy—accompanied by a dozen men and women—ran through the emergency-room exit and out into the parking lot. They'd done it! They'd actually stopped Michael motherfucking Myers! Evil really *had* died here tonight at Haddonfield Hospital, and now no one in town would have to live under the shadow of the Boogeyman ever again. He'd fantasized about this night, or at least different versions of it, since he'd been eight years old, and he'd begun to think that he would never get the chance to take out the bastard who had haunted him like a knife-wielding ghost all these years. But it had finally happened, and the only bad thing was Lonnie was going to be royally pissed that he hadn't been here to get in on the action.

Several of Tommy's group—including Brackett—had made it outside already, and they stood around Michael's body, looking down at it solemnly. Tommy didn't get it. They should be whooping it up, celebrating! Ding-dong the witch is dead, and all that. But they didn't look happy. If anything, they looked upset.

Tommy slowed to a jog as he approached, and the people accompanying did the same, as if they too sensed something was wrong. When they reached the body, Brackett turned to look at Tommy, clearly distraught.

"It's not him," Brackett said. "It's not *him*, Tommy."

Tommy frowned. What the fuck was Brackett talking about? Of *course* it was him! He pushed past the man to get a look at Michael's corpse for himself. Michael lay on his back, staring sightlessly up at the stars. His body was broken, limbs bent at sickening angles, blood trailing from his nose, mouth, and ears, brain matter spread out around his bashed-in head.

And yet…

There weren't many photographs of Michael Myers' face. Not adult Michael. His parents had taken pictures of him while he was growing up, images of a little boy who never smiled, whose eyes never seemed to focus on anything in particular. But after he killed his sister and was sent to Smith's Grove, the picture-taking stopped. When he was captured after the murders in '78, he'd been returned to Smith's Grove right away, so there were no mug shots, and he'd never stood trial for his crimes, so there were no photos taken by courthouse reporters, no video news footage. But there were a *few* pictures of adult Michael out there, taken by staff at Smith's Grove looking to make some money on the side. These images were easily found with a quick Internet search, and Lonnie had used several of them in his book. Most people wouldn't recognize Michael, of course, but for those whose lives had been irrevocably changed by encounters with the Boogeyman, his face was as familiar to them as their own. How many hours had he stared at images of that face, gazed into those eyes, trying to understand the vast Nothing that dwelled within them?

The face he was looking at now wasn't that face. Tommy had never seen this man before in his… Wait. He remembered now. In Mick's, the news bulletin: two photographs displayed on the TV screen side by side, one of Michael, and one of another patient who'd escaped when the transport bus crashed. *That* was who this man was. Not Michael. Not the Boogeyman.

Tommy felt as if he'd been kicked in the stomach. This man was dead because of him, because he'd been so desperate to stop Michael, to pay Laurie back for protecting him forty years ago. He'd created a fucking lynch mob and led them straight to the poor sonofabitch, and the man—god, how *terrified* he must've been—jumped out of a window rather than let them get their hands on him.

Brackett looked at Tommy, eyes filled with sorrow. "Now he's turning *us* into monsters," he said.

Tommy gazed upon the man he'd, for all intents and purposes, killed this night.

Some of us have been monsters all along, he thought.

*

The chaos in the hospital corridors had subsided somewhat, and Laurie began to hope that Karen had done it, that she'd managed to convince Tommy's mob that the man they were chasing wasn't Michael Myers. But when Karen came limping down to Laurie's room, hair mussed, cuts, scrapes, and newly forming bruises on her body, she knew what had happened.

"Oh, baby… I'm so sorry."

"Goddammit," Frank said, shaking his head.

Karen stood in the doorway, leaning on it for support, looking defeated. "We all thought he was coming here for you," she said, as if this could explain the madness that had taken hold of so many people.

"Let me find him," Laurie said. "He's after *me*!"

"No, he's not!" Frank shouted.

Laurie and Karen looked at him, startled by his outburst.

"It was that doctor that took him to your house tonight. It wasn't Michael. It's not about you, Laurie."

While Karen had been gone, Frank had told her how he had ended up as her hospital roommate. She pictured it now, Frank and Dr. Sartain standing over Michael, who lay on the ground stunned after Frank had rammed him with his cruiser. Sartain suddenly whirling around and stabbing his penknife into Frank's neck...

"It's not personal," Frank continued. "Michael is a six-year-old boy with the strength of a man and the mind of an animal."

Laurie thought there was more to it than that. "I've seen his face. I've looked into his eyes."

Frank nodded, as if she'd agreed with his point. "When he was a child, he would stand in his sister's bedroom and stare out the window. My partner told me in '78. He used to play with Michael when they were kids."

Laurie frowned. She'd always had difficulty imagining Michael as a child. To her, he would always be an ominous shape emerging from shadow, an inhuman creature surfacing on a vast dark ocean.

"What was he looking for?" she asked. She leaned forward, listening intently. Karen stepped into the room, drew closer to Frank's bed, eager to learn Michael's secret.

"That's the mystery," Frank said. "My partner died the night he stood in that spot. For an instant before his death, I think he knew. Maybe Michael wasn't looking *out*. Maybe he was looking *in*. At his reflection. At himself."

Karen turned away then. A mirror hung on the wall near the bathroom, and she stepped toward it, looked at herself in its glass. Laurie wondered what she saw there. Her own darkness reflected, the desire to avenge her husband's death that had driven her to help create a mob that had ultimately killed the wrong man? She wanted to tell Karen that any darkness she thought lay within herself had come from her mother. Laurie had raised her daughter to be afraid, to be ready to battle the Boogeyman at a moment's notice. Karen may have helped Tommy spur on the mob, but her motivation for doing so had come directly from Laurie. Since Karen's birth, Laurie had done everything she could to prepare her to face the evils of the world. But she hadn't been able to protect Karen from the toll darkness took on a person's mind and spirit.

Frank went on.

"Who knows what makes him kill, what motivates him? But in his heart, it always seemed to me, he wants one thing."

Karen turned away from the mirror then and walked to Laurie's bedside. She took her mother's hand and squeezed it tight. As she did, Laurie looked into her daughter's eyes, and she didn't like what she saw there.

"I've got to go, Mom. I love you."

She released Laurie's hand and hurried out of the room before either Laurie or Frank could stop her.

"Karen!" Laurie cried. *"Karen!"*

*

Allyson wished she had her phone. She wanted to know how her grandmother was doing, and how her mother was holding up. She was beginning to think that she'd made a mistake joining Cameron and his father on their hunt for Michael Myers. She'd lost her father tonight, but her mom had lost her husband. Her parents met in college and had been married for nineteen years. They'd had their ups and downs like all couples, but they deeply loved each other, and what's more, they *liked* each other. They enjoyed spending time together, had been best friends as much as spouses. What would it be like to lose someone that close to you, who was your whole world?

Normally, her mom was so strong that Allyson didn't think of her as needing anyone's help. She was the one always helping others, listening to people's problems, giving advice. *Occupational hazard*, she'd joke. But tonight she was the one in need, and what had Allyson done? Instead of remaining at the hospital to give her mom the emotional support she needed, that she *deserved*, she was driving up and down the streets of Haddonfield, playing monster hunter. She'd told herself that by helping to track down Michael, she'd not only be avenging her father, but she'd be helping ease her mom's pain. Her mom would know that Michael wasn't roaming free anymore, that he couldn't hurt anyone else. And if Michael really was focused on killing her grandmother, Allyson would help save her life too. If nothing else, it would help Laurie put the demon that had haunted her most of her life to rest.

Cameron had been looking at an old-fashioned paper map for the last several minutes, reading it by the dashboard's light. Now he held it in front of her so she could see it. He traced Michael's route for her with his index finger, naming the locations as he did so.

"Michael's going home," Lonnie realized. "He went from Laurie's compound to victims in her neighborhood, to the park... If you track those locations, it's a straight line."

During their long drive, Lonnie had been in periodic phone contact with friends in the sheriff's department, who'd kept him up to date on Michael's activity.

Despite her earlier determination to return to the hospital, Allyson was intrigued.

"What does that mean?" Cameron asked.

Lonnie answered him. "It's basically an arrow pointing right to Lampkin Lane. Michael's childhood home. I came face to face with this asshole when I was a kid. He creeps, he kills, he goes home."

If that was true, then they knew exactly where Michael was right this minute. No more driving around aimlessly, hoping to get lucky. They could go straight to Lampkin Lane and kill the Boogeyman himself.

Allyson made a decision. "Then that's where we're going."

*

It had taken some effort, but sheriff's deputies—assisted by the officers from Russellville and Eaton County who had finally arrived, as well as former Sheriff Brackett—had gotten the situation in the hospital parking lot under control. More or less.

They'd cordoned off what was now officially a crime scene, surrounded the body with orange parking cones connected by yellow tape, and they'd managed to disperse most of the crowd. The medical examiner was on her way, as well as a forensic unit, but for now guards had been stationed around the body of the man Tommy and his mob had driven to commit suicide. The police had been forced to take a few of the more belligerent people into custody until they could cool down, but so far they hadn't made any actual arrests. Tommy figured it was only a matter of time, though, and he planned to remain in the lot until the officers got everything sorted out and began assigning blame for what had taken place here tonight. When that time came, Tommy intended to be the first to confess his role in the riot, and he was prepared to accept whatever punishment he'd eventually get. Whatever it was, it wouldn't be enough.

He kept hearing the sound of a window shattering, kept seeing the face of the dead man looking up at the sky, blood running from his eyes like tears. He paced back and forth, unable to remain still, wanted to scream and keep screaming until his vocal cords snapped like too-tight guitar strings. He almost did it, but then he saw Karen coming across the parking lot toward him, moving through the remnants of the crowd. She limped slightly on one leg, and he knew she'd been injured. He had a flash of their confrontation on the hospital's fifth floor: her standing in front of him, arms spread wide; him moving forward, pushing past her, forgetting about her the instant she was out of his sight... Shame overwhelmed him, and he stepped forward to meet her, eyes wet with tears.

"I'm sorry, Karen. I'm so sorry."

Karen didn't acknowledge his apology. Maybe because she was furious with him—and she had every right to be—or maybe because she had something else on her mind.

"Just because you try to do the right thing, doesn't mean it always works out. Look at me! If we're going to go down, let's go swinging!"

Tommy frowned, confused. "I... don't understand."

Karen gave him a grim smile.

"I know where Michael is—and I think it's time we made a plan."

23

Lonnie pulled his Altima up to the curb in front of the Myers house. He parked, then turned off the headlights and killed the ignition. None of the lights were on, including the porchlight, but that wasn't necessarily a bad sign. It *was* late, after all. The house looked nothing like it had forty years ago, when he'd tried to enter it on a dare and was scared away by a mysterious voice. Years later, when he'd been interviewing Samuel Loomis for his book on the Boogeyman, the doctor had confessed that it had been him hiding in the bushes, waiting to see if Michael would return to his childhood home before dawn, and he'd been the one who'd frightened off Lonnie. They'd had a good laugh about it.

The house had been completely renovated in the decades since, making it look like it had only recently been built, even though the damn thing was over a century old. The realtors, Big John and Little John, had purchased it and fixed it up, and while to certain older folks in town it would always be the Myers house, it no longer held the same stigma as when Lonnie had been a child. It was hard for a haunted house to keep its spooky reputation when it didn't *look* haunted anymore. At one point, Lonnie had been considering releasing an updated version of his book, and he'd tried to interview the two Johns, wanted to ask them what it was like to live in the most infamous house in Haddonfield. They'd politely declined, however, saying they didn't want to stir up their home's *lurid past*, as they called it. Lonnie had understood and hadn't bothered them again. They were nice guys, and now that he was here, he hoped like hell that their theory about where Michael was headed was wrong. He didn't want to think of anything bad happening to the two Johns.

He turned to Cameron and Allyson. Both were doing their best to put on brave faces, but he could see they were trembling. They were scared shitless, and he couldn't blame them. He was too. He regretted throwing his booze out the window earlier. He sure as hell could use a drink right now.

"The key is that we stick together," Allyson said. "He can't take us all at once."

Despite how frightened she was, Lonnie was impressed by how steady she managed to keep her voice. She was a tough kid, and he was glad his son had found her. She'd be good for Cameron, would help smooth off some of his rough edges.

Lonnie came to a decision then.

"I'm going in alone."

"What?" Cameron said.

"Mr. Elam, *please*…" Allyson said.

"Fucking dummy," he muttered to himself. "Bringing your kid to the belly of the beast."

Too many people had died tonight. Marion, Vanessa, Marcus… and Lindsey had been severely injured. He couldn't let Cameron and Allyson go up against a killing machine like Michael Myers. They had too much to live for. Now him, on the other hand…

Cameron gave Allyson a look, as if he was worried that Lonnie was losing it.

"Dad?" he said.

Lonnie stared straight ahead as he spoke. "I don't want you to live the way I have, Cameron. Never feeling like you're enough. Drinking away your fear and self-hatred." He let out a long sigh. "Driving away the girl you love because you're living in the past. Obsession can kill as effectively as any knife—it just takes longer."

The three of them were silent for several moments after that. Finally, Allyson spoke.

"With all due respect, Mr. Elam, do you really expect me to sit by and watch while you go into that house and confront the man who killed my father?"

He turned and gave the girl a weary smile.

"No, I don't expect you to do it. But I'm asking, Allyson. For your sake—and for my son's. Just stay here. Honk if you see anything suspicious. And protect yourself." He nodded toward the sawed-off shotgun nestled between Allyson's end of the front seat and the door. He then placed his hand on

286

Cameron's shoulder, and it was his turn to try and put on a brave face.

"See you at the finish line, buddy."

Before either Cameron or Allyson could say anything, Lonnie got out of the car, gun gripped tightly in his right hand, flashlight in his left, and started walking toward the house.

*

Allyson and Cameron watched nervously as Lonnie went up the front walk and onto the porch. Allyson had been by the place numerous times before, and she was well familiar with what it looked like these days. How could she not check out the Myers house from time to time? She *was* Laurie Strode's granddaughter, after all. This place loomed large in her family's history, was practically a holy site in a twisted way.

Lonnie turned on his flashlight and shined it on the porch, looking left and right, making sure it was clear. The current owners had erected Halloween decorations: a zombie woman in an old-fashioned black dress standing next to a red-skinned devil in a black suit holding a pitchfork. Normally, she might have thought them cute, but not tonight. Tonight they seemed sinister, ominous.

Lonnie rang the doorbell, which Allyson thought was absurd, but then she remembered that the house had new owners. Lonnie couldn't exactly break the door down and go charging into the house looking for Michael. Not only might he scare the owners, what if they had guns? Lonnie could end up getting shot as an intruder. No one answered the bell, though, and a moment later, Lonnie tried the door. It was unlocked, and he pushed it open and—after giving Cameron and Allyson a last look—went inside. He didn't close the door behind him, which Allyson thought was smart. If he needed to get out of the house in a hurry, he didn't want to have to screw around with trying to open the door again.

Now there was nothing for her and Cameron to do but wait.

"I'm sorry about my dad," Cameron said. "He's just a little…"

Allyson couldn't take her eyes off the front door. Inside, the house was dark, and all she could see was a great blackness.

"If Michael's in that house, your dad is gonna be dead in five seconds," she said.

She continued looking at the house, counting down in her mind. *Five, four, three, two…*

They heard the crack of a gunshot.

Allyson didn't hesitate. "Go!"

She grabbed the sawed-off shotgun, threw open the Altima's passenger door, and jumped out of the car, Cameron—pistol in one hand, flashlight in the other—right behind her. They ran onto the porch and paused at the open doorway.

"Dad?" Cameron called into the darkness.

Lonnie didn't answer.

Cameron stepped toward the doorway, but Allyson grabbed his arm to stop him.

288

"Stop. Listen to me. We can run. We can wake the neighbors. We can call the cops. 'Cause if we go through that door right now, we might never come out."

She was scared, yes, but she'd already lost her father tonight. She didn't want Cameron to die as well.

"I can't wait," Cameron said, almost apologetic. "It's my father."

Allyson understood. She gave him a nod. Cameron turned on his flashlight, and together they entered the Myers house.

*

Cameron's flashlight illuminated their way, but its feeble beam only did so much to hold back the darkness. Shadows surrounded them, and Allyson imagined Michael Myers standing in every one of them, hidden, watching, waiting for the opportunity to strike. Cameron held his pistol in firing position, and Allyson had the shotgun shouldered and ready to blast the first thing that moved. She swung her weapon back and forth as they proceeded, scanning the darkness, searching for a hint of white among the black, for Michael's mask—his true face. The hall closet door was open a crack, and a faint orange light flickered from within.

Allyson had a sudden sick feeling.

"Dad?" Cameron said.

He walked slowly toward the closet door, Allyson at his side. When he reached the door, he stretched out his hand, hesitated, then swung it quickly open.

Allyson had a flash of a grotesque face staring at her, and without thinking, she pulled the shotgun's trigger. The weapon roared, the stock kicked back into her shoulder, and the face exploded into a hundred fragments.

Cameron shined his flashlight on the carnage. Sitting atop a mound of junk were the remains of a jack-o'-lantern, among the pieces a small broken candle, a thin line of smoke curling from its wick.

"Goddammit," Allyson swore. So much for stealth. If Michael *was* in the house, he knew they were here now.

From upstairs, they heard the sound of a phonograph needle scratching across a vinyl record, followed by music—an upbeat jazz tune, a Halloween song that Allyson didn't recognize. Then came three loud thuds, as if someone was striking something with a heavy object.

Cameron looked to Allyson. She nodded, and they headed toward the stairs.

They ascended slowly, weapons ready, Cameron illuminating their way with his flashlight. The music became louder as they drew closer to the second floor, and in this context, Allyson found the singer's cheerful voice to be one of the creepiest things she'd ever heard. It was almost like he was inviting them up, and she thought of the line from an old children's poem—*Come into my parlor, said the spider to the fly*. She shivered and gripped the shotgun tighter.

When they reached the second-floor landing, they saw a crack of light coming from a partially open door. They slowly walked toward it, and as before, Cameron opened it quickly. This time, however, Allyson made sure to get a good look at the scene before blasting away with the shotgun.

It was a study—bookcases, secretary desk, stereo system—and two-middle aged men sat on a love seat, as if they were enjoying the music. One wore a pirate costume, the other a pair of pajamas with small pumpkins on them. The handle of a carving knife protruded from the pirate's chest, and the other man had a paring knife jammed in his neck. There was no sign of Michael.

Both men's eyes were wide and staring, and Allyson knew they were dead. Still, she had to make sure. She lowered the shotgun, stepped to the love seat, and reached a trembling hand toward the pirate's neck. She placed two fingers against his skin. No pulse. She did the same for the other man, touching the undamaged side of his neck. He also didn't have pulse.

"I'm so sorry," she whispered.

The music was driving her insane, so she went over to the turntable and switched it off. The silence came as an immediate relief. She turned back to the doorway, expecting to see Cameron, but he was gone.

*

Cameron could see that there was no danger in the study. Michael had been here, done his gruesome work, and moved on. Cameron stepped out of the room and directed his flashlight beam down the

291

hallway, the light shaking in his hand. He couldn't get the image of the two dead men out of his mind. Michael had killed them, then posed their bodies in a grotesque parody of domestic coziness. What might he have done to Cameron's father? What if Michael was attacking him right now, and he needed help?

The flashlight illuminated a closet at the far end of the hallway. Michael had put a jack-o'-lantern in the closet downstairs. What might he have put in this one?

Cameron raised his gun and walked slowly toward the closet.

When he was halfway there, he felt something warm and wet strike the hand that held the pistol. He looked and saw a dot of blood on his skin. It was quickly followed by another, and then a third. Cameron swung his flashlight beam toward the ceiling and saw an attic access door. Crushed between the door and the frame was his father's face—half of it, anyway—one eye wide, mouth open in a silent scream, blood running from one of his nostrils, dripping like thick, crimson rain.

"Dad!" Cameron shouted.

Now he knew what had caused that series of heavy thuds he and Allyson had heard from downstairs. Michael had pulled his father into the attic and crushed his head using the access door. *See you at the finish line, buddy*, his dad had said. For Lonnie Elam, *this* was the finish line.

Cameron heard a soft creaking noise then. He lowered his head, turned, saw the closet door open, and then Michael was coming at him, moving with inhuman speed. Cameron had lowered his gun when he saw his dad, but he raised it again now, ready to blow away the bastard maniac that had killed his father. But he was too slow. Michael got to him first, wrapped a hand around his throat, drove him backward, and slammed him against the wall next to the staircase. The impact knocked the breath out of Cameron, his hand sprang open, and the gun hit the floor and slid away. Michael lifted him off his feet then, and Cameron clawed at the man's hand, trying to free himself. But it was no use. Michael's grip was like iron.

Cameron saw Allyson then. She emerged from the study, sawed-off shotgun in her right hand, blood-stained butcher knife in her other. She'd pulled the blade from the pirate's chest, he realized. Smart. She approached Michael, aimed the shotgun, tightened her finger on the trigger…

Michael wasn't facing her, but somehow he was aware of her presence. Still holding onto Cameron's throat with one hand, he spun around and knocked the shotgun out of Allyson's grip with the other. The weapon fired, but the pellets struck the wall, leaving Michael unharmed. Undeterred, Allyson gritted her teeth, lunged toward Michael, and stabbed the butcher knife into his gut three times in rapid succession.

In that moment, Cameron thought he'd never seen anything more magnificent.

Michael let go of Cameron's throat then, and he fell to the floor. Before Allyson could strike a fourth time, Michael grabbed the back of her head and slammed her face into the stair railing. She gasped in pain, and then he lifted her up—she seemed to weigh nothing to him—and hurled her down the staircase. She managed to keep hold of the knife as she tumbled downward, but when she hit the bottom floor, Cameron heard a sickening *snap*, and Allyson screamed in pain. She dropped the knife, took hold of her left leg with both hands and shouted, "Fuck!"

Michael stood at the railing, gazing down at her. She attempted to stand, but her left leg bent back at an unnatural angle, and with a cry of pain she collapsed to the floor. She was injured, badly, and Cameron knew there was no way she could outrun Michael now.

His throat felt as if it was on fire, and breathing was an effort, but he knew he had to do something fast if he was to have any chance of saving Allyson's life. His gun lay on the floor several feet away, and he reached for it now. Michael, again with that uncanny sense of his, spun around to see what Cameron was doing. He stepped forward and stomped down on the gun before Cameron could get his fingers on it. He then leaned down and picked the weapon up. He straightened and looked at Cameron, and for an instant Cameron thought the killer was going to shoot him. But Michael tossed the gun through the open door of the study. He then returned to the railing to gaze down at Allyson once more.

She'd managed to rise and was supporting

herself by holding onto the stair railing and keeping her weight on her right leg. Even now, she was still fighting, and Cameron had never loved her more than he did right then.

Without taking his eyes off Allyson, Michael reached down, grabbed the collar of Cameron's coat, and pulled him toward the railing. He took hold of the back of his head, and before Cameron could even attempt to resist, Michael slammed his head between two of the railing's wooden supports, breaking them. They tumbled downward and struck the floor close to where Allyson stood.

Cameron thought he might've blacked out for an instant, but then his vision cleared, and he saw Allyson pull herself up onto the first step. She was trying to get to him, to help him. But he was stuck in the railing, unable to free himself, and he knew there was no help for him now.

"Allyson, get out of here!" he shouted.

Michael still gripped the back of Cameron's head, and he felt the man begin pulling his neck backward, exerting enormous pressure. He didn't understand how this was possible. Allyson had stabbed the motherfucker in the stomach three times, and he was still going strong. Maybe, he thought, his father had been right all along. Maybe Michael Myers really *was* the Boogeyman.

Then his neck snapped, and he fell into eternal night.

24

Allyson cried out when she heard Cameron's neck break, and hot tears rolled down her cheeks. Michael released his grip on Cameron's head, and it flopped forward, nothing but dead weight now. Michael pounded his fist on Cameron's head one last time, as if to make sure he was dead. Then he put one hand on the railing and slowly began descending the staircase toward Allyson.

If she could've run, she would have, but as it was, all she could do was hop on her uninjured leg. She hopped into the living room, desperately trying to maintain her balance. Michael reached the bottom of the stairs and, without slowing, continued toward her. When he got close, she swung the knife through the air several times, not out of any expectation of actually striking him, but more as a warning gesture. Michael, however, was not intimidated. He stepped forward quickly and grabbed her knife hand by the wrist. His grip was so strong, she felt bones grind together, and then he turned the blade to her face and began pushing it toward her. She fought him, but it was no use. He was unbelievably strong, and the point of the knife moved inexorably closer to her left eye.

Michael's masked face was only inches from her own now, and she could hear his heavy breathing muffled by the latex. It was steady, calm even, and she realized that he felt nothing—no thrill at the prospect of ending her life, no sense of victory at besting an opponent. He was as simple as a one-celled organism mindlessly fulfilling its genetic programming. He killed because he was made to kill; no more, no less. She looked into his good eye—her grandmother had told her how she'd injured the other using a coat hanger back in '78—and she thought she saw *something* there... She didn't understand what it was, but she knew one thing—it was absolutely, utterly inhuman.

She stood in her grandmother's place now. Forty years ago this very night, Michael Myers had tried to end Laurie Strode's life and failed. What he couldn't do to her, he was about to do to her granddaughter.

The knife point was a fraction of an inch from her eye.

"Do it!" she challenged him. *"Do it!"*

Allyson saw sudden movement behind Michael, and then her mother was there, gripping the pitchfork from the porch Halloween display tight in both hands. Karen charged and drove the tines into Michael's back. He stiffened, released his grip on Allyson's wrist, flung her away from him. She stumbled, came down on her bad leg, cried out in pain as it gave out beneath her. She landed hard on her rear, the impact causing her to lose her grip on the knife. The blade hit the floor and slid away from her.

Karen leaned forward, shoving the tines deeper into Michael's back, driving him to his knees. Karen shoved again, harder, and this time she drove Michael all the way to the floor. He raised his head, tried to push himself up, but Karen held him down with the pitchfork and kicked him in the back of the head. He lay there, stunned, and she reached down and with a single violent motion yanked the mask off his head.

He's an old man, Allyson thought when she saw his face. *Just an old man.*

Karen stepped back then, holding the mask with one hand while pulling the pitchfork out of Michael's back with the other. The tines were slick with blood, and a dark strain spread on the back of his coveralls. Despite his injury, he rose to his hands and knees, covering his face with one hand while swiping the other toward Karen, desperately trying to get hold of the pitchfork. *Or maybe*, Allyson thought, *his mask*. But Karen wasn't close enough for him to reach either.

"That's right," Karen said, taking another step backward. "You want your mask? Come and get it! You want to fucking kill someone? Take *me*."

The knife lay a couple feet from where Michael crouched. Still keeping his face covered with one hand, he reached out with the other, snatched up the knife, and then rose to his feet. He swayed unsteadily, but he didn't fall. And then he began to limp toward Allyson's mother. Karen backed toward the front door, holding the mask out in front of her like a lure, taunting Michael with it. She backed out onto the porch, and Michael, moving weakly but steadily, followed.

Allyson pushed herself to a standing position, wincing as her broken knee screamed with pain. She ignored it and hopped to the front door on her good leg. Once there, she gripped the sides of the doorway to support herself and watched as her mother drew Michael out into the night.

Karen ran down the front steps, turned, and hurled the pitchfork at Michael. It missed and clattered harmlessly to the porch.

"I'm an innocent woman like your sister was!" Karen said. "She was in her bedroom. It was Halloween night. Just like tonight. And it was right here. Your *home*. Can you feel it?"

Michael stepped over the pitchfork and began making his way down the steps. Karen backed across the lawn, still holding out Michael's mask, him following her, his gaze fixed upon his other face, his *true* face, as if it were a magic talisman with an irresistible hold on him. They continued this way—Karen backing up, Michael following his mask—until she reached the other side of the street. Then she turned and ran across a neighboring lawn, disappearing between that house and the one next to it. Michael, his stride becoming stronger and steadier with each step, pursued her. Allyson watched until he too was swallowed by the shadows between the two houses and was gone.

What the hell was her mother doing?

*

The Shape hurts, but pain means nothing to him, whether it's his own or someone else's. There's only one thing that's important to him now: regaining his face. He feels the cool night air on his skin, and he finds the sensation revolting. His true face protects him from the outer world, helps him control the maelstrom that rages inside him. It gives him focus, purpose. Without it he is diminished. With it, he's unstoppable.

He emerges from between the houses, crosses a lawn, finds himself standing on a sidewalk. And there, waiting for him in the middle of the street, is his face. He stands there for a moment, head cocked to the side, contemplating. This does not seem right to him, but there is no way he can resist the call of his face—nor does he wish to—and so he steps into the street and starts toward it. When he reaches it, he stops, senses something, looks to his right. He sees only an empty street, but an instant later he hears the sound of a bird's song. He looks to his left and sees three people standing there: Tommy, Brackett, and between them, Karen. Tommy grips a baseball bat in his hand, the words Old Huckleberry *burnt into its side. Nails have been hammered through the word to create a makeshift morning star. Two vehicles are parked on the street behind the trio— an SUV and a catering van with the words* Mick's Bar and Grill *painted on the sides. The headlights of both vehicles click on, flooding the street with light. Mick gets out of the SUV, and a group of tough-looking men exit the van.*

The Shape hears the sound of roaring engines and squealing tires then, and he looks over his shoulder to see two pickup trucks round the corner and come toward him at high speed. When the trucks are close enough, they screech to a halt, and men and women disembark. They are armed—crowbars, tire irons, axe handles—and their faces shine with dark anticipation.

The Shape is blocked from both sides now.

The porchlight of the house directly across from him turns on. Then the one of the house next to it. Then the one next to that. Another and another and another come on, until every house on both sides of the street is lit. Faces appear in windows, and occupants step onto their porches to bear witness to what is about to happen.

Brackett grins, says, "It's Halloween, Michael. Everyone's entitled to one good scare."

Then they come for the Shape, striking with their weapons, raining blow after blow upon him, faces aflame with savage delight. The Shape goes down under the assault, hits the ground, loses the knife. Karen steps forward, snatches it up, and slams the blade into his back. She leaves it there as she straightens, grim satisfaction on her face.

"We got this, Karen," Tommy says. "Go be with your daughter."

The Shape sees the woman nod to Tommy. She leaves, heading back toward the Shape's home. He wants to follow her, but the crowd falls upon him again, a raging tornado of vigilante justice.

*

Karen felt dazed, lost in a fog. She sat on the porch of the Myers house while a helpful neighbor—a woman in her early sixties wearing a white shirt and jeans—stood close by, gazing with concern at Allyson's broken leg.

"Just hold still and stay calm," the woman told Allyson. "You're going to be just fine. I'm not a doctor, but I do have some training in first aid." She smiled. "I used to be a summer camp counselor when I was younger."

The sound of sirens cut through the air, and an EMT van came zooming down the street, lights flashing. Karen had called 911 on her way back to the house, and she was glad to see the EMTs arrive so quickly. Allyson was doing her best not to show it, but she knew her daughter was in a tremendous amount of pain. The sooner she got medical attention, the better.

Allyson spoke then. "He'll always be here, won't he? Even when you can't see him."

Karen recognized the words she'd said to her daughter in the hospital. She'd been speaking of Allyson's father, wanting to reassure her that he would always remain a part of their lives as long as they kept him in their hearts and minds. But she knew Allyson wasn't speaking of Ray now. She was referring to Michael.

The EMTs pulled up to the curb, parked, and immediately turned the siren off, leaving the lights on. A man and woman, both in their thirties, jogged up the front walk. The woman carried a duffle bag that Karen assumed contained medical supplies. The friendly neighbor in the white shirt moved aside, and Karen did the same, standing and stepping off the porch so the EMTs had plenty of room to tend to her daughter.

The EMTs crouched down so they were both at Allyson's eye level.

"Did you fall?" the woman asked. "Did someone hurt you?"

The EMTs continued their assessment of Allyson's condition, but Karen tuned them out. She looked up at the second floor of the Myers house—the place that had always been the heart of darkness for her family—and fixed her gaze on one of the windows. *That's her window*, she thought. *Judith's*. The one Sheriff Hawkins had said Michael used to silently gaze out of when he was a child. Somehow, in a way she didn't understand, that room was the key to everything.

As the EMTs began to prepare Allyson for transport, Karen walked back onto the porch, careful to step around them. She glanced at Allyson, said, "I'll be right back."

Allyson was in too much pain to reply verbally, so she gave her mother a quick nod.

Karen turned away from her daughter and walked into the house where Michael Myers first killed.

*

The Shape has sustained so much physical damage that even he feels it, and the pain is an alien sensation to him,

303

one for which he has no name. He does not like it.

His attackers are blurs of motion around him, a series of fragmented images. Hate-filled eyes, bared teeth, hands wrapped tight around weapons… He hears sounds as well. Feet shuffling, rapid breathing, grunts of effort, invectives hurled at him as if they're weapons themselves… And of course he hears the solid, meaty thuds of the blows landing on his body, one after the other without letup.

The Shape senses something then, a familiar, welcome presence. He turns his head to the side and finds himself looking at his other face, his real face, lying on the asphalt, forgotten by the crowd. Blood pools on the ground between them, his blood, but it is of no importance. His face is just out of reach, but if he can stretch his hand far enough… The three fingers remaining on his left hand brush the mask's edge, fumble at it, finally get a grip. He yanks his face toward him, drawing it through his blood, and in a single fluid motion, he slips the gore-slick mask over his head and springs to his feet. He draws in a deep breath, feeling the pain of his injuries recede. He is strong again.

He is whole.

His attackers pull back in surprise, shocked that the cowering creature they'd been in the process of killing now stands before them, pain-free and unafraid. Tommy is the first to recover, and he steps forward and swings his bat, the nails wet with the Shape's blood. The Shape merely looks at Tommy as the bat strikes his head. He doesn't feel the blow. He doesn't feel anything. His hand shoots out and snatches the bat from Tommy's hand. Tommy looks at the Shape in stunned disbelief as he grips the bat in two hands, swings, and slams it into the side of the man's head.

Tommy is dead before he hits the ground.

The Shape drops the bat, grabs a crowbar out of another man's hands, and drives the chiseled end into his throat with such force that the neckbone snaps and metal bursts out of the back in a spray of blood. The man drops like a puppet whose strings have been cut, taking the crowbar down with him. The loss of this weapon is of no concern to the Shape. There are other weapons within reach. Many of them.

Now it is the Shape's turn to become a blur of motion. He moves through the crowd like a whirlwind of death, killing his attackers with their own weapons, felling them one by one. One of his attackers—a woman—holds his favorite weapon, a beautiful large knife. The blade Karen rammed into his back was dislodged during the crowd's attack, so he grabs it out of her hand, and uses it to flay open her throat. He then wields it to finish off the last of his attackers, and the final man to fall is an older man in a uniform whose nametag reads Brackett. The Shape has no idea who this man is, nor does he care.

He stands in the middle of the street, breathing evenly, and surveys the carnage he's created. It might be his finest work yet.

The residents of the street, the ones who came out of their houses to witness the Shape's execution, have seen something they did not expect and could not have imagined. Now that it is done, they withdraw into their homes, lock their doors, turn out their porchlights, and tremble in the dark, praying the Boogeyman doesn't decide to pay them a visit next.

25

Karen stood at the bottom of the staircase in the Myers house, gazing upward at the second floor, almost in a trance. She placed her hand on the banister and used it for support and she began ascending the steps. She hadn't brought a flashlight with her and the house was dark, so she didn't notice Cameron's body at first. But just before she reached the second-floor landing, she saw him, and she stopped to look. She felt no sorrow, no disgust, only a distant numbness, as if she'd been dosed with a strong tranquilizer. *I'm in shock,* she thought. But considering what she'd been through in the last twelve hours, she was lucky she hadn't fallen into complete catatonia. Cameron's head protruded through a broken space in the railing, lolled to the side, eyes open and staring. Michael had taken the life of Allyson's boyfriend, just as he'd taken Karen's husband. *Like mother, like daughter,* she thought.

When she reached the second floor, she paused for a moment. Her eyes had adjusted to the dark by now, and she was able to make out several doors in the hallway. The question was, which one led to Judith's room? She imagined herself standing outside on the lawn, looking up at the second floor, and she decided Judith's room must be the one at the end of the hall on the right, just before what she took to be the linen closet.

She started toward it.

Halfway down the hall, her foot slipped in a patch of wetness. She braced a hand against the wall to keep from falling, and she looked up to see Lonnie's face crushed between the attic access door and the ceiling.

Like father, like son, she thought, and continued walking.

When she reached Judith's room, she stepped inside, found the wall switch, and flipped on the light. The illumination momentarily dazzled her, and she squinted her eyes half shut until they'd adjusted. When she could open them all the way once more, she took in the room's contents. This was hardly a teenage girl's room—brass bed, sophisticated furniture, and that godawful painting of a cat in Elizabethan dress. Michael must have found the décor as jarring as she did, for he'd done his best to destroy it. The furniture had been overturned, the duvet and mattress had been slashed to ribbons, and the anthropomorphic cat now had large gaping holes where its eyes had once been, and a long slash mark in place of a mouth.

Looks like a jack-o'-lantern, she thought.

The only item in the bedroom that hadn't been touched was the antique vanity resting next to the window. She walked toward the window now, pulled as if by a magnetic force. It was closed, and as she reached it, she looked out and saw that the EMTs had gotten Allyson onto a stretcher, covered her with a silver foil blanket, and were carrying her to their vehicle. She watched them lift the stretcher onto the bed in the back, and one of the women hopped inside. Her partner then closed the door, ran around to the front of the vehicle, and climbed into the driver's seat. A moment later the van pulled away from the curb and raced down the street, lights flashing. Karen watched until they were gone.

She was relieved that Allyson was going to be taken care of. She'd get to the hospital as soon as she could so she could be at her daughter's side, but right now she had something she wanted—no, *needed*—to understand.

This was the window that Michael had gazed through when he was a child. She stood in the same place now, peering through the glass, trying to see whatever it was he had seen, whatever had fascinated him so. She saw nothing but darkness, though. That, and her own reflection. She thought of something Sheriff Hawkins had said to her mother earlier at the hospital.

My partner died the night he stood in that spot. For an instant before his death, I think he knew. Maybe he wasn't looking out… *Maybe he was looking* in. *At his reflection… At himself.*

She focused on her own reflection now, closed her eyes, took a deep breath, and tried to feel what

Michael must've felt when he'd stood here last.

When she opened her eyes, she no longer saw her reflection. Instead she saw the blood-covered face of a monster. And in his hands was a knife—a very large one.

She turned, screamed, and Michael rammed that knife into her chest again and again. And if she had any last insight into her killer's psyche before she died, she carried it into the darkness with her.

*

Laurie looked at the device monitoring Frank's vitals. She was no nurse, but it looked like his readings were steady. That was good. She could use some steadiness right about now.

The two of them held hands between their beds. Frank looked relaxed, peaceful, but Laurie was anything but. She gazed at the room's open doorway. Staff still ran by from time to time, looking stressed and harried. Perhaps the worst of the chaos that had ruled the hospital for the better part of the night had subsided, but it was clear that things were far from normal yet. They might not be normal for anyone who was here tonight for a long time, maybe not ever.

A tear rolled down her cheek as she began speaking, talking to herself more than to Frank.

"Michael Myers was formed from a mother and a father. Flesh and blood. Like you and me. But a man couldn't have survived that fire. The more he kills, the more he transcends. He becomes legend which is passed among us. And that's when he becomes something impossible to defeat. That's the true curse of Michael.

"He is the fear that incites us. The panic that radicalizes us. He is the terror that follows us wherever we go. If they don't stop him tonight, maybe we'll find him tomorrow. Or next Halloween when the sun sets and someone is alone..."

Frank had been listening intently as she spoke, but now he said, "If only we knew then what we know now."

Laurie went on as if he hadn't said anything.

"Never turn your back on him. The secret of Michael... He's the essence of evil. You can't defeat it with brute force. You can't study it like Loomis tried. This is a spiritual fight. Never underestimate it. You can't close your eyes and pretend it isn't there. It is. It always will be."

She let go of Frank's hand, and she suppressed a moan as she got out of bed. She walked slowly over to the window, looked out at the parking lot, and saw hundreds of people gathered outside. Many of them held candles, and she knew they were mourning the victims that had fallen to Michael's blade. Television news crews were on the scene, documenting their sorrow, broadcasting it to the world at large.

"It's all happening," she said, her voice thick with anger. "Michael's masterpiece."

What he'd done to her and her friends back in 1978 had only been practice, she realized, just as killing his sister in '63 had been. He'd been preparing for *this* night, for this blood-soaked rampage that would take the Haddonfield Boogeyman and transform him into a legend the world over.

Frustrated, feeling helpless, she pounded a fist against the glass, once, twice, three times… If only her trap had worked, if Michael had just lain down and let the flames devour him, the parking lot would be empty now, and all of these people would be in their homes, safe.

Frank spoke then. "He needs to die, Laurie."

You're preaching to the choir, she thought.

She heard Karen's voice in her mind.

We all thought he was coming here for you.

Laurie wished Michael *had* come for her. She would've confronted him again, finally finished this. But he was still out there somewhere…

Karen…

Laurie turned and slowly walked toward the front of the recovery room. On the way, she stopped at her bed, reached beneath the blanket, and withdrew the knife that Allyson had left for her. Its solidness felt comforting, reassuring. Holding the blade tight, she continued toward the room's entrance. A hospital phone was mounted on the wall next to the door. She lifted the receiver, tucked it between her cheek and shoulder, and began pressing digits. She knew Karen's cell phone number by heart.

*

The Shape stands at his sister's window as he did so many years ago, blood-splattered mask reflected in the glass before him. He does not see himself, though. He sees something else. Something beyond... *something* greater. *He sees—*

A series of musical tones plays then, distracting him. He turns toward the sound, sees the woman—Her daughter—lying dead on the floor, Christmas sweater in tatters, her chest a ragged mess of blood and torn meat. The music is coming from one of her pockets. The Shape tilts his head to the side, considers. Then he kneels, reaches into the front pocket of the woman's jeans with his three-fingered hand, and pulls out her phone. He stands, looks at the display, pushes a button, and raises the device to his head.

*

Laurie was relieved when the call was answered. She was about to speak when she heard heavy breathing on the other end, sick and distorted, as if whoever it was had been seriously injured. This wasn't Karen. She *knew* that breathing, knew it as well as her own. She felt a tearing sensation deep inside then, as if a vital piece of her had been suddenly, violently ripped away.

Karen...

Her hand trembled, but when she spoke her voice was as cold as a windswept Arctic plain.

"I'm coming for you, Michael."

ACKNOWLEDGMENTS

Thanks to my amazing agent Cherry Weiner, my equally amazing editor Joanna Harwood, fellow *Halloween* geek Tasha Qureshi, and copyeditor supreme Hayley Shepherd. Thanks to Scott Teems, Danny McBride, and David Gordon Green for writing a kick-ass script and continuing to breathe sinister new life into Michael Myers. Most of all, thanks to maestro John Carpenter, whose gloriously dark imagination changed horror forever.

ABOUT THE AUTHOR

Bestselling author Tim Waggoner has published close to fifty novels and seven collections of short stories. He writes original dark fantasy and horror, as well as media tie-ins, and he's recently released a book on writing horror fiction called *Writing in the Dark*. He's won the Bram Stoker Award and been a finalist for the Shirley Jackson Award, the Scribe Award, and the Splatterpunk Award. He's also a full-time tenured professor who teaches creative writing and composition at Sinclair Community College in Dayton, Ohio.